Amelia Thorn

By Richard J. Alley

MAY 2020

BEACON
PUBLISHING GROUP

For information, or to order additional copies, please contact:

Beacon Publishing Group
P.O. Box 41573 Charleston, S.C. 29423
800.817.8480| beaconpublishinggroup.com

Publisher's catalog available by request.

ISBN-13: 978-1-949472-10-3

ISBN-10: 1-949472-10-3

Published in 2020. New York, NY 10001.

First Edition. Printed in the USA.

Lyrics from "Soldier's Heart" courtesy of Caleb Sweazy.

For Kristy

ACKNOWLEDGMENTS

I want to thank Kristy for her guidance and encouragement over so many years, and our kids – Calvin, Joshua, Somerset, and Genevieve – for their understanding and curiosity about the worlds their dad escapes into from time to time.

My friends and family are endless sources of inspiration and I thank them, but especially the strong women I've known throughout my life. Their confidence and persistence make this world a better place.

And finally, thank you to the Crosstown Artist Residency program for the time and space to realize Amelia's strengths.

MEMPHIS

Chapter One

Daddy
Palmetto, Florida. 1931

Kodak film instaprint, 7.62 x 12.7 cm
(3 x 5 in.)

Courtesy, private collection of
Ms. Elizabeth Templeton.

"It's the first photograph I ever took with the first camera I ever owned," she says. "A Kodak Brownie. It was little more than a box, but it winked out at the world in a way that made me see things differently. I remember that day on the beach at Palmetto when Daddy sat and stared for hours at the horizon where sea met the sky. The colors were the most vibrant I'd ever seen, but it would be years before color made it into my photography.

"I also remember what was just outside of the frame of my viewfinder — a marina full of boats bobbing in the soft wake of a trawler heading out, fishermen readying their gear, a woman popping tops off of cold beers and one Coca-Cola, for me. It's the details that photographs don't reveal that make them so special to me. I came to learn that in a career that's spanned my lifetime. I was *there*. I played witness, Mr. Severs, when few dared to go where I did. Certainly few women. I know the secrets and surprises, the unknowns in the shadows that could never be revealed in the development process. I've always known there was more to be seen and it's what kept me looking all those years.

"I carried that photo with me on the train the day I left home. It was tucked into a book of children's fables taken from the Mourning Public Library. I'd stolen that book. Grandmother warned me of the dangers and threats that awaited me in the world, yet I was already a thief.

"The camera was with me that day as well and I remember fingering its lens and knobs, the scarred leatherette cover. I took comfort in the familiarity and memories of my first photo and my dead Daddy, and in the camera itself, which had already become an extension of my body. My other hand was folded neatly into Edward's, our palms sweaty from the heat of the day and the nerves that plague every young couple on the threshold of marriage."

Chapter Two

I'd never been to Memphis. Grandmother Reynolds had filled my head with stories of gray buildings like tombstones that overlooked the river, and of wicked music oozing from every weedy crevice. She admired her purled stitch while warning Mother and me about shirtless Negroes loading barges and paddle boats and unloading goods onto cobblestones as they sang their dirges like a funeral procession. She'd made the city into a cemetery, a back alley full of shadow and danger, a place all young and decent women should beware. Grandmother talked about crowds and swarms of automobiles like locusts, their noise an assault on the ears. The women, she'd warned, were out of place and the blacks didn't know theirs. "Danger lives there." She meant it as deterrence, but that's just how little the old woman knew of her granddaughter, for those warnings only heightened my curiosity.

The Tennessean pulled into Central Station and we disembarked into hissing steam and humidity and crowds. Men with briefcases and newspapers tucked neatly in their armpits. Women overloaded with bags and pulling resistant children along by limp wrists. This was the crowd Grandmother had cursed? This was merely humanity, a seamless flow of faces and voices that I found more thrilling than frightening.

The country's part in the war was not yet six months old and at every turn I saw military uniforms and flags and posters hawking war bonds; a small brass band played patriotic songs in one darkened corner. Edward nodded to passing men and stopped to offer a match for a cigarette and to ask where we might eat. "The Italian, across the street," answered an infantryman who said he was headed to Europe. I wondered whether this boy, his duffel slung over his shoulder and hand cupped to Edward's flame, would be alive a year from then. It was a morbid thought and one I never would have visited upon Edward.

I was in denial of the danger he would be in, I know that now. Yet that very danger had a permanent home buried deep in the back of both of our minds. It was the reason we'd traveled to Memphis as quickly as we had in the first place. Marriage would make him a whole man, he'd said. Having a bride back home waiting for him would give him a drive, the fight to survive he feared was not in him as instinct. He had no other family, both parents dead since he was a boy. "I need someone to care if I even return at all," he said.

Still, I didn't think of Edward's war as the same being reported on the radio and written about in newspapers. I was such a young and naïve girl back then, barely out of school and with clothes bought by my mother packed in my bag. Talk of war was on everyone's lips, carried on locomotive steam and in the duffel bags of young boys, but that wasn't Edward's fight. He would leave for a while as if on a business trip, I told myself. And then he would return again, whole, and eager for our life together.

The plan was for me to accompany him to San Diego and then wait there for his tour to end. There would be cheap housing for us and other Navy wives close by to keep me company. I would be safe and secure there, Edward assured me, but I'd never been to California as he had. He'd worked with the Civilian Conservation Corps, lying about his age to leave home at sixteen. He told me stories, how he'd traveled north to Ohio and Chicago before heading west to Oregon and down the deckled edge of the West Coast. "You'll like California," he promised. "The sun shines gold there."

I was seventeen years old the day I stepped off the train, unafraid of my adventure that lay ahead of me. But I feared for Edward's. He was twenty and had so much on his mind I felt I should keep my fears to myself, so his last days before going to war might be spent in peace. He wanted to write books and stories and awoke every morning at 5 a.m. in his room over the post office to write at a small wooden table. He kept a hunting knife stuck in the maple tabletop and each day the sun from the window would cast its shadow across the surface, ticking away time like a sundial. When the thinning shadow reached for a mark scratched in the wood, his day of writing was over. I admired his discipline and, maybe, was a little envious as well, wishing I had something I might care for just as deeply.

I sensed Edward was as scared as I was about the future. He never said so, and wouldn't, courage being a point of pride with him, part of being a man as he'd learned it through mismatched role models and in books over the years: gleaned from the sharpened edge of a hunting knife, a talisman and the only thing of his father's he still owned. His fear became transparent only in the stories he wrote, stories of fear and death. He wrote of loneliness and being trapped in the woods or as the sole surviving passenger on a doomed freighter passing around the Cape of Good Hope. I was supportive, but curious why he would write about tragedy and abandonment. "It's cathartic," he said.

I looked up that word — *cathartic* — in Daddy's *Oxford English Dictionary*, the big one, bigger than any Bible, that was kept open on a pedestal in his study. My curiosity knew no bounds then, and there were times as a child when I thought I might become lost in it, falling down a well of stories and facts and details the way Alice had fallen down her rabbit hole. As a child, I thought Daddy's dictionary had been written in Oxford, Mississippi, where Grandmother took me to shop. The town square had seemed ancient then with its chipped red brick and weathered wood façades old enough to have produced a book of the English language.

Even the people had been old. I wasn't used to that age; Mourning didn't have a lot of old people. Grandmother was the oldest by far, the matriarch of a town full of youngsters who'd moved in for cheap land made available when the suddenly childless left or died off. My grandfather bought up much of that land, more than anyone else for miles around.

It was Daddy who eventually told me there was another Oxford, where he promised to take me one day. I'd spent the whole rest of that afternoon in the library reading about England and royalty and crusades. I'd missed an appointment to have a dress fitted with Grandmother and had been in trouble when I arrived home. It was worth it. I knew then about kings and queens and pageantry, even if Daddy never did take me to see it all.

But our minds can't stay full of war and power grabs and distant lands, and those thoughts vanished from my mind on the top step of a wide staircase that soared above the main concourse of Central Station. Light cascaded from windows that rose to the ceiling and glinted off the terrazzo floor, burning like fire in the empty spaces among the crowd assembling to read arrival and departure times on overhead timetables handwritten by men floating above us all on ladders. With sleeves rolled over their elbows, they looked down on the crowd and dusted it in a fine, white chalk powder like fairy dust. People scattered as quickly as they'd come together, rushing for the tracks and ticket counters. Others sat on long wooden benches worn smooth over the years and polished by the trouser seats of thousands. Chairs like thrones were set up along one wall where shoeshines stooped against the boots of men hidden behind newspapers. Everywhere was the air of expectation carried aloft on cigar, pipe, and cigarette smoke as if the train's steam had seeped into the building.

We descended the stairs and something swelled within me as it had on the Ferris wheel when the carnival came to town. It was a hint of the unknown, a first step on the tip of an iceberg, a mere hint at the opportunities available in life.

There were voices in the air that spoke of everyone who had passed through the grand hall before, of deals made and promises whispered. The intention of a wedding. I believed Edward and I added something to the story. I felt as though I was giving myself over to fate and to the crowd that would carry me aloft, and I was more than willing to allow it to do so.

Chapter Three

My name is Amelia Thorn and I'm from Mourning, Mississippi. Such a sad name. No one recalls the town's original name. At least, no one I know has ever spoken it. If anyone were going to, it would be Grandmother, either for nostalgia's sake or spite. Surely, it must be written down, I thought, and as a girl I'd searched the dusty stacks of the library, my refuge and the tallest and grandest building in Mourning. Taller, even, than the Presbyterian church of my people, the only church I'd been in until that day in Memphis. My wedding day had also been my first time in a Catholic church, though it had been this religion's steeple in Mourning that would best the Presbyterian's by a mere eighteen inches, a fact my Grandmother clipped like a coupon and kept in her pocketbook of slights. "Papists," she hissed, the *sts* at the flinty end of that word running together and dripping from her tongue like a hex.

Mourning is at a point in Mississippi so centrally located as to be invisible, like the tip of your nose you can't see in front of your own eyes. Equal distance from the state's borders, it is far enough from Tennessee that Edward and I were anonymous as we crossed its boundary line, and far enough from the coast of the Gulf of Mexico that the salt air dried up and fell to the ground before it reached the town's limits.

Fifty years before my birth, Mourning had been little more than a hamlet with a dry goods store and post office, both still there today, serving farmers and those on their way to someplace else — Jackson, Oxford, or the gulf coast. A schoolhouse at the center of town was attended by twenty-eight children of all ages during the growing season with the long weeks of harvest given over to their small hands helping in the fields. One year, hard rains hampered the planting season, though no one thought much of reaping on the dawn after the accident. A dirt road, rutted and dusty on most days, shot through farmland and fields where a wagon, bouncing along and stopping at farmhouses, picked up children for school. It was a latter-day school bus with two mules driven by an old Negro who had at one time been the property of my family. The road, where it crossed a creek swollen from days of rain, was washed out and the wagon, carrying twenty-seven children, turned in the mud, slid from the road, and overturned in the creek. Every child on board, along with the driver and his two mules, drowned.

No one may recall what the town was called before, but after the day of the tragedy, those in neighboring towns — family members who came from far and wide to console mothers and bury the dead, who lay awake at night on makeshift beds in parlors and barns unable to sleep for the wailing that carried across the fields, down that mud-slick road, from one side of the state to the other and all the way down to the coast on salt air — called it Mourning.

My grandmother was six years old. She'd missed school that day, having told her mother she was sick. It was a lie. She'd been given new shoes by her father who'd just returned from Memphis, and she hadn't wanted to get them wet. All four of her older siblings — a sister named Amelia and three brothers — were on that wagon.

Chapter Four

The Timeless Café was across the street from the train station at the corner of Main Street and Calhoun. Voices from the station and sounds of the street — the noise Grandmother had groused about — filled the air and mingled with the scent of cars and horses, restaurant kitchens, and open-air cafés. Metal against metal, squealing brakes, car horns, trolley bells, men and women shouting for each other, shouting to be heard over the din, merchants barking their wares, and voices high and low calling out, "Aboard! Aboard! Aboard!" I stopped in my tracks to take it all in. It raised gooseflesh on my arms and burned my ears. Edward, walking ahead, held the door before turning to collect me where I stood on the corner, my head still in the music of the city.

Indoors was quieter, though sounds from the kitchen and the hum of conversation, punctuated by spoons in coffee cups and the incessant ding of a cash register drawer, bounced off wood and tile. Light from windows and overhead fixtures gleamed off polished chrome and caught the face of a clock over the front counter. I sat staring through the window at the throngs passing by, marveling at the clothes and cars and movement like the river's current. I didn't notice as Edward took two menus, held in place by a red and white napkin dispenser promising that a Coca-Cola would refresh, and handed one to me. "Coffee. Amelia, dear? What will you have?"

A waitress tapped her pad impatiently with the eraser of a pencil.

"Hm? Oh, I'm sorry. Coffee, please. Isn't it amazing, Edward? Have you ever seen so many people?"

"It puts a strange smell in the air."

"What does?"

"I don't know, but that's what struck me as we stepped from the train — the smell."

"Well, what does it smell like?"

"What doesn't it smell like?" he laughed and took a cigarette from his breast pocket, tapping it on the heel of his thumb one, two, three times, as was his habit before lighting. "Animals, men, a beef brisket over heat, automobile exhaust . . . But then there's something else."

"What is it? What's that something else, dear?"

He took the cigarette from his mouth and plucked a piece of tobacco from the tip of his tongue. "Magnolia blooms. I can smell it through the white noise of odor."

I laughed. "Oh, Edward, that's on you, and on me. We brought that along with us from Mississippi."

"Perhaps you're right, darling. What will you eat?" The waitress had returned with our coffee and we both ordered eggs, bacon, and grits, with toast for me and biscuits with gravy for Edward.

"I don't know why I ordered all that," I said once the waitress had gone. "I'm not hungry in the least."

"You've got to eat."

"I'm too nervous." My eyes went back to the window.

"The wedding?"

"Of course the wedding!"

Edward laughed at me then.

"Have you got the address?"

"Yes, dear, I told you on the train. Cooper wrote it all down for me and I've kept it here with my enlistment papers." He patted his chest, the same side from which he'd drawn the cigarette.

We were to be at St. Mary's Cathedral at 3 p.m. Mr. Cooper, whom Edward had worked for at the Mourning post office, had arranged it all. Father Hollahan was a priest who would marry men heading to war without the required waiting period and counseling. Had Edward asked his own priest, word surely would have made its way to Mother and Grandmother. My people weren't Catholic, but the town's grapevine was nondenominational and would have raced toward the women ahead of me like a wisteria root searching for daylight. Mr. Cooper had even taken care of the marriage license through a network of postmasters that Edward said he hadn't even known existed.

In the moments before our lives would change forever, we talked excitedly about the wedding and how it might go. I was concerned it might all fall through, that the priest might ask me if I'm Catholic and I might be made to prove it. I was such a nervous, silly girl that morning in the restaurant, and I suppose there was some part of me that wished my mother could be there, and even Grandmother, and — Oh! — Lizzie, too. She'd have made such a fine maid of honor, and so pretty in sunflower yellow. That's the color I would have chosen had a proper wedding been planned.

Oh, but it was proper. I would be marrying Edward, whom I'd known since we were children and loved nearly as long. We'd hoped to have a family wedding, of course, but then there was the attack on Pearl Harbor and everything got put on hold. Everything. Time, even in Mourning, Mississippi, a town that moves so slowly it seems only a day since those children died, stopped and all anyone could talk about was war. Everywhere, everyone was outraged, and how can you plan a wedding in such an atmosphere? Who would want to? Who thinks of cakes and fabric and vows when boys are leaving their homes by the thousands, leaving all they've ever known for an unknown a world away? It was madness just trying to wrap my head around my own happiness. And then, without consulting me, Edward had enlisted. Was I angry? Of course I was, though it wouldn't last for long. Young men everywhere were doing the same thing. Mr. Cooper was in charge of enlistment for the county, a special emissary was sent from Jackson just to swear him in. I wondered if the old postmaster had tried to talk Edward out of it; Edward was like a son to the confirmed bachelor. Deep down, though, I knew that Mr. Cooper must've been proud. I could imagine him taking his bifocals from his nose to wipe his eyes with the embroidered handkerchief I'd given him at Christmas.

And so there we were in Memphis to be married. I without my family, such as it was, and Edward without his, which consisted only of Mr. Cooper. We were beginning our lives together alone in a city neither of us knew. It was all at once thrilling and frightening and, if I had to pick one, and could keep that feeling all to myself, folded into the handkerchief Mr. Cooper had given back to me as a remembrance as we'd boarded the train that morning, I would choose thrilled.

"My valise," Edward said, pulling my attention once again from the rush beyond the window. "Amelia?"

"Your what? What's the problem, Edward?"

"My valise, it's gone. I had it right here on the floor by my feet. I only left for the men's room. Did you see anyone down here?"

I'd been lost in thoughts of Mourning and war and Mr. Cooper, and so it took me a minute to catch up to what he was saying and what had happened. "Why I . . . no, I didn't see a thing. It must be here." I folded myself into the booth to search the floor. Edward was standing now and looking beneath other tables, becoming frantic.

"Ma'am? Is there a problem?" It was the waitress.

"My husband's bag, it was right here beneath our table with the suitcases, but it's gone now."

"The suitcase?"

"What? No, his valise. It has our money in it. All of our money." The reality of it hit me like a locomotive and the full breakfast I'd just eaten heaved inside me. "Every cent we own is in there."

The waitress dropped to the floor and crawled beneath the table as Edward went from table to table asking if anyone had seen anything. They hadn't. He was stopped by a short, pudgy man with a nose like a beak who wore a greasy apron and wiped his hands on an equally greasy towel. Edward spoke, gesturing back to me and running a hand across his brow. The man patted him on the shoulder and took his leave when a table of businessmen called him over. Edward continued his search, even stepping out the front door to look up and down the block.

"Anything?"

He fell into his seat. "Nothing. Everything is in there, Amelia."

"Your papers?"

"No, I keep them here." Again, he patted his breast pocket. "My enlistment papers, train tickets, . . ."

"Marriage license?"

He must have seen the fear in my eyes because his face softened and he took my hands in his. "The marriage papers are safe, darling."

Mesmerized by all around us, we'd dropped our guard, assuming we had it up to begin with, and were robbed. It was just that simple. We'd looked away from our possessions

19

and the city had taken them, swallowed up what was meant to get us to California. "What will we do?" I asked.

He shrugged and wiped his face with his hands. "My pay should be processed and waiting for us when we get to San Diego. We'll have to make do until we get there."

"Make do? But how, Edward?"

Again he shrugged.

The short man slid into the booth beside me, startling us. "Excuse me, please, mister . . .?"

"Oh, I'm sorry. I'm Edward Thorn and this is my fiancée, Amelia Reynolds. Amelia, this is Mr. Zaccone, the restaurant's owner."

"Oh, the Italian?"

"Yes."

I blushed at my informality. "I'm sorry, it's just that when we asked directions to a restaurant, we were told to go to the Italian's and, well . . ."

"Yes, I'm Italian, from Lucca. You know it?"

I blushed again at my lack of world knowledge. "Well, no."

"It is beautiful and I miss it. Sometimes I miss it, but Memphis, it is a beautiful city, too. Ah, in her own way. There is the river and there are trees, oh, you've never seen so much trees . . ."

"Mr. Zaccone," Edward cut the man's speech short. "Sir, I'm very sorry but all of our money was in that valise, and I just don't know how we'll pay . . ."

"Shhh," Mr. Zaccone waved his hand as though brushing Edward's words to the side. "Memphis, my home, much like Italy, my home, has beautiful people as well, just like the trees. Mr. Edward, people know what happened to you and Miss Amelia. No, nobody saw who it was. Thieves here, like in Lucca, they slip like, ah . . ."

"Oil?" I offered.

"Yes, Miss Amelia, oil. Nobody knows where your bag is, but people call me to their tables — man, man and woman, woman and child, maybe somebody from my kitchen, maybe man delivering lamb and eggs in the back door — and they say to Charlie, 'Give this.'" He slid the greasy towel he'd used on his hands across the table and when Edward lifted it up, we were both surprised to see a pile of cash. Edward quickly put the towel back.

"Mr. Zaccone, I can't. I just . . ."

Again, Zaccone waved the words away. "For you, a young soldier, a beautiful bride. For you."

"But . . ."

"What you want to do? Give it back? To who? Whose money is that?"

21

I searched the faces of the restaurant, yet no one looked back. Edward slipped some bills from beneath the towel for the food we'd eaten, but Mr. Zaccone pushed it back. "No, Mr. Edward, you go off and you come back safe. You hear? That's payment enough at The Timeless Café. Il Caffè Senza Tempo."

"Oh, Mr. Zaccone," I cried, unable to contain myself, and put my arms around his shoulders. "Thank you so much."

He smiled wide. "So you see, Memphis not so bad. People not so bad. Please, don't think so bad of us."

"They're beautiful. You're all just so beautiful."

Chapter Five

The wedding was a small one — Edward and me, the priest, and the caretaker of the rectory, happy to be pulled from polishing wood and brass in the sacristy to act as witness. She'd held up the ceremony to run to the church's small garden for a hasty bouquet of flowers. I was grateful to her for that, as the bouquet formalized the event and leant an authenticity to what we were about to do. Our small group there on the altar smelled like gardenia, azalea, and lemon polish.

Edward and I were nervous, childlike despite the sacrament. We must have looked as though we were playing at being adults, a game of dress-up with me in my oyster-colored skirt and jacket, pillbox hat with just a hint of veil over my newly opened eyes, and Edward looking dashing in his pressed Navy uniform. The sun streaming through a stained-glass window bathed us in tints of red and yellow.

There was nothing childlike about anything we were doing or where our lives were heading. Edward was due to ship out in a week and we'd wanted to be married first. We'd traveled alone and had only each other, anxious already for the day we'd again board a train for California where Edward would continue by ship for the South Pacific.

The train from Mourning had only been our first great adventure that day. We arrived in Memphis not knowing a soul in the city. After we found ourselves unexpectedly without money and with no place to stay, Father Hollahan called upon his network and found us a room in the home of a parishioner.

The trolley ride lasted longer than the wedding ceremony itself and I was nearly overcome by the heat and excitement of the day. Sitting on a slat wood seat, I felt a sense of dreaminess I'd had since the train departed from home that morning, added to by the gentle rocking of the car. Beside me stood my new husband holding fast to a leather strap with one hand, his other on my shoulder, so familiar. My head swam at the change a single day could bring. Did I ever think a day would end this way? A train, a wedding, a trolley ride across a city I didn't know to stay with people I'd never met? It was an unlikely and exciting start to something that had always been presented by Mother and Daddy as benign and rote: marriage. Edward had promised more since we were kids, but that was just the way of kids and their hopes and dreams like balloons set loose in the wind. They floated and danced before falling to Earth and bursting. So much fun, so dazzling while it lasted. That's what I'd hoped it would be and that's what the day had offered so far.

The house Father Hollahan had arranged for us to stay in was in a new neighborhood close to the limits where Memphis was pushing itself up against fields of soybean and cotton. The walk from the trolley stop was beneath a leafy canopy, sunshine following us like a spotlight. The church's caretaker hadn't wanted us showing up empty-handed at this stranger's house and took a cooling loaf of bread from the priests' quarters. I carried it wrapped in a towel beneath my arm, its warmth and weight like a baby at my elbow. Children ran in front yards and neighbors visited on porches, and I wondered if those people could tell Edward and I were husband and wife. Had the brief ceremony at St. Mary's Catholic Church changed something in my face? In the way I walked? Did I carry myself in the manner of Mother browsing aisles at Lloyd's Dry Goods while I, a toddler, clutched her hem? Or in the manner of Ms. Fielder, a young widow whose husband died in the Great War, as she walked the main street of Mourning, turning the heads of husbands and fathers? Most likely those neighbors only saw Edward, handsome in his uniform and a grip in each hand, as he walked flanked by the nation's colors draping every porch. Maybe I wasn't even there beneath the green canopy backlit like the stain glass of church. I've thought in the years since that the girl I once was must have vanished behind a veil of marriage.

The house was warm and comfortable and my senses were assaulted as Edward's had been downtown when we'd stepped off the train. There was food cooking — meat and something tangy, a cake as well, or pie. It was sweet, anyway. And there was the smell of cleaning products beneath it all — lemon, like the woman at the church — and bleach, not unpleasant, but like home. I was smelling a home.

Eleanor was tall and fingered an earring beneath flame-red hair as she welcomed us into her house. From behind her legs peeked a boy of six or seven, and she nearly tripped trying to take a step backward. "Run along, Jimmy," she said. And then to us, "Grandson."

"We can't thank you enough, ma'am," Edward said. "Really, we never expected this. I had a valise, it was my father's, actually, one of the only items of his left to me . . . Anyway, all of our money was in there, every blamed cent, and it was stolen right out from under us as we ate."

"Oh, heavens," she said. "How awful. And the thief left you with only your luggage and a loaf of bread?"

"Oh, I'm sorry," I said, blushing. "This is for you."

"You bake?" Eleanor took the parcel and turned to the kitchen, gesturing for us to follow. "Leave your bags, we'll get them later."

"No. No, ma'am, I don't bake. Well, I've tried. Pies, mostly, when Lizzie had the patience to teach me." I was flustered. "The caretaker at St. Mary's sent this. It's all so embarrassing."

"Nonsense. If this is what it takes for me to get a loaf of Gertrude's bread then so be it. She's the best baker in the city."

In Mourning, we had a brick barbecue pit behind the house and it was there, surrounded by other men — neighbors, friends from town, business associates — that Daddy would strike a fire and slow roast thick slabs of pork ribs. Other than the fields when he stopped the tractor to adjust a spring or plug, or the times I spied on him and saw him in the barn passing a bottle with the field hands, it was the most relaxed and natural I'd ever seen him. Tending that brick barbecue was also the only time I'd ever seen him, or any man for that matter, approach anything even close to cooking. So it was a shock for me to see a man standing at Eleanor's stove clad in a plaid apron over dress pants and collared shirt rolled at the sleeves.

He stood stirring a great, steaming pot and he grinned at us when he turned around. The floor fell away beneath my feet and, with it, all reality. Even Edward gasped as it dawned on him that Mr. Zaccone was standing there at the stove.

"Charlie?" I managed to say.

"Miss Amelia. Edward. Welcome to our home!"

Chapter Six

Eleanor, with martini
1942

Kodak film instaprint, 7.62 x 12.7 cm
(3 x 5 in.)

Courtesy, private collection of the
Zaccone family estate.

Grandmother's husband, twenty-two
years older than she, had served while scarcely
older than a boy under Captain Finley in the 10th
Mississippi Infantry during the Civil War. She'd
been sixteen when she married Colonel
Reynolds, a child bride whose betrothal had also
married together two of the largest land-owning

families in Mississippi. She'd been raised to bear the brunt of a Victorian patriarchy, while her mother and father (a cavalry leader himself) were consumed by seasons of inconsistent crops, war, and the untimely death of four children. The young wife of an older man, Grandmother had the sole expectation to bear children — sons, specifically — to carry on a legacy as decorative as the medals on the Colonel's gray, woolen coat. It was the duty of all Reynolds women to extend that legacy, as it would become the duty of all women of Mourning to fill the beds left empty by the rains.

What Grandmother bore, alone, was the brunt of one miscarriage after another. She was made to try again and again, the Colonel's hot breath stinking of cigar and whisky in her face as he methodically pummeled his seed into her until, at long last, that sticky kernel took root.

The boy was small and blue and it was a half-hour before the doula could coax a wail from him. Even then, it was thin and reedy, and the Colonel pronounced his son, all of an hour old, to be weak. It was less than a month before he mounted his wife again, drunk, badgering her for the thistle of offspring she'd pushed out. She did little but lay there and bleed, and nothing else would ever spring from her womb.

She'd expected to die young, thought that would be her legacy, and hoped for it on lonely nights when survivor's guilt over new shoes and slick mud ate at her insides. In those early days of motherhood, she found comfort only when her son latched and kneaded her breast with his tiny fist. But she outran death and strengthened in her resolve to survive if only for the sake of the boy. Years passed and a new storm blew in from the horizon. The Colonel died, his heart torn open by a withering income as drought and recession circled the South. The Widow Reynolds, not understanding just what was happening until it was too late, until cotton prices had sunk so low there was but a trickle coming in, blamed her misfortune — the loss of income, the death of her husband, the demise of the South, as she saw it — on "Yankee bankers." She carried on the only way she knew how, the only way she'd ever known, and picked up the flag of entitlement and high expectations to march it across the scarred, lonely battlefield of motherhood. Over time, her resolve strengthened and she vowed to make the Reynolds name — now hers alone — great again. This, she would do through her son, and promised so to the tombstone, as gray as the man and his coat buried beneath it in the shade of a massive oak.

Her son grew strong. He grew tall and lean and the sun tanned his skin from hours spent outdoors, first playing with dogs and piglets and, later, working in the fields. He preferred the outdoors and its lack of boundaries because, once inside, his mother hounded him to be a gentleman, to consider the society she insisted was just beyond the gate, and to try, though no one ever could, to live up to the legacy left by the Colonel.

After my grandfather's death, the family continued to live on means that kept us comfortable, though guarded and ever on edge, leasing out more than three-hundred acres to someone else to farm. Grandmother presumed Mourning looked up to her and her station. She expected the world to come into her house, blown in on the wind, and compliment her on her new drapes. She still had credit at the grander department stores in Jackson and Mobile and would not hesitate to use it if something caught her eye.

I could tell from our first moments together in the Zaccone home Eleanor knew nothing of such entitlement. Surely she'd never waited for anyone to knock on her door. She'd walked right out of that door, gotten herself a job — more than that, a career — and worked her way through the Depression to support her family when the café on Main Street fell on hard times. She ate lunch with men she worked with. More, again, they worked *for* her! She drove her own car, something Mother and Grandmother had never done. She knew fashion, as Grandmother had, but she also knew budgets and when she could and could not afford the latest styles. She had four children, raised in the ecliptic, overbearing dynamic and bored detachment of her Irish ancestry. Love was on display in the Zaccone home. I could see it in the way Eleanor touched her granddaughter on the shoulder and kissed her grandson's forehead when they came to her where she sat at the kitchen table smoking a cigarette and drinking a cloudy martini.

"Run along," she said, eager for her own space. The kitchen filled with bodies and conversation and Charlie stood at the stove, stirring the thick, red sauce he called gravy, and laughing with the kids as Eleanor sunk into the deep end of her own thoughts. I lifted the camera to my eye and snapped a picture. "You're a photographer?" she said.

"Hobby."

"I'd love to see your work sometime." She held her glass out for Charlie to refill. "I'm dear friends with Don Newman, who makes good money with his photography. Perhaps you should pursue it as a career?"

At that point I'd never thought of photography as a way to make money and couldn't comprehend that someone might pay me to take a picture. I'd only hoped to capture what I saw in Eleanor, that thing I still couldn't name.

A young girl, Anna Marie, went to her grandmother, yet kept her eyes on Edward and me, unsure of who these new people were. She whispered in her Nonna's ear and Eleanor shook her head no. Again she whispered. "No." Anna Marie stomped a defiant foot and Eleanor sipped from her glass. As the girl left the room, she stopped at her grandfather who tore a hunk from Gertrude's loaf, drew it through his gravy, and handed it to her. She ran from the room with a smile on her face.

"She wanted to know if y'all are related to us. She thinks everybody is family. Most people are — aunts and uncles are always stopping by and she goes to school with cousins. Mama Zaccone lived with us during the Depression. Shared a room with Peter and Dean. Do you have siblings, Edward?"

"My parents died when I was a boy."

"Oh dear." Eleanor lit another cigarette, punctuation at the end of an unpleasant topic.

I was lost in the smell of the kitchen — pasta gravy and tobacco and coffee bubbling on the stove. There was still a sweetness as well and I looked for its source, finding a cake under glass on the counter, its frosting a dark chocolate that looked nearly black.

"Eleanor made that," Charlie said. He pulled a slab of brisket from the gravy and dropped it on a butcher block, its juices running red with tomato. He cut the meat into long, thin slices. The smell was overwhelming and my empty stomach lurched. "She makes one every morning before work."

It made me wonder again at this woman with her kids and career, her martini and mornings spent baking before it all began. A whole cake every day? Where does it all go?

As if on cue, as if it happened every day just this way (I would come to learn it did), the back door opened and we were introduced to Eleanor and Charlie's son, Peter, and daughter-in-law, Jean. Not long after, Dean came in, followed by neighbors and introductions were once again passed around with glasses of wine and plates of cheese.

It was the most boisterous dinner I'd ever been a part of, and it was what I would come to expect in a meal. Eleanor hovered around Edward in a way that had me wondering if I might ever be able to. She served us as though we'd never been offered food before, then slipped from the dining room to the kitchen for more pasta, more gravy, more bread. Wine was gulped and spilled over Eleanor's tablecloth, a sin that would not be forgiven, though it was soon forgotten, and toast after toast was made for the newlyweds. I ate and drank (it was my first taste of wine) and watched the ease with which my hostess dealt with men, women, and children alike. The feast was old-world, a tradition brought from across an ocean and a century past — one in which you take care of guests first, yourself second, and you never, ever turn anyone away. Yet there was also a glimpse of the future as when Eleanor ordered the men to move over, to help her, to clear the table or clear out altogether and watch after their children. There was a side dish of the coming women's liberation on the table and the promise of it was like dessert for me.

And there was actual dessert as well: chocolate cake, the best I'd ever tasted.

Chapter Seven

"The Timeless Café. Such a unique name, what's its story, Charlie?" Edward said as dinner wound down and plates were picked over for any morsel left behind. He was so curious and I could see him fidgeting, wanting to take notes. He'd often talked about working in journalism after the war as a way to pay bills while working on his stories and novels.

The café's story had been told and retold, as much a prayer as the blessing Charlie rushed through before eating. And though it was Charlie's story, it was Eleanor who told it. She'd heard it all her adult life, as had most guests at the table. But this telling was for us.

"The Timeless Café," she said, "was once a place where time was measured to the second." Charlie came from a long line of clock and watchmakers. In Lucca, his father and uncles ran the family business and people came from across the region for their precision. "Charlie's papa, the eldest of the Zaccone brothers, was meticulous in all things — from the way his house was run and his children behaved, to the cleanliness of his shop and orderliness of his tools."

"He was very precise in all things, yes." Charlie peppered Eleanor's story with asides and silent nods. Though men think their actions define the world, it is women who are storytellers and the facts and lore of the world will always be born from them.

From a very young age, Charlie apprenticed under the eyes of his father and uncles. He began by sweeping and dusting, but his responsibilities soon grew to inventorying and sorting hairsprings and screws, crown wheels and ratchet cocks. Every morning before the day's business began, Charlie was expected to have these parts and instruments in place at the worktables. "These were not Charlie's favorite chores, of course. He was bored with wheels and screws and yokes, he'll tell you."

"It's true," he said.

"What was your favorite part?" I asked.

He spread his hands out as though the answer was right there in front of me, a side dish on my dinner plate. "Talking to the customers."

"He met people from all over Italy and asked them about their journey, their lives, much as he does today in the café. And just as today, just as I'm sure you did, they opened up to him. I laugh to think of it now, what it must have looked like — little boy Charlie among adults in conversation while all around him were tick-tocks and clicks and chimes. What did you ask them about, Charlie? Their difficulties and joys, their families and lovers and regrets?"

Charlie brushed the thoughts back into the past with a wave of his hand. "Papa called me lazy."

"Oh, he was anything but!" Eleanor said, squeezing Edward's forearm. "He served those customers and made them feel like part of the family. There was an espresso machine kept in back . . ."

"As precise as any timepiece," Charlie interjected.

" . . . and Charlie offered a doppio and conversation while they waited. He brought them bread and cheese and olives meant for his uncles' lunches, and they cursed him. I like to picture the scene with light filtering in through the front glass and steam rising up to meet it. And I believe, while they sipped and chatted, time stopped for Charlie." She was looking at her husband now and I wondered if, after so many years of marriage, I would look at Edward in the same adoring way. Would I tell his stories for him? "I hear the silence as the ticking and chiming fade into the background until it disappears altogether."

"My Eleanor, she is a romantic," Charlie said. "It is the wine, I believe." And everyone laughed, including Eleanor.

The truth was that when Charlie sat at his workbench in the darkest corner of the shop and was made to disassemble and reassemble a cuckoo clock again and again as practice, time became finite and immovable. The thought of a lifetime spent bent over heirlooms and antiques depressed Charlie and, several years later, as a young man, he told his father he was moving to America. A man had come through town, a man from Memphis, Tennessee, and told Charlie about a school there — the Southern College of Watchmaking — and they needed instructors. By then, Charlie's work was as good as his father's and uncles. "Papa Zaccone died shortly after and his widow made the journey to Memphis to be with Charlie. By then, though, he'd left the school to open his own shop on Main Street." She squeezed Charlie's hand. "But he became disillusioned with it, and who can blame him? Once again he was depressed that he might see the same fate as his father whose life had been meted out in ticks of the second hand."

"America is the land of dreams, no?" Charlie said.

"And he chased his. He closed the shop one day and reopened a week later as The Timeless Café."

"I was with people again, hearing heartbeats, not tick-tocks," he said.

"But then Mama Zaccone arrived in Memphis," Eleanor continued. "And when she walked from the station across the street, she expected to see workbenches and men hunched over pocket watches with loupes affixed to their eyes. It would have been a comforting sight, no doubt — bit of the old world in the new where she would feel at home. What she found that day, though, were families and businessmen and travelers hunched over lunch plates. And I was who greeted her at the door that first day."

Chapter Eight

After Eleanor's story, after dessert and more wine, Eleanor assigned Jean and me to dish duty. Eleanor pronounced herself finished with the ritual of supper and wandered off with a martini in her hand, looking for a quiet place to sit and rest her eyes. "She's playing cards," Jean said.

"Who?"

"Mama. She complains about being tired but I don't think that woman ever sleeps."

"Does she eat? She never sat long enough to take a plate for herself."

Jean waved a soapy hand in answer.

"What's the occasion, by the way?" I said. "I never got the chance to ask."

"Occasion? No occasion, this is just supper. A small one, too, really."

"I feel as though we've imposed."

"Oh, honey, no. Hand me that towel. Dinner at the Zaccones' is a given. And if you hadn't been here then someone would've been in those seats — a cousin, a neighbor, a friend of a friend passing through town. It's all family."

"Do you come every night?"

"No, but Peter loves his papa's brisket. We only live around the block and I think that man can smell brisket cooking from our back porch. How'd you happen here?"

"Friend of a friend. Father Hollahan arranged it."

I reached for the next dish and it was the cake plate, empty, its crumbs and smears of icing the only evidence there ever was a cake. An entire cake gone, and tomorrow there would be another with another group of people, or the same people, coming together to finish it off.

"Aha, that's the golden ticket. No request from Hollahan will be denied. They're hedging all their bets that he'll write them one of those tickets into Heaven."

I looked at my reflection in the vanity mirror where I sat brushing my hair as I had every night before bed, many times with Mother or Lizzie chatting or fussing over the state of my bedroom. I tried to see what the neighbors might have seen as Edward and I walked from the trolley, or what Eleanor or Jean might have taken from the blush in my cheek and knowing smile on my lips. Was it a little girl or a grown bride? I was foolish in those days, eager to know what others saw in me, what they took me for. Grandmother had planted that seed early. "You reflect the Reynoldses when you leave this house, young lady." It was why she was mortified the first time she saw Edward and me walking back from the meadow where we'd go to be alone. The memory came back to me with wine swirling in my head and soft brush bristles massaging my scalp, the whisper of an old friend. The meadow was down a dirt lane running from the front gate of our property, past the big house, through the shotgun shacks where Lizzie's people lived, alongside the barn and through a copse of slim and straight pine trees. The thrill of going from light to the dusk beneath the canopy, and back into light again, made my head spin just as the wine had tonight. Edward took my hand as we came out into sunlight and it was the first time. I blinked and looked down to see our skin pressed together. But then there was something else, a sight I will never forget — in the meadow of wildflowers and clover unlike any patch of earth on the farm was a rising kaleidoscope of butterflies as the flowers appeared to lift into the air. "They're migrating," he said. "They're going out into the world." My heart, already racing from Edward's touch, fell into the rhythm of a thousand beating wings.

Edward lingered in the den, finishing a game of bridge, drinking, passing stories back and forth through cigar smoke. He stood to leave when I'd passed through talking of being tired, but I told him to stay, finish his cigar, his whisky. He leaned in and kissed my cheek and I blushed for the third time that day as the others in the room basked in our affection.

I brushed my hair and thought of what Jean had said about Father Hollahan. The priest was handsome, I agreed with her on that, and his church was impressive. I'd never been inside a Catholic church, not even Edward's back home. Grandmother had warned against Protestants crossing that threshold. A "cathedral," Edward called it, and images from picture books leapt into my mind of castles with stained-glass windows, turrets, and chandeliers. I'd felt unworthy of Edward's church, though I don't know why. It was the serpent hiss from Grandmother's lips that spoke of misunderstanding. Edward dipped his finger in a bowl of water and touched it to his forehead as statues and robed characters trapped in thin, painted glass looked on. The church had been cold and my skin rose to it. It was the unknown becoming known, two-thousand years of mystery unfolding before me with each step down the aisle.

I never did know if Hollahan knew I wasn't Catholic. He never asked. Could he see it in the way I moved, in the angle I held my head just as I'd felt the Zaccones' neighbors had known I was a newly married woman? I searched the vanity mirror for any hint of my soul and spirituality. I repeated Hollahan's words back to him and, when offered, took the stale, tasteless wafer on my tongue just as Edward had. My worthiness to be in that building, to marry, had never been called into question and, in that trust, I'd felt more worthy than ever. Father Hollahan smiled and placed his hands on both of our backs as if to push us together to begin our lives. Just like that, we were husband and wife.

Chapter Nine

"Where will you live?" Mother had asked, clutching the collar of her housecoat as I packed for this trip, for this life.

"California."

"But for how long?"

I didn't have an answer for that and felt like a little girl again, standing among childhood things in my pink and purple bedroom, scared to say the word "forever" for its finality, its fully encompassing time and all that could not be known about it. "Until my husband comes home." There. I'd said it. "Husband" and "home" and all that they imply — marriage and war and womanhood and forever. Still, there was so much unknown to me in those days, and I picked up my hairbrush and packed it into the suitcase.

My eyes fluttered open to morning light streaked across the guest room walls, blue like the linens of the bed. The furniture was white so I felt as though we floated among clouds in a cerulean sky. It was all so unfamiliar, sunlight streaming through curtains I hadn't bought and tracking across wallpaper I hadn't hung and furniture I hadn't picked out myself. I found I was eager to make my own home.

The idea of it all was a flutter in my chest and I couldn't believe it was happening to me, waking next to the love of my life, feeling another's body pressed against my own, both hard and soft at the same time. I'd known so little about those feelings only hours before. Grandmother had tried to teach me what it was all about, throwing a torch into the vast, midnight expanse of the unknown so that I might see. "Men need both," she warned, equating sex with violence as I brushed her long, silver hair. "They take both whenever they want, however they want."

It was a memory that had come back to me in the cramped coach seat on the way to Memphis, smothered by the heat of the day beside Edward in his military best, a soldier going off to battle, going off to marry and enter his virgin bride. The train rocked like the chairs on our porch and my eyelids grew heavy. Not so much, though, that I didn't see the other soldiers, young men from Tupelo and Vicksburg, watching me like hungry wolves. Their eyes took my body in a flash and I wondered how many of those boys would never return to Mississippi. How many would be killed instead? How many would kill others?

Though this journey had been planned — a wedding in Memphis, a life in San Diego — so much was still unknown. But how much of life can we really plan? Edward had sensed my apprehension and tried to soothe me with stories of California. He told me there were Chinamen doing most of the work there. "Oh, there are Negroes, too," he said as we ate sandwiches I'd made and packed for the trip. I didn't finish mine and gave half to a little boy who watched with hungry interest as I'd unwrapped it from the wax paper. "But it's Chinamen who built the railroad and infrastructure, bridges and roads and such. Had one as a foreman when I worked on the dam. Can you imagine that here? In Mississippi? An Oriental telling a white man what to do? They're good workers, though, I'll tell you that. Smart, too. California is the future, Amelia."

The boy wiped his mouth with his shirtsleeve when his mother wasn't looking and I laughed. He knew nothing of war or violence, nothing of smart Chinamen or broken-backed Negroes or entitled whites. I watched him finish the sandwich, taking bites so big that his cheeks inflated and eyes bulged, and welcomed the adventure ahead whatever it held. I wanted only to be married to Edward, and I wanted to see Memphis.

The blue walls talked, murmuring from rooms beyond the guest bedroom. Footsteps. Conversation. I thought for a moment Edward must be up and put my hand out to feel the warmth of him. I fingered the gold cross resting on his chest and mimicked his slow, rhythmic breathing. Edward hadn't been violent. Not at all. I had a sudden urge to write to Grandmother and tell her how he'd touched me lightly, tenderly, and seemed to sense when I was ready. And I was. Beneath his body, I felt everything I'd hoped marriage would be as we rocked together gently like the train, like the meadow flowers in a breeze. "Are you okay?" he asked over and over until I put my finger to his lips, kissed him with my tongue silencing his. I pulled him deeper and faster, felt the pain and was glad I'd thought to put a towel down on Eleanor's fine, soft sheets. I saw the faces of those soldiers on the train only for an instant. Like a flash, their dull, dead expressions entered and left my mind, taking the violence and Grandmother's fear with them. Edward tensed and the world stopped — the train, the butterflies, the long strokes of a hairbrush — and in that dark, unknown space of time, he said my name and it was as if it were the first time it had ever been spoken aloud.

No, there was no violence, Grandmother, and perhaps there never would be again. Not anywhere. Was it the naiveté of a new bride to think love could put an end to all war everywhere? To think I'd just spared the lives of those boys on the train with one selfish act of passion?

Chapter Ten

Broken Horse
Main Street, Memphis. 1942

Kodak film instaprint, 7.62 x 12.7
cm (3 x 5 in.)

From the artist's private collection.

The Chisca Hotel on Main Street at Linden Avenue was not the nicest hotel in town. There were others more regal — the Gayoso, The Peabody, of course, and the smaller, newer, modern-era William Len with its deco features like a Hollywood movie set. But the Chisca was the loveliest I'd ever seen. Better than any in Jackson, grander than the Oxford square itself. It sat on the corner like a sentinel, both gatekeeper and greeter to anyone entering the southern end of Main Street. In our room, where I could see clear to Central Station to the south, I checked my makeup while Edward changed shirts.

"They must have heard," I said.

"Oh, I'm sure they didn't hear a thing. They only said they wanted to give us this gift."

"Dinner was a gift. All that wine was a gift. 'We just feel that newlyweds need their own space.' Oh, I'm so embarrassed, Edward." Had I cried out in pain? In ecstasy? Had bed springs moaned through those blue walls? I went over the night again in my head as I had the whole trolley ride downtown and, again, felt my cheeks flush. I hated to think of the Zaccones passing judgment on us, on me. I was still so new to the world, so fragile in a way I wouldn't be for much longer.

We walked back through the plush lobby with its bellmen running back and forth and travelers from all parts of the country asking directions. From the awning's shade I saw grocers, jewelers, tobacconists, boarding houses, dress shops, haberdashers, and produce stands lining the street.

"You're overthinking it, dear," he assured me once again as he lit a cigarette. "Charlie understood. He assumed we wouldn't want to be cramped by so many children and strangers."

"We're banished," I said, and didn't want to say after only one night I already felt closer to the Zaccone family than I had my own.

"Don't be silly. Now run along, don't keep Eleanor waiting."

Despite my embarrassment, I found myself excited by the notion of lunch and more time spent with her. "I suppose she'll pay for that, too," I said. "It's all just too much."

He waved the talk away, a gesture he'd quickly picked up from Charlie, and kissed my cheek. "Don't think of it. As soon as my check comes in we'll send them something, but they insisted this is a wedding gift."

Edward went his way to the enlistment office to take care of paperwork and see about his pay, and then to the post office to get a letter off to Cooper, and I went mine, following the trolley line north on Main as Eleanor had instructed. She suggested I take a trolley, but I preferred to walk. I squinted up through gingko trees at terracotta roofs and looked in large and welcoming windows of furniture shops, boutiques, and pharmacies. Everywhere were advertisements for soda and booze, shaving cream and war bonds. I stopped below a second-floor music store to listen to piano trills falling from an open window.

There seemed to be music everywhere as Grandmother had said. I walked on.

At the corner of Union Avenue there was a commotion; a crowd was swelling and people were shouting. My heart pounded, not knowing if this was normal or something everyone was seeing for the first time, an experience we all shared, these strangers and I. "What is it?"

"Horse," a man answered over his shoulder, not taking his eyes off the animal.

"It's dead," a woman added, her hand at her mouth.

"Ain't dead," said another man in overalls. His hat was in his hands and perspiration beaded across his bald head. "Not yet."

"What happened?"

"Lit out, unbuckled from its dray up the road there. Lit out."

I could see the horse, lying on the ground with its foreleg bent at a wrong angle. It was trying to stand but its hooves wouldn't make purchase against the cobblestone and oil-slick trolley track. A trolley car blared its horn, impatient for the crowd to move. The mob turned on the conductor, waving him back, shouting in unison about animals and broken bones and blood. There was blood from the horse's nose, I saw then. "It's bleeding."

"Hit her head on the bricks there," the second man said.

I lifted my camera and snapped a picture. All around us, nothing but buildings. Concrete crept block by block, floor by floor. "Where was she going?"

He nodded to the west, to the hill where Union Avenue crested then disappeared. "Look like a canyon, don't it? Look like freedom to her and she damn sure gonna make a run for it."

"Where does it go?"

"River. She'd a drowned. Either way, she dead now, just don't know it yet."

A policeman in white gloves showed up, shouting, shoving people out of the way. The horse whinnied and I felt sick at the sound. I turned and walked toward the canyon, and as I topped the hill that would lead to the river I heard the crack of a single gunshot.

Eleanor was waiting at the big, brass lobby doors of a building on Madison Avenue. She knew immediately something was wrong. "Oh, dear, what is it? The heat? You're as pale as the moon."

"I'm so sorry," I said as I searched my bag for a handkerchief. I could feel sweat trickle down my spine. "I just saw the most terrible thing. A horse was broken."

"Broken?"

"Hurt. She had a broken leg and was bleeding from her nose and mouth. Oh, Eleanor . . ."

She held me and we must have looked a sight there on the sidewalk, an island for the current of rushing people to move around. "Let's get you inside."

At Anderton's Cafeteria just around the corner, Eleanor urged me to eat. "I'm afraid the sight of it all took my appetite," I said.

"It must have been awful. Here, let's get you a drink." She ordered champagne cocktails for both of us and I gulped mine to her amusement. "There! Now you'll feel better." She ordered another, and a shrimp cocktail as well. My appetite returned, carried on bubbles.

Chapter Eleven

On the day my Daddy died, he'd gone out to the fields early, just before sunup. The rumbling of the thresher's engine woke me and I rushed downstairs to see him, but only caught the cotton dander left swimming in summer sunlight with his leaving. Lizzie came into the house minutes later; she must have passed him on the way.

I recognized the trouble first. "What you staring at?" Lizzie asked me.

I could only stand there, motionless, on the top step of the wide front porch. "Daddy," I whispered.

We stood and watched for what felt like an hour as the thresher, puffing smoke, alive, sat idle in the golden field like a giant, red island. I squinted in the morning sun with Lizzie at my shoulder, motionless, a shadow catching my thoughts. She finally broke away and turned inside, the creaking screen door breaking the silence.

Mother ran from the house moments later and didn't stop, the door slamming shut like a shotgun blast. "Henry." She spoke his name quietly at first, growing ever louder, the syllables following behind her like a kite's streamer. As she reached the field, swallowed by wheat stalks, her voice receded until I was once again enveloped in silence. In that silence I heard a cat beneath the porch, scratching, looking for its morning meal. It was the big female, I knew, pregnant again and making a home for her litter in the cool shade beneath the house.

Mother's scream filled the air between the field and house. The cat stopped scratching. Lizzie ran in again to get Grandmother from bed.

"A tragic accident. So much awful, angry death in the South, don't you think?" Eleanor said. We sat in the dressing room of Goldsmith's Department Store, having window shopped at Lowenstein's, Kress, and Gerber's department stores after lunch. She'd been intent on taking my mind from the horrible event of the morning yet had asked about Daddy and I'd answered with the story of his death. Tragedy was on my mind, the image of the dying horse still so fresh. Shrimp and champagne turned over in my stomach.

At Goldsmith's, the clerks knew Eleanor by name and I was passed around as a novelty, a small town girl in the big city. I tried on dress after dress, each more elegant than the last. With every new garment brought to me, I insisted it was not necessary and Eleanor had done enough, more than enough, already. "Nonsense," she said from the sofa where she sat cross-legged, flipping through a fashion magazine and smoking one cigarette after another.

"He was tender and caring for a man who worked the fields until sundown," I quickly added. "I could never really figure that out, you know? He had these large, calloused hands, lined and like leather, yet he was so soft at the same time. I would open his hand and trace my finger along those crevices like gorges. It was as rough as the terrain he'd just plowed. But then, you know, when he touched my face his hand was soft, it felt like a baby's."

I stood beneath harsh lights on a small stage in the prettiest underwear I had and felt ill at ease talking about Daddy, as though he were there in the fitting room with us. I wanted to cover my pale, white shoulders and breasts, but the salesgirl was slow in coming with a new dress.

"He was quiet," I continued, "but he said a lot with his face, his eyes. I'd sit across the living room, getting an earful from Mother about my grades or the tattered hem of a dress or something, and he would just look at me, raise an eyebrow, you know, or puff out his cheeks, and all of that bad air would go out of the room. Sometimes I'd laugh. I didn't mean to, but I couldn't help it. Mother didn't like that."

"They sound like night and day," Eleanor said.

"They were. They could be. Mother is kind, though, I don't mean to give the wrong impression. I think she just had an idea of how she should be, how the world should be, how I should be. And if that path wasn't being followed, well, then she was at a loss for what to do. The wind would blow and Mother would let it take her, like a dandelion. She lacked backbone. I think I've always thought that, but never could say it. But there it is — my mother is weak."

"And you?"

"Oh, I hope I'm not."

"Hope?"

"Well, I don't guess a person ever really knows, not until she's tested. I haven't been, I don't think."

"What about your daddy's death?"

"Mother was there for me, and Grandmother. And Lizzie."

"Sister?"

"Sort of. Grandmother's caretaker, but we grew up together mostly."

"Well, you came to Memphis, got married, and you're on your way now to California. That takes backbone, young lady."

She tossed the magazine down beside her and looked up at me then.

"Maybe." I shrugged and turned to the mirror to see the back of a dress. I liked what I saw. "What about your family? As big as it is, you must have trouble keeping them all straight."

"Oh, I know them all. I've got their numbers right up here."

"What about your mother-in-law? I don't have one, you know, Edward's parents both died."

"You're lucky." She bent to an ashtray on the coffee table in front of her. "My mother-in-law hates me."

"Oh, that's awful."

"It's mutual, I assure you."

"But why?"

"Isn't it obvious, dear?" Eleanor laughed, as did the salesgirl. I felt as though I were left out of a joke, or I was the joke, and even more naked than I already was. "Look at this hair, Amelia. This isn't Italian, this is Galway-red. A red so hot it burns Mama Zaccone's eyes just to gaze upon it." She threw her head back and laughed.

"You're Irish and Charlie's mother doesn't like you because of that?"

"The Italians don't cook with ginger, dear. She also never forgave me for Charlie opening the café in what should have been a watchmaker's shop like her husband's family for generations."

"She blamed you for that?"

"Of course. It was easier that way, her boy never would have sabotaged his own destiny. She forbade us to get married."

"But you did."

"Backbone. Took backbone, too, for me to let her live with us during the Depression."

"Why did you?"

"It was the Depression, dear, and you did for your own. She isn't mine, be sure of that, but she is Mr. Zaccone's."

"Is she still alive?"

"Amelia, she's too goddamn mean to die."

Chapter Twelve

I'm still not sure just what we buried beneath the old oak tree beside the house; the teeth of a wheat thresher are ferocious, unforgiving implements. The soil that day was damp and as cool in the sunlight as it was beneath the porch where the cat, in the days between death and burial, had given birth to four kittens. On the day of the funeral, the thresher was still in the field, left to run itself out of gas where it stood.

I recalled two things about the funeral as I walked from Goldsmith's down Main Street, past the scene of the horse's accident, cleared now and as if it'd never happened. The first was Lizzie standing in the picture window of the house, framed there like a portrait. The men who worked for Daddy, and with whom he ate his supper after long afternoons in the field, stood just inside the barn door, hats in hands and heads bowed. Neither they nor Lizzie had been invited to the service. Yet Lizzie was expected to prepare food for guests and serve it, see to it that no one was in need of sweet tea or coffee. It was the first time Lizzie had been denied; the second would be the day I left for Memphis and slipped into her room for a private goodbye.

The other thing I remember, and it's what I would think of later, during long days when I walked to the river's edge with the bluff above me and the water below, was Edward arriving at the funeral on a horse. He would not be sent away by Grandmother, not that day. It was the same day he left town with the Conservation Corps. His horse grazed nearby with the very duffel bag he'd carry with him later to Memphis and the South Pacific. I looked from the horse to Lizzie and then to Edward, who stood near the back of the throng of family and neighbors. He nodded to me when our eyes met. He winked and smiled and I'd taken that simple, kind gesture to mean that everything would be alright, nothing more.

Chapter Thirteen

Lizzie once told me she wished to be free. It was Christmas day and we sat at the kitchen table stringing popcorn with sewing needles for the tree Daddy was expected to drag into the house soon just as family and friends would arrive to help decorate. It was a rare instance of Lizzie dropping her guard and I would think later it must have been the time of year, the warm kitchen, and the smell of pies in the oven. "But Lizzie, you are free. There ain't no slaves no more," I said, laughing. I liked to talk that way when it was just Lizzie and me, and neither Mother nor Grandmother were around to correct my grammar.

Lizzie told me her idea of freedom was running through wide-open spaces with those closest to you, able to spread your arms wide and feel the wind in your hair and laugh and yell at the top of your lungs. "You could just keep on running, too. Run away if you wanted, up and leave. But you wouldn't because there would be so much love right there so close by, just buzzing at everyone's fingertips."

Lizzie hadn't known anything outside Greenlaw County ever. Her daddy, they said, ran off. Her people were sharecroppers, her grandparents had been the property of Reynolds. Her mama left her, too, or died, nobody ever did know the story. Lizzie was left behind, told by Grandmother there was nothing out there for her, that the great wide world was no place for an orphan Negro girl. What she was telling me on Christmas Day in the kitchen was she only wanted the opportunity to leave. In that choice to go or stay would be her freedom.

How odd, I thought, my own idea of freedom was. No wide-open fields or miles of nothingness for me. No Mourning, either, where I couldn't walk through town without being known and without women telling me to straighten my hem or sit up straight at the ice cream parlor where they'd also *tsk* at the pounds that treat would add to my frame. Mrs. Florentine once told me to use my inside voice when I'd called to my friend, Camilla, that I'd found the brass button she'd been looking for. I had an inside voice, of course, but it was not any of Mrs. Florentine's business and I said so. I got the switch later that evening. Grandmother's eyes were everywhere in Mourning and when she wasn't around, I was looked after in a way that made me feel restricted, claustrophobic almost. The townspeople seemed to have the same expectations for me as Grandmother had. But then, the whole town had expectations for the Reynolds family. They looked up and saw the white farmhouse rising in the distance like a temple, they saw what they wanted to see: *Austerity. Wealth. Respectability.* But there was something else, too — Grandmother had survived the storm, the overturned wagon, the muddy water where her classmates' and siblings' bodies writhed like catfish. Sure, she wasn't there, but there was something mystical even in that. There had long been tales she was told not to leave the house by some whisper on the wind, by a voice as rich and baritone as the Colonel's would turn out to be. My Grandmother was a survivor, the lone survivor, and this meant she, and by extension the Reynolds legacy, held promise. It was as if the Reynoldses were meant to lift the whole town up from its deathbed and onto the gray, woolen shoulders of a long-dead war hero.

The expectation was too much and one I didn't want. One I know Daddy didn't want. It's why I craved the anonymity of an unfamiliar city and walking shoulder-to-shoulder among strangers, free to re-imagine myself, to try on a new personality just as I'd tried on gown after gown at Goldsmith's. That anonymity would be the freest I'd ever felt. I wasn't even a Reynolds in Memphis, I was a Thorn. I was free.

I was twelve years old and Lizzie sixteen when she shared her freedom with me. Despite the age difference, we were sisters that Christmas Day when we stuck sewing needles into our forefingers and touched the red blood together, swearing to each other on forever.

Chapter Fourteen

I spent the rest of the afternoon strolling along sidewalks and through alleyways, exploring Memphis. It was a tapestry at once gritty and polished, a labyrinth peopled, not by Grandmother's monsters, but by field hands far from home, businessmen, housewives, troubadours, the old and the young. As I made my way to the Mississippi River, sunlight glinted off the water so I had to shield my eyes. I thought about the day Edward returned from his travels with the Conservation Corps and the way the sunlight landed on him as he stepped off the train in Mourning. Had it been the same light he'd known in the West? A calliope sounded and down the cobblestone bank men sang their work songs. I closed my eyes to feel warmth on my face and found it was both inside and outside of me.

From somewhere deep inside, I found something else as well — I did not want to go to

California. I did not want to climb back aboard that train. Edward had promised a trip I'd never forget. "Sights of a lifetime as the country rolls past," he said like a radio advertisement. The fields of Arkansas turn into mountains, to the windswept plains of Texas and Oklahoma. Gold becomes red becomes brown until the sun of California burns it all away to cool your eyes with the bluest blue you've ever seen in the Pacific Ocean. I wanted none of it. There were blues enough in Memphis, be sure of that, yellow trees and brown faces and hearts of gold. Streets teeming with enough sights to last a lifetime, the good and vibrant going in and out of office buildings and barbecue joints and jazz clubs on Beale Street. Oh, Beale, with a power I'd never known. It had an electricity that could've driven Daddy's tractor. It created steam enough to push that locomotive all the way to California. And the way I was feeling in those moments alone, it could go on without me, for all I cared. I knew the moment I stepped onto Beale that my life would never be the same. It was as if I had never climbed from the platform of the Mourning depot onto a train and then down again into Central Station in Memphis. It was, instead, as though I'd stepped from Grandmother's wide, shaded front porch directly onto the whiskey-soaked paving stones of Beale. I wondered for a moment if I'd lost my shoes, such was the past of the street against the soles of my feet — all its years and characters, sadness and happiness squished between my toes like fallen apples in the Owen's orchard back home. I loved it from the very first step, from the very first brush of liquored breath on my cheek, the way I used to love running through that orchard barefoot even though Mother forbade it. I loved the freedom of the people on Beale, the true freedom of a people who have found the one place they are allowed to let go of themselves, of their worries and fear of those around them. It infected me and I felt myself swaying with a piano and brass horns. I eased into the sway of the crowd and its smiling faces so much darker than my own. They paid me no mind, this small, white girl from Smalltown, Mississippi. Probably from the same fields they'd escaped, just happy to be themselves on the only street that would allow it.

The men would come to pay me mind eventually with the same looks as I'd had from soldiers aboard the train, bloodshot eyeballs the same, whether red from fear and homesickness or liquor and cigarette smoke. Those eyes followed the curved lines of my young body as I swayed with the music and the Kodak Brownie bumped against my belly. I was pulled into a saloon in three-fourths time. Gazes flowed like waterfalls from the top down, losing interest somewhere around the shallow pool of my hips. I developed early, my period coming at eleven with breasts not far behind (Mother would die if she heard me talk so). "Lord, Miss Amelia, them girls grow overnight?" Lizzie said at breakfast before the older women had come to table. I blushed and folded my arms in an attempt to hide. "But where the rest at? You want a man one day, you better get something round back. Men want hips. Babies need hips, too, girlie. Now you eat every bit of this food." The women on Beale had hips. They knew how to use them, too, bumping and rubbing against their men so eager to get closer and closer to their own promised land.

The women didn't smile so much, not at me. Not like Lizzie smiled. I would write to her later: *Dear Lizzie, I wish you could have been here with me on Beale Street to feel what I felt, to know the freedom in the music, my sister.* My sister. "You hush," Grandmother said, whispering as though the night might carry the notion off and share it with neighbors. I was eight or nine years old, brushing her hair and saying my prayers. "… and bless my sister Lizzie." She tugged on my hair to get my attention. "We're white, you know that. She is *not* your kin." I didn't let that stop me thinking it, though. I loved Lizzie as much as any blood relative.

And I loved the people on Beale as well. Somebody handed me a glass and what was in it burned my throat, made me feel love for those strangers. I was hungry and wanted to eat,

73

wishing I still had the half of sandwich from the train. But I didn't want to leave the crowd. The piano was like nothing I'd ever heard, certainly not the staid old instrument from church on Sundays or in Grandmother's parlor. I can picture her sitting on the bench, rail straight and with a high collar buttoned to her chin. When I hear the time-traveled echo of Grandmother's music in my head today, it sounds like age and smells like powder. I couldn't reconcile that music with what was in my ears that day, chased from my memory by the man at the piano. He was darker than the keys he touched, sweating and moving all over the bench, his tie undone and shirt collar opened so I could see the gold rope at his collarbone. There was no crucifix there as on Edward's. A panatela cigar stuck in his teeth, he pounded the keyboard like a man gone mad.

"Marcus Longstreet, up from New Orleans," I heard a man shout when his woman asked who the pianist was. I wondered if Marcus Longstreet had ever heard of Mourning, Mississippi. I wondered if that was what the piano sounded like in Lizzie's church, a small clapboard building built up against the bank of the creek that took those children and Lizzie's grandpa home. Was it the same music heard in Edward's church with its medieval steeple rising so high that I could see it from any place in town, even from Grandmother's front porch? "Papists,"

Grandmother said. "Don't they study their Bible? Haven't they heard of Babel's tower?"

My head swam in a different language, hunger, liquor, and reflection, and I looked around at the men who watched me, their women with skirts pulled up over glistening brown flesh. It was Marcus Longstreet, the sorcerer up from New Orleans, who made it all happen and I thought, in that brief interlude, that I might just understand the idolatry Grandmother warned against. The saloon was Babylon itself.

I left, pushed out by the crowd and a need for air, and walked to the Timeless Café because it was the only place I knew. It wasn't nearly as full as it had been when Edward and I first arrived in town. When was that? I felt disoriented. Was it the day before? A lifetime ago? I'd been unmarried then, a virgin. A lifetime. I sat in the same booth and watched an old man at the counter, his rumpled hat resting on the countertop beside him. He was just as rumpled himself and looked sad or broken. A soldier in uniform sat alone at a table, an olive duffel sitting across from him like his date. He didn't look my way as the men on the train had and I wondered if it was obvious I was now wed. The young man squinted at the bill and reached for his billfold but the rumpled man had already whispered in the waitress' ear and she pushed the soldier's money away. What is this place where no boy going off to combat has to pay for bacon and eggs? A premonition sent shivers through me — this was every soldier's last meal. The bitter taste on my tongue wasn't coffee, but a taste of what it might be like once my husband was gone. I longed for Edward even more. I could only pick at the eggs, yet I devoured the bacon. I added more sugar to the coffee and gulped it, signaling the waitress for more. The soldier stood to leave and shook hands with the rumpled man who brightened and found a smile for this boy going off into the world. I was left feeling empty and the void was filled with thoughts of Edward. I missed him and thought I should go back to the hotel. There were things to be resolved.

Richard J. Alley

Chapter Fifteen

White lights strung corner-to-corner reminded us of dew on a spider's web. The setting sun cast pinks and purples against a canvas of darkening blue. My day in Memphis had been a kaleidoscope with each turn of the prism lovelier than the next. The only comparison I was capable of then was to storybooks I'd spent hours with as a child. Even with that background, though, my imagination had been ill-formed to conjure up tables laid in white cloths and real silver sparkling in candlelight. As the sun sank, Arkansas, glimpsed across the river from the rooftop of the Chisca Hotel, was as inky as the river that separated us. Black men in gloves and white coats with hand towels draped over forearms delivered and took away dishes, poured wine, and used a special tool to whisk crumbs from the already pristine tablecloths. I was sure to thank them at every turn and they nodded their welcome with formal grimness.

"You're so polite, Amelia."

"You make fun of me."

"Not at all, it's one of the things I love about you."

"There are others?" The fact I'd even had to ask the question of Edward, I see now, said more about my insecurities than the words themselves. I'm surprised I said them aloud at all. Edward told me again and again that he loved me. We'd grown up together, the outer circles of our groups touching each other in a Venn diagram of church socials, sport fields, and swimming holes. I was being groomed for something better, a station above my own mother, somewhere closer to the place that Grandmother believed her name and husband's legacy still floated. An orphan — Grandmother never would have approved of any union, whether it be childhood friendship or marriage. Edward grew up in the town's post office with Mr. Cooper and, for me, there was something alluring about such ambiguity in a person's life. He wasn't tied to any spit of land or a graying name. He was elusive, like the coyotes that stalked the tree line of our property.

When I was old enough — when I believed myself old enough — I asked about him. Somewhere near the root of the Mourning grapevine, I inquired as to his aspirations, what he had planned after leaving school, and whether he planned to leave Mourning as so many did. The vine did its work and within the week he'd come around to ask about me. It was Mother who first ran him off, asking if he had a parcel from the P.O. to deliver. When he said he didn't, she said, "Well, then, run along. Come back when you do." The next time it was Grandmother, who had no pretense towards what his intentions might be. She leaned in on her cane and, from the porch, when she was sure he was in hearing distance, shouted, "Sic him, dog! Get him!" Edward turned tail and ran, unaware the Reynolds dogs had all died of distemper the previous summer. When Edward found out, he bypassed the adults and met me after school, walking me all the way to the end of the drive leading to our house. And it was there he left me until the following day when he retraced his steps, this time carrying my books. And then again the day after and every day for almost the entire frigid month of February until, finally, the world thawed, we skirted the big house, and he took me to the meadow behind the barn.

And then he left. It was in the meadow, with butterflies tickling my ankles, as spring was just beginning to melt into summer when he said he'd be heading west with Roosevelt's Corps. I missed him. I didn't tell anyone — not my friends, not even Lizzie. Instead, I waited, and the waiting irked me. Sitting on the porch, helping Lizzie snap beans, I'd find myself watching the road where it met the long drive, where he'd left me those days after school, looking for any sign of a horse and rider. I'd throw a bean down and stomp into the house, frustrated at my powerlessness against the memory of a boy. I took a letter to the post office for Grandmother and asked, casually, as though I were asking whether it might rain soon, how Edward was doing. Any word? Yes, we were in school together, I said. (Had he even told Cooper about me?) I shrugged at his answer and sauntered away in case he might seal my faux apathy in an envelope, stamp it, and send it off to Edward, care of Franklin Delano Roosevelt.

He was gone for two years and a young lady's life moves forward, doesn't it? Shouldn't it? Through force of will, I managed to push Edward aside and focus on school and the novels I'd grown into while sitting in the library's tower. He'd been placed on a shelf with the storybooks of my childhood. Not gone or forgotten, for I could go to them and pull them from the stacks any time I felt to be reminded. But I didn't.

And then one day he came back. And I was there, quite by accident. Sent to the train depot to retrieve a package, a window dressing Grandmother had ordered all the way from Atlanta, there was Edward Thorn stepping to the street side of the depot, a head taller, leaner, and more handsome than I'd remembered. He squinted up at the sun, a smile curling on his lips as though that sun were a long lost friend. I knew in that moment I loved him and would forever.

He said those words to me when he returned to Mourning and he told me as he looked up from his bended knee in our meadow beneath a star-filled sky. He told me again beneath the same sky that night on the rooftop of the Chisca as a five-piece band played soft music to fill the gaps between the stars. But why? I was so different from the elegant women at Goldsmith's or even headstrong Eleanor. I watched women dance on Beale Street that very day with their plump, swaying hips and knowing hands, and they were just that: *women*. I felt sheltered, kept like a little girl behind her mother's skirt, caged even in the wide-open fields from which I'd come. The soybean and cotton back home knew nothing of the concrete and asphalt of Memphis. Grandmother and Mother showed me Oxford and Jackson, and the bits and pieces of society in Mourning that only hinted at a great wide world beyond its limits.

I wanted more and there, atop the Chisca, I felt uneasy, seasick, as though the table and chairs we sat in were in motion. I didn't want to ruin the night for Edward, but by the time I'd made it to the rooftop of the Chisca Hotel, my decision had been made. I would make Memphis my home. At least for a little while. At least while Edward was a world away. "I'll need that comfort," I told myself. "This friendliness the city has shown me." It wasn't a fear of the unknown, but simply that California held no promise for me. I could've gone home to Mourning, I knew, and the safety of Grandmother's house with Mother fussing over my hair and dress, but I was quit of that. Such a prospect held as little promise for me as San Diego without Edward.

The table was set with the things I'd seen that day and a stain spread the river's India ink across white linen. I felt as though I were keeping something from Edward and knew I'd tell him about shopping with Eleanor and about the broken horse. I'd tell him about the marquee lights of movie theatres and storefronts of Main Street decorated for war. But not about Beale Street, nor the young, doomed soldier I'd seen accepting a meal from a stranger at the café. What I wanted was to tell him I felt drawn to the city as I'd never been drawn to any place before. But the Chisca's rooftop was ready-made for romance and I felt so grown up, so pretty in my new dress. It was like a second skin, one I'd never worn before. And Edward, in his Sunday suit, looked so handsome that I saw him as he would be — a successful writer in a hotel in a foreign city celebrating the release of his latest novel. I didn't want to take that from him, not before he shipped to war. I would wait, I told myself, and, instead, took his hand and related a truncated, whitewashed version of my day. It was the only instance of dishonesty in our short relationship at the time.

Chapter Sixteen

There were long and humid summer nights when I sat on the roof outside my bedroom window listening to owls and the far-off lows of coyotes. And some nights I'd catch Lizzie as she left the house in her good dress hemmed up special, short and sassy. I could see it twitch even from my lofty perch. Her shadow grew long as she escaped the reach of the house lights where bats swooped and darted, into the darkness and down the long driveway to where a car waited. I couldn't see a car, but there was music coming from the night above the angry rumble of an engine, and the peal of laughter was blown back on pine-scented wind.

What did Lizzie do on those warm evenings? I thought I knew. I thought maybe Lizzie was searching for the freedom she craved, but I ached to know for sure. The next morning, as Lizzie rolled out dough for a pie, I dragged a fingertip through the excess flour and asked, "You ever kissed a boy, Lizzie?"

"Sure," she said.

"Anything   else?"

"Never you mind, little girl."

I'd hoped to embarrass Lizzie into answering, but I'd been the one embarrassed, chastened like a child told to wipe the flour from her dress. So I pushed. "I saw you last night, leaving."

"That so?"

"Might tell Grandmother."

"And so what if you do? I don't belong to nobody. I work for your Grandmama but I come and go as I please." She was angry; the pie crust would be too thin.

"I only want to know where it is y'all go."

"Run along, Amelia Reynolds. Find your baby dolls to occupy you."

In our bed that night, after dinner and drinks overlooking Main Street and the river far below, Edward and I made love. It was different. I was different. More confident and emboldened from a single night of experience or from my day spent dancing and drinking, I can't be sure. With Lizzie's blood flowing through my veins that night at the Chisca, I wondered if she knew about the pianos and brass of Beale Street, the swaying and saloons and sex. I held Edward's hand and guided him, we moved together, swaying to the finish. I remember thinking, "This is what it's supposed to be." It wasn't as Grandmother had told me, nothing of violence or fear here, not with this man. Neither did Mother know anything of the love I felt. She could teach me to bake a cake — one step at a time, never over-pouring, never overlooking an ingredient — but I knew it was Lizzie who could teach me how to eat a cake, how to hold it in my hands and devour it while sitting on the floor without a stitch on.

Edward and I held each other afterward and I thought those sheets might be the most comfortable I'd ever known. More so even than Eleanor's. We opened windows so trumpet and guitar carried in on warm spring air that left drapes fluttering in the breeze. It was perfect, more perfect than the dinner had been and I knew then I had to say something. The thing I'd carried back with me from Beale had played in my head over and over as accompaniment to the tune Marcus Longstreet rolled from his fingertips. I put my hand on Edward's bare chest, felt the crucifix against my palm and saw his eyes flutter. Before he drifted to sleep, I took a deep breath full of night air and the melody from below and told him what I wanted.

Later that day years earlier when I'd told Lizzie of spying on her, and once her pie was in the oven and the morning chores complete, I slipped into her bedroom where she bathed sitting in a small metal washtub with her knees drawn up to her chest. In Lizzie's bedroom we were equals, she in the bath while I washed her hair. "Hand me that cloth," she said.

"What's it like, Lizzie? To kiss a boy?"

"It's warm and soft, mostly, like bath water. But they can be rough, too. Not too rough now, don't let them be too rough. They just unaware like men are about most things."

"It was a man kissed you?"

"Mhm. Soap?"

I handed her the cake soap from its wax paper package and watched her run it under her arms and over the back of her neck. "Anything else?"

"Anything what else?"

"You do anything else with that man? Did he put it in you? Love you?"

"He loved me, yes."

"Was that rough?"

Lizzie smiled and poured clean water from a pitcher over her hair. For years I longed to know what was behind that smile.

Chapter Seventeen

Edward By Moonlight
Chisca Hotel, Memphis. 1942

Kodak film instaprint, 7.62 x 12.7 cm
(3 x 5 in.)

From the artist's private collection.

Edward was already awake, fully dressed and bent over the small writing desk at work with sleeves rolled up his forearms. His thoughts were elsewhere and ink stained his wrist like a birthmark. Outside, the sky was dark and the window was pulled down to just a crevice. Still, the drapes danced. "A bad cloud blowing up," Grandmother would have said and gone to her family Bible for comfort and safety with memories of floodwater filling her head.

"Why didn't you wake me?" I said.

"You need your rest," he answered without turning.

"How long have you been up?"

"I never went to sleep."

"What time is it?"

He picked his wristwatch from the table and read its face. "Eight o'clock."

"Edward! You'll be late!" I threw the covers aside and leapt from the bed, naked, the humid air clinging to my body. "I need to pack."

"I've packed for you."

I walked to where he sat and put my hands on his shoulders, leaning in to kiss him on the top of his head. "You're mad."

"I'm not."

"You haven't slept, though."

"There were things to be taken care of. I've taken care of them." He stood abruptly, shrugging me off and disappeared into the other room. "Now, get yourself dressed and we'll go," he said before closing the door and leaving me alone in the gray morning light.

Downstairs, Edward commiserated with the concierge who scribbled on a pad and nodded while I stood in the center of the hotel lobby, watching a sundry store clerk reach up high for a box of talcum while another jerked a soda for a woman who searched through her purse for change. When Edward finished, he took my arm through his and we walked out to Main Street, the day looming dark with rain. Almost immediately, I wished for the white glow of the light globes in the lobby or, even better, the warmth of the bed I'd just left.

"Our bags," I said after walking several blocks.

"Mine is being delivered to the station. Yours will be delivered here." Edward had abruptly stopped us.

"Where?"

"Here." He pointed to a weathered doorway, a step up from the wide sidewalk. People bustled all around, threatening to push us from our path. He guided me through the door.

The woman who showed us to the room was heavy and blocked the view to the top of the narrow staircase. She squeaked when she walked and, as we ascended the stairs, I couldn't help but want to laugh. I held it in, though, and pinched Edward who, I could see, was turning red with laughter as well. The room at the landing was sparse — a bed, table with two chairs, countertop with a hot plate, and a wash basin on a bureau — and I was still confused about just where it was I was standing.

The previous night had not gone well, though I'd managed to tell Edward what I'd been thinking and feeling since arriving in Memphis. "I don't want to go," I said and he looked more confused than hurt. We lay on top of the bed's covers, sticky with sweat. "To California. I want to stay here, in Memphis."

"But, Amelia . . ." He leaned up on his elbow and reached for a cigarette on the bedside table, tapping it against the base of his thumb. One. Two. Three. "Our plan is for you to go to San Diego and wait there. We've discussed this."

"I know, but it seems like a world away. I'm only a hundred-fifty miles from home and already I feel a world away. What's the difference, Edward? What's the difference if I'm here or there when you're in the middle of an ocean? I think I can be happier here, and won't that ease your mind?"

It would give him one less thing to worry about while on his crusade, I'd considered as I'd nibbled on a piece of bacon at the Timeless earlier that day. I wouldn't be able to hide my misery in California, I knew that. He would see the loneliness in my irises, reflected in the gold of the California sun before boarding his ship. Though I'd try to cover it up, he'd read it between the lines of my letters. It would be mixed in the ink, nestled within every looping pen stroke. Better to tell him goodbye in Memphis with its flurry of activity and the changes the river itself brings.

"I'll wait here for you and, when you return, if you wish, I'll go to you in California," I said, and then didn't say, *If you return home to me alive and whole, then I'll move where it is you want, wherever you can write, Edward, whether that be California or Texas or Chicago. Even here in Memphis or back to Mourning.* I hoped it wouldn't be Mourning; the smallness of that town had long closed in on me. Perhaps we would go to Oxford, England, if there was such a place after this hellish, brutal war. But I wouldn't live a continent away on my own. The loneliness would push against me in the same way the smallness of Mourning had with its predictability and familiarity, its dusty veins pumping little but hot air and cotton dander. I feared my very body would become its own town square, its diners, its side streets. I carried my home inside of me and when left so alone I would live only within it. It wouldn't be any life at all. In Memphis there were people coming and going. It was the crossroads of the South with train tracks and paved roads for miles, Zaccones, and men of commerce and music and politics passing as if going someplace, seeking *something.* Going slowly, to be sure, in this late spring heat. Sauntering, yet with a destination, a purpose. The end goal might only be a plate of fried chicken and cold iced tea, but it was a goal nonetheless.

Edward described his war as a crusade and memories of sitting in the Mourning Public Library reading about England and kings and queens would come racing back to me. In Edward's crusade, though, there would be Nazis and Japs spreading hate and fear and fire, and he and the other G.I.s — boys, really — would march in to stop them. They wouldn't be on horseback, but on foot and by boat, in the air and cocooned within tanks. In books I'd read, queens and princesses waited for their warriors in gilded palaces and faraway castles. *The sun shines like gold.* But in the tiny, gray room of the boarding house my head swam and I steadied myself against the wall as I looked from the only window to the people below, going, moving like a current.

"Are you alright, dear?"

"I'm fine. Where are we?"

"This is where you'll stay. At least for now. I worked it out with the concierge at the hotel. This is his sister-in-law." He gestured to the woman standing by the door, tapping her foot impatiently.

"It's good?" the woman asked. She was German and I wondered if this upset Edward. I wondered at the hard life the woman would have in this country from then on.

Edward nodded. "Leave us, please."

The woman did as she was told, closing the door behind her.

"Edward ..."

"Listen," he cut me off. "You made your point clear last night; this is what you want. You'll lead your own life while I'm gone, I can't stop you nor would I want to."

I fell into him and he held me tightly. Looking into his eyes I could sense distance between us that hadn't existed the night before. We'd come to an impasse then and he'd leapt from bed to light another cigarette — one, two, three — and stood in front of the open window. I watched his naked body and wondered if anyone from the street or the buildings across the way could see my husband. My camera was on the bedside table, and he never heard the click of the shutter. He was still standing, looking, searching, brooding when I fell asleep, unable to keep my eyes open any longer.

Remembering his body today, I think I can feel its heat against me and it's lovely. But that day in the boarding house he held me too tightly so I could feel his every breath, his heartbeat, his hardness. He kissed me and wouldn't let me up for air, his hands all over, pulling my skirt up over my thighs. I let him. Of course I let him, I didn't know better. He turned me around and put his hands between my legs, testing, and it was all so new for me. I was anxious, unsure of what I should do. It was rougher than the night before and I didn't enjoy it, it wasn't for me, had nothing to do with us as husband and wife. The thought of Grandmother's warnings came back to me as I felt Edward's violence with each thrust until he pulled me back against his hips one last time and finished. That would be how he left me there in that room with its scent of sex and force. He left all of the violence and anger and frustration there with me, nothing left for the war itself.

I adjusted myself, spreading my skirt smooth and paying some attention to my hair before going to him where he stood smoking and looking from the window. I stretched up to kiss him and that's when I noticed the tear on his cheek.

Chapter Eighteen

What was it like when Edward left? Was the sky rent open and did the rains come like tears? Yes. It was the heaviest rain anyone had seen in a year's time. As I sat and wrote later in my small room, it was still beating against the window and lightning flashes stole the night away. I jumped with each crack of thunder. It was a strange, new city that rain came down in curtains and ran thick and muddy into the river, carrying with it whole trees, garbage cans, and produce carts, and took me closest to what Mourning must have felt the night before the death of those children. Baggage porters on South Main looked up wide-eyed, wondering if one of the Pullman coaches might be buoyed like Noah's Ark. They wondered aloud if their lives might be spared.

Edward clutched my hand and I let him, grateful for his strength and what I felt might be my last moments of stability. He was still angry, I could sense that as well, and I felt the soreness of it between my legs making the warmth of his hand all the more welcome. He pulled me through the crushing crowd, fording the way as though across a river, his broad shoulders creating a wake for my safe passage. The air was thick with the odor moisture pulls from people and sound traveled through the air just as it had on the day we arrived in Memphis. When was that? I couldn't recall, but it seemed like weeks ago. How long does it take to imagine a new life? Perhaps ruin the old? Promise of adventure had been in the air upon our arrival. On the day Edward left, it was acrid with fear and, again, the unknown. There was dread inside me put there by Edward. It would sit in my belly and ferment as his train snaked across the country and his ship cut a wake across an ocean. It would consume me until I was able to hold him in my arms again.

He asked if I was hungry as we passed the Timeless Café, but I couldn't think about food. Instead, I hurried him to the station. Why? Was I eager to be rid of him? Back at the hotel, I'd watched him put his watch on and seal envelopes to be sent off with the morning mail; at the boarding house, I watched as he wiped himself clean on a towel from the sink. The way his body moved in everyday tasks was already so familiar and had become part of him in my eyes and a part of us and would be added to the list of what I'd miss when he was gone.

The dread I felt in the pit of my stomach wasn't for myself, for there was still the aftertaste of excitement in my mouth, even after the chilled silence from the night to the soft violence of the morning. No, my anxiety belonged to Edward. He was going off to war and I was sending him there. As though I was Roosevelt himself and had ordered that young man to go alone into hell. I will never forgive myself for those final moments together. I will never forget the feel of steam against my skin, hot and moist; the sound of the rain like a snare drum on the tin roof of the platform; the baritone voice that cried out, "Aboard!"; and the softer, quieter crying all around as wives, lovers, sisters, mothers, and children said goodbye to their men. There was too much sorrow and I found myself wishing for a flood to come and wash it all away, for the muddy river to overflow its banks and fill the wailing, plaintive lungs with brackish water. I felt the storm upon me, the rain on my cheeks and chin. But it wasn't rain. Edward had stopped and was looking down into my eyes as he had in the rooming house, though softer and kinder. He turned to glance up at the conductor who cried out again — "Aboard!" — and in his profile I saw the boy he was, the scar from some childhood accident white at the corner of his eye, a lock of hair curled against his forehead. He'd removed his hat. When had he done that? How could I not have noticed? I wanted to remember it all, every detail. And I would. Or so I thought. The rain, the red caps of the porters, the din of feet, and spark of flint lighters, and crying and crying and crying. Yet I hadn't seen Edward remove his hat. I wasn't watching. And now he was watching me, looking down at me, into me, and his lips were on mine. I drank him in as though for the last time. He squeezed me, crushed my body against his so I couldn't breathe. He was breathing for the both of us. "I love you." I heard myself say it but I must have been the only one. I wasn't even sure I'd said it or if it was the rain on the roof.

"I love you," Edward said. "I always will, no matter where you are."

"Aboard!"

I said it again — "I love you" — but it was drowned out by the calls, by the hiss of brakes and catching of metal. Standing on the step and holding to the train's door, Edward disappeared into a cloud of steam.

Chapter Nineteen

Clouds folded over themselves like Mother's quilts and still the rain came in sheets. I walked without knowing where, my clothes becoming soaked until I felt my stockings grow heavy, tugging at their garters. Porters offered me umbrellas, businessmen their cabs. I ignored them.

Only minutes earlier I'd clung to Edward's hand like a schoolgirl as he led me through the suffocating crowd pushing toward trains, toward exits, toward loved ones waiting with open arms. Now I wandered, aimless and rudderless. The streets were slick and glistened beneath streetlamps, their white reflections reaching for the opposite curb. Standing at the window of the Timeless, I peered through rain-streaked glass at diners inside. Everywhere there were couples and groups laughing, eating, sipping the coffee I'd thought so bitter. I'd never felt so alone as I did in that moment. I had never felt that I'd made a mistake so big that it would take a piece from my middle. My focus shifted so I glimpsed my reflection in the window and it was a face I didn't recognize. I'd spent an hour on my hair that morning, nearly making Edward late for his train, and yet it hung limply, plastered against my forehead smudged with soot. Makeup ran from my eyes, casting ghastly shadows and running to my neck where it stained the collar of my shirt. I didn't recognize myself. I was a stranger echoing the hollowness inside.

Back in Mourning I had hugged Mother goodbye on the front porch, pulling her close. Over her shoulder I could see Daddy's grave beneath the shade oak. Mother smelled like the house, it was in her hair and on her clothes — apples and allspice. Lizzie had been baking all day, keeping her hands busy in flour and eggs, her mind occupied with pinches and teaspoons. We'd said our goodbyes. I slipped into her small bedroom in the back of the house, a walled-in corner of the sleeping porch, and we held each other like sisters. I tried not to cry. Standing on the other side of the bedroom door, I'd told myself not to cry, but the truth was she was what I would miss the most. Lizzie was my home. Covered in flour and with skin hot from the oven, she was home.

"Don't you cry, Amelia."

"I'm not."

But I had. I spent so much energy projecting myself into Grandmother's vision of the future and fretting over when a man might hurt me, when he might leave — I was determined not to let it get inside of me and turn me inside out — the prospect of leaving that house of women hadn't even factored into my being. But I was *of* them. It didn't anger me; it upset me. I'd hidden away to hold my best friend, to feel her warm black cheek against my own, and hear our mingled blood coursing through my ears. It was wrong, scampering under the door like a mouse just to be with my family. There was no shame, nor should there have been. Nor should my affection for Lizzie have been hidden away. "She is not your kin," Grandmother had said. Guilt would forever wrack my brain and heart.

I'd hugged Grandmother in the parlor where the old woman sat fingering her Bible enveloped in dust and age, and I'd held Mother there on the porch in full sun. Mr. Cooper pulled into the drive in the postmaster's Jeep, his pride and joy built in New Orleans for the war, painted canary yellow by Cooper himself, to carry me to the depot.

The night Edward left Memphis, I sat in my barren room, my new home, alone. In my posture and my being, I saw Grandmother and Mother as they'd sat in the swing that hung from the tree over Daddy's grave. Hugging my stomach, I rocked myself, unprepared for loneliness. My suitcase had been delivered from the Chisca but I had no interest in opening it and seeing the things I'd worn on my wedding day, on my wedding night. I had no interest in unpacking those memories and facing my freedom, the exact freedom that was so like what Lizzie had wished for yet was so different in reality. So I sat with rainwater pooling on the floor beneath me. I took Mr. Cooper's handkerchief to catch a tear at the corner of my eye. In a vase on the windowsill was a single red rose Edward had asked the German woman to leave. Just past the flower, the only dot of color in the otherwise sepia room, out the window and down a grassy slope, was a motel. It was where Edward and I would have stayed when we first arrived in Memphis had we not lost our money. I watched through the night as visitors came and went, everyone eventually disappearing behind their own closed doors.

MAIN STREET

Chapter Twenty

"It wasn't forty days and forty nights of rain, but I assure you, Mr. Severs, it was biblical." He shifted in his seat and glanced at the voice recorder between them. Amelia pulled a tissue from the sleeve of her housecoat. They'd become like a married couple — or mother and child, at any rate — in a short time. "The river swelled over its bank and buildings all around were washed in watercolor reds, yellows, and blues. And I was alone in a one-room boarding house regretting my decision to stay. I was sure I'd made a mistake. At my age now, when I look back at the young woman sitting at a table set for two, water dripping from her hair, elbows, and the tip of her nose, as though her very insides were leaking through her skin, I pity her. I do. And I hate that for that young woman and this old one. It was the most alone I'd ever been. I feared the loneliness might eat me alive. Have you ever felt so lonely and lost, Mr. Severs? No? I can tell you, it gives you the time and space to second guess every decision you've ever made. It gives you time to wonder if you ever had any control over any decisions at all in the first place. In the hours, days, weeks after Edward left, in my solitude, I examined every inch of my character to try and understand just who this new girl — this Amelia Thorn — was."

Chapter Twenty-One

Produce Stand, Blind Woman
Main Street, Memphis. 1942

Kodak film instaprint, 7.62 x 12.7 cm
(3 x 5 in.)

From the artist's private collection.

It was a week or more — time had become timeless — before I needed air and stepped through the front door to find a new world at my feet. The rain had stopped and the sun was out and my new world was South Main Street — from the train station to the south stretching to the Chisca Hotel on the north — a half-mile, the distance from the Reynolds' front gate to the barn and meadow was a longer walk. The buildings were short and narrow and lined the street at the sidewalk like the spines of books on a shelf. The hotel and train station stood as bookends rising into the sky like sentinels to watch over the activities on the street. Storefronts, with inviting windows, drew me into scenes unfolding within — a couple sitting at a small table to enjoy a dessert and each other, a woman with her child shopping among colorful displays of stationery, linens, kitchen utensils, and shoes. Every address made up a patchwork quilt of doors and window trimmings, awnings and brick. I ate in the cafés and browsed in the stores. There was music Grandmother had warned against, but which quickly became the soundtrack to my days. I wandered among the people and came to know them intimately. More, I came to think of them — the lawyers, bartenders, shop owners, porters, washerwomen, and whores — as family. They claimed a place in my life and are still with me.

I wished to be the writer that Edward was so I might share with him the stories unfolding — disputes over property lines, lovers arguing and reconciling, drunks tossed out and arrested, a dog stealing ham from the butcher. I tried to put the feel of the street and the emotions I was going through into letters. I filled page after page with the names of people I'd met, their situations, the things I'd seen and overheard. He would have no context, I knew, other than the few days we'd spent together here, so I included photos as footnotes to better illustrate my new life. I suppose, looking back, I was trying to make Memphis seem as much of a home to him as it was to me. I described my attempts to make the tiny room where I lived into a home with paragraphs that ran longer and deeper than the apartment itself. I wrote to him of mundane things — hand towels I bought, curtains, how the table at which I sat had one leg shorter than the others so it wobbled with each page I turned.

On that table were fresh flowers, a luxury I permitted myself. They were bought from Tony Podesta's produce cart between the Wagenschutz Bakery and Phillips' Stationer. The Podestas had a truck farm to the north of town in Frayser (an area I wasn't wholly sure about, either where it was or if it was its own city). Each morning, Tony's old Ford truck rattled down Main and stopped in front of his stand and, when the truck rattled away again, the sidewalk was filled with the greens, reds, purples, oranges, and yellows of his labor. The most beautiful and sweet-smelling flowers I'd ever seen framed the cart, bees and butterflies added to the canvas.

"Beautiful bunch today, Tony."

"Thank you, dear. You take what you like, I throw in a cabbage. One cabbage for you, Miss Amelia."

"What would I do with so much cabbage? It's only me."

"Maybe you find a man," the old woman said. Tony's mother sat beside the stand in a worn easy chair Tony loaded up every morning and night into his truck with his wares. She was blind and claimed to know only Italian yet offered her opinion in English when it suited her. She was consumed by the notion I didn't have a husband at my age.

"I don't need to find a man, Mrs. Podesta, I'm married. My husband, Edward, is in the Pacific right now."

"Eh?" she shrugged, suddenly unclear of the language, and turned her unseeing eyes back to the rosary she worried with arthritic fingers.

As friendly and exciting as the days could be, the nights were just the opposite. Loneliness took over as the sun dipped behind the boarding house and the motel at the bottom of the hill outside my window became swallowed up by the purple sky. Sometimes, when the quiet in my room threatened madness, I would show my memories in and ask them to take a seat. Then I held conversations with Edward or Mother or Lizzie. They weren't there, of course, but I needed to hear my voice and reassure myself I was alive. Sleep would eventually come and, with it, spectral images of Mother and Grandmother beseeching me to return to Mourning.

Though I might have considered going back to Mississippi, it never occurred to me to go on to California. Edward wasn't there. He'd shipped off into the Pacific — to "an unknown destination," as he'd written — so there was nothing for me on that coast. California might have been Mars, a no-man's land left harsh and inhospitable with a population I couldn't know.

His checks continued to find me at the boarding house and it was enough for me to live, keeping me relatively comfortable in that uncomfortable room. But something I learned about myself in the quiet time after Edward left is I had no interest in being kept. And that's just what I'd become — kept — an unlikely princess in her turreted cell. I wanted to work and make my own way in the world as Eleanor had, and with the independent streak Daddy left me.

By the last day of my first month alone, I'd had enough of measuring time against the death of a rose on the windowsill. I gathered myself up and walked down to the Timeless Café to ask Charlie for work. Oh, I was full of steam as I stepped onto the sidewalk and turned toward the restaurant. I marched — I believe I actually marched — waiting impatiently for traffic and the light to change, tapping my foot and thrumming my fingers on my thigh the while, until finally I continued my parade across the street and right up to the door. In the little entrance vestibule with its tiled floor beneath the neon TIMELESS sign, though, I halted. I was seized with panic. I'd been so full of ambition, so full of myself as I fussed with my hair in the smudged mirror and applied lipstick and gathered up my purse, that I hadn't considered what I might say, how I might present myself, what my qualifications might be. An image of Mother flashed through my mind. Would any businessman have hired such a quiet, timid field mouse? Why would one hire me? Then I conjured the face of Eleanor with dancing green eyes beneath fire, her knowing grin, the fierce lines of her forehead that bespoke wisdom and concern. I took the confidence of Eleanor into the café with me and right up to the lunch counter.

"Table for one?" the waitress said, pulling a menu from below.

"A job," I answered, holding my chin up the way I thought a confident woman might. It was pejorative, I see now. It was as though I were daring that poor, young girl to deny me a job.

"Pardon?"

"I need one." I wasn't making sense. It must have seemed to those around me that I was suffering a stroke right there at the lunch counter. I felt the eyes of diners on me. "I can work," I stammered, too loudly.

"Would you like to speak with Mr. Z?" she finally, compassionately, asked me.

It's funny now to think of how scared I was, how unsure I was that morning. Charlie asked me about my experience, asked if I'd ever waited tables in a dining establishment before. I'd been waited on my entire life by Mother, Grandmother, Lizzie, and Edward. "No," I said. He waved my answer away and told me I would start work that day and that he would be my first customer, ordering coffee with heavy cream. And then he made me sit and drink with him.

Chapter Twenty-Two

So much has happened to me since the day I began working at the Timeless and I'm not the same woman I was then. Was I a woman at all? When I cast my mind's eye back to that scene with Charlie, I see a girl, barely a month removed from my grandmother's house, from the watchful gaze of Mother: two women who couldn't look after themselves charged with raising a girl into a woman in a world that was changing by the day. Where would I be now had I stayed? What would the rural life have brought me up to be? Mrs. Bowers, the Mourning Public Library librarian, had ten children — most in Mourning felt duty-bound to reproduce as quickly and as prodigiously as possible — and yet I'd never seen one of them in the library.

"They ain't smart, either," I said to Lizzie one day as we snapped peas at the kitchen table.

She did most of the work, I spent much of the time looking out the window and talking.

"Why you say that?"

"Can't read. And the librarian's children, too. Ain't no way they know about irony."

"That don't make 'em dumb."

"Don't make 'em smart."

Lizzie snatched up the bowl and scooped piles of beans — snapped and unsnapped — into it. "Go on and get your bath now. Go on! Get!"

I had no idea what had set Lizzie off like that. I sat in the bath and recounted the conversation again and again, until the water went cold and my fingers wrinkled like raisins. Lizzie didn't even know the Bowers children as far as I knew, as colored folks weren't let into the library.

That night, once I'd gone to bed and turned out the light, Lizzie pushed the door open and eased into my room. "Amelia," she whispered. "You asleep?"

"No."

"Wanted to offer my apologies." The moonlight coming through the window cut Lizzie in half so I might never completely know her. The words seemed to come from the night.

"What for?"

"Earlier, when we was snapping beans and you talked about them kids, calling 'em dumb cause they can't read?"

"Yeah."

"Amelia?"

"Yeah?"

"I can't read neither."

She didn't ask, but I started teaching her to read the very next day. First by my reading to her under the pretense I needed to practice for school, then by letting her read along and teaching her the alphabet at the same time. I was sensitive to Lizzie not being embarrassed. She was full of pride, even as she cooked and cleaned for a house full of white women who were certainly capable of cooking and cleaning for themselves. I realized the next morning, as I read Louisa May Alcott aloud and Lizzie cooked breakfast, that I'd never seen Lizzie using a recipe or looking through a cookbook even though they lined an entire shelf in the kitchen. She was smart and resourceful and a quick study, and it wasn't long before she could read basic sentences with confidence. It made me feel good, I felt maybe we were equals, though I still looked up to her like an older sister.

She stayed home nights for weeks after that first lesson, choosing reading over going out. I would sit on the roof outside my bedroom window, waiting to see Lizzie run off into the night, her dress hem shortened and holding shoes by her fingers. I could hear music from the car radio at the end of the driveway, but after a time it would drive off without Lizzie. Instead, a rectangle of light spread from her bedroom window onto the ground below. She stayed up late practicing the alphabet and the words in books I'd lent her. She practiced at copying words onto brown butcher paper that had held pork chops and lamb shank only hours before. The letters she sent me later were only slightly neater than those early exercises.

My dear Amelia,
I wonder how you are doing in Memphis Tennessee? I can say it was a shok when you wrote to say youd be staying put in Memphis. But then it was not all at the same time. you always was a strongheded gurl. how is it? you must tell. are the peeple nice? are they many? I do not know how you do it. evrything here is just the same. grandmother is as sour as ever, a bitter old women. what is it makes her so bitter? she has a big house and money far as i can tell. she does not lift a finger i can tell you that much. your ma sits by the window most days just staring out. if the weather is nice shill sit outside on the porch. she just stares there to. do not know what it is she waits on. you? your pa? somebody we do not no. you stay there in Memphis, Amelia. nothing for you here. any word from mister Edward yet? i hope he is safe and sound. i cannot imajin what the oshun is like. you have seen it, i have not. maybe I'll find a book on it altho old missus

Bowers does not like me coming round the library. i do not think she cares much for colords. i will ask mister Cooper to look for me. mister cooper asks after you all the time. i will tell him you sed hello. you take care of yorself my dear Amelia. miss you like a sister.
Lizzie

Thank God I had Lizzie. Dear Lizzie. She watched over all of us. I've missed her and wish that I could see her again, make it up to her for the fact that she was treated as less than family in our home. As less than a woman. I wonder at how different she would look from when we sat and talked in the kitchen and giggled at night in her bedroom. She's an old woman now, like me. But a mother, a grandmother many times over, and a great-grandmother at the end. A tree blossomed in Mourning, its branches heavy with the fruit of my dear Lizzie.

Chapter Twenty-Three

During the Great Depression I traveled with Daddy to Pascagoula, on the Mississippi Gulf Coast, to see if there might be some work in the shipyard for the men of Mourning. I was seven years old. Cotton prices had plummeted that year and the farmers were beat, having a hard time making ends meet. It bled over into town where merchants saw goods sit on their shelves, covered in dust and going bad. People were scared. My family felt the pinch, too, as the weight of the farm bent Daddy's shoulders. He hadn't wanted any of it, I knew that, I could sense it even at my young age and see it in his tired eyes and the resignation in his gait when he left the house in the morning, returning at dusk weary and dust-covered.

So we made that trip, he and I, to see if there might be something to be done while the government went about its plans to make the country whole again. I remember standing on the dock of the shipyard as Daddy talked to the foreman in his glass-walled office. I leaned back, looking up at the towering gray whale, all metal and might above me. The country was gearing up for a war of which it wasn't yet aware. It would be more than a decade before that ship I gazed up at would carry young sailors to the Pacific Ocean. Edward would be aboard it when it did. The sun was harsh and I shielded my eyes and squinted up at men hanging over the sides like spiders, suspended on ropes swaying in the breeze. They were shirtless and tanned a deep brown, their arms and chests strong and spotted with the gunmetal gray they slathered on the hull. From where I stood I could hear their calls, whistles, and laughter falling on me like rain. The sounds became confused with those of gulls floating low in the sky, waiting for the men to flick their cigarette butts to the water below.

I would never see anything like that towering ship again until years later when I stood on cobblestones lining the harbor banks of Memphis with the Mississippi River lapping at its moss-slicked surface and gazed up at the riverboats docked there. Those boats, with their stilled paddles and gleaming black calliopes, were as tall as the Mourning Public Library's turreted tower and, when I turned to look up the bluff at Cotton Row, the blocks-long hedge of buildings that was the center of the cotton-trading world, it was again like looking up at that great, gray battleship. That day in Memphis, I wondered if Daddy had ever sent his bales to the warehouses along the bluff. Had he ever leaned against those brick buildings, smoking, and talking business with the men there?

Before leaving Pascagoula, we stopped at a tobacconist so Daddy could get a box of cigars. The shop was warm and the scent of aged tobacco and wood hit me in the face like a soft pillow. The shopkeeper and Daddy talked about the Depression, as everyone did in those days, and change was made. When Daddy asked a question, the man pulled a map from a drawer and unfolded it on the counter. Daddy followed the man's finger as it slid along a winding black line.

"What are you looking at there, young lady?" the shopkeeper said. I stood by the register staring into a display case, its glass cloudy and yellowed with nicotine.

"What is that?" I said. It was a black box with a peephole in it like an eyeball. The advertising placard behind it showed a jolly-faced boy looking like one half of Tweedle-Dee and Tweedle-Dum, the word Brownie emblazoned above his multi-colored cap.

Daddy bent with his hands on his knees to see from my level and I heard him mouth to himself, "Eastman Kodak." Then, to me, "That's a camera, sweetheart."

We left the tobacconist and rolled down the two-lane blacktop that wound through Alabama with briny swamps on one side and blue sky and water on the other. Crossing a long bridge outside Mobile, I tasted the air like broth.

The trip to Pascagoula was supposed to be overnight, but Daddy had heard all he needed from the foreman in the first ten minutes. "No work. Not for an entire town's worth of men." He'd offered Daddy a job, saying he admired his gumption to travel so far, but Daddy said no thank you. Said he was acting in the interest of others.

Before that, though, the man had asked Daddy to repeat where it was we were from and then repeated it back, "Mourning." He tipped his hat back and scratched at his forehead. "My grandmama's uncle was from those parts," he'd said, and spit into the water off the docks. Fish the size of a man's shoe swirled around that floating mess.

The name of Mourning was spoken like a hex by some, whispered from the side of mouths. Tales of bad luck had spread like a spider's web after the day those children drowned. And like any rumor, or lie, it grew in size and scope. Dozens of boys and girls had drowned or were crushed by the wagon and trampled by horses. Their bodies were left to rot, the parents too distraught — the people of Mourning too uncaring — to do anything about it. Some said it was done on purpose. I never did understand the logic behind that one. Regardless, with that much time passed, and that much weight given to an event from another century, people figured they'd be better off keeping their distance. Salesmen erased the town from their routes. Travelers willed their cars to make it to the next exit for gas. Even Mr. Cooper had to fight with the Postmaster General of Mississippi to get mail delivered. These were people with small minds and with a religion that catered to superstition. It was no wonder Daddy wanted to get away.

He drove east and for a long time neither of us spoke. I imagined he was thinking about the men back home and their plight, maybe about his own. I just watched the sun dipping to my right and knew it was on the wrong side of the truck. Finally I couldn't hold back any longer. "Where we going, Daddy?"

He cupped the top of the steering wheel with one hand, a thin cigar at home in the crook of his middle and ring finger, smoke trailing out the open window like a river boat's calliope. His left arm rested on the open window; it was nut brown, a shade darker than the other, and the tendons and muscle rippled in the onrush of air.

He pointed forward with his steering hand. "East."

I looked to the east. "Why?"

He sighed and shrugged and that's when he said, "Sometimes I just need to step out of Mississippi, Amelia, even if it's only for a minute." He looked over at me and smiled. "What do you say? Want to come with me?"

I was already with him there in the truck, but I smiled and nodded just the same.

Palmetto City was hardly that. Little more than a village on the edge of Florida, really, until the night a drunken local thought it would be clever to paint the word "City" underneath the hand-painted sign welcoming the world to Palmetto. It was linear, that town, a narrow swath that existed between the cracked concrete of the highway and the blue waters of the Gulf of Mexico. Its size depended on the reach of the tide every night. The white sand beach made a switchback, a comma in the state forming a small bay and natural barrier, a serene piece of water so full of docks and boats it looked like a city unto itself. A diner sat on a spit of land jutting into the bay and the beach was bookended on the eastern side by a motel. That was it. It was a hamlet somewhere between its sister fishing villages of Destin and Apalachicola, someplace between today and whenever.

Daddy got us a platter of oysters and crab legs, himself a cold beer and me a Coca-Cola from a bucket of ice, and we sat at a picnic table on the pointy tip of the comma. The sun was hot but a breeze from the water refreshed us and slapped the lines of boats against their masts. It was one of the most pleasant days I ever spent as a child.

We talked about nothing, really — what we saw from our perch, what we thought those men on the boats might be fishing for out in all that blue-green water. I didn't ask about the work at the shipyard in Pascagoula or the Depression going on or what it might all mean for Mourning and for us. I didn't want to invite real life to our lunch table.

And I don't think Daddy did, either. After we ate, I wandered around, looking at the small fish and hermit crabs that lived at the edge of the water. I dug in the sand and made a half-hearted attempt at a castle. I spit into the water to see if fish would swarm as they had back at the shipyard. I remember looking over at Daddy from the beach. He sat on the table part of the picnic table, smoking his cigar, and looked out at the horizon. The sun was on his face and I wondered what he might be thinking. I had my new Kodak Brownie camera around my neck, careful to keep it from the water, and I held it up and snapped the shutter at what I saw. It was the beginning of

looking at life through a viewfinder. Years later,
I would point it at the buildings and people of
Main Street in Memphis and wrap those images
in tissue to send to Edward to help tell the story
of who I was becoming. I think of those snapshots
today washing up on beaches around the world,
maybe even in Palmetto. I can still see the picture
of Daddy, the first picture I ever took. In his face
I saw those boats in the harbor and the fishermen
working their nets and I can recall there may have
been something more in his voice than just simple
curiosity about their catch. I think maybe there
was a longing, maybe even a hint of envy for the
men who would soon sail away.

I think, too, of the simple boys I'd come
to know in Mourning. My father wasn't simple —
he was smart and well-read, and I know he had
dreams — yet he stayed where he was. What is it
that makes a person stay where they don't belong,
do what they don't want? Why that plot of land in
Mourning? Just because his daddy had done the
same thing? Could legacy hold so much promise?
I thought it too simple. Seeing my Daddy through
the viewfinder that day, the sun on his face, I
became aware of his features in a way I never had
before. There is Cherokee blood somewhere in
our lineage, someplace far back from when our
people first made their way to the South. In many
ways, I suppose, it was diluted over the years but
for the face. My Daddy's nose was flattened and

wide, the same nose I'd see in history textbooks and in the mural at the Mourning Public Library depicting a meeting between settlers and the natives of the area. It was the same nose as my grandfather. Mine is smaller, that of Mother's people, though perhaps a bit pressed like a Reynolds. His was a nose I'd seen on someone else, though, and I'd never considered it until the day I looked at him through the camera, and I would spend nights studying the photo held beneath the light of my bedside lamp. I think that day was the start of my understanding, of my knowing the unknown, a secret washed up with the tide. It only registered for a second before washing back out to sea. In that instant, Daddy turned to me and smiled. It was as though he knew what I was thinking and could hear my thoughts. But his bright smile jarred it from me again and I only smiled back and nodded when he said, "Well, we better be getting home." It would be years before such familiarity again entered my mind.

On the drive back I watched the sun dip lower and lower, turning the sky into a painting of reds and purples. I must have fallen asleep because as we arrived home, bouncing up the long, rutted driveway, I was roused enough to watch Daddy through my half-closed lids as he cut the motor and sat looking up at the farmhouse. He didn't say anything or shift to step down from the truck, but only stared. A deep, cigar-rattled sigh preceded silence and kept time with the cooling of the truck's ticking engine.

Chapter Twenty-Four

Today, I'm an old woman, older by scores than my Daddy was that day on the beach. My face sags, my arms sag, my breasts sag. I have lines in my face that may not be as austere as I first imagined the wizened wrinkle on Eleanor's forehead to be. I try to walk upright, I do. I see my fellow senior citizens, whitened and thinned over time, walking with a stoop, and it makes me sad. I find them pitiful. So I walk as straight as my spine will allow, hold my head up and, yes, even jut my jaw the way I did that morning in the Timeless as I stammered through asking for a job. It's prideful, I know, but at my age, with my body and mind drying up, I think my pride is all I have left. That pride and the fleeting memories of all I've been through, a life that puts lines in the face and a bow in the back.

My body mostly complies with the demands of my waning mind, a feat at my age.

But my body has seen so much, been through so many trials of violence and loss and love. My tree doesn't stand so full and lush as Lizzie's once did. It was in the dawning of summer that my body blossomed into full womanhood, when life became a butterfly flutter in my belly that, I believed, could be felt all the way across a continent and out to sea where a sailor stood watch on the deck of a destroyer, scanning the horizon for the enemy.

The realization of what was happening came over me slowly after only two weeks of working for Charlie. I was not a very good waitress in the beginning, I might add. I'd been waited on by Lizzie for so long that the motions of serving others didn't come naturally. It was early June when I overheard Big Bobby, one of the cooks in the kitchen, talking about being short with his rent.

"Due today," he said. "Where the time go? Seems like when I ain't got money, first of the month rushes to get here. When I do have money, the weekend rolls by so slow all I can do is lose it all on dice and drink."

He'd laughed, but the awareness of the date sparked something in me. I went to the calendar hanging over the phone beside the kitchen door. It was from a kitchen equipment supply company and the new page hadn't yet built up the layer of grease that would coat it by month's end, making it hard to read the notes reminding Charlie of deliveries and payments due.

I took it from the tack in the wall and counted back through May's grime. The lateness washed over me like a fever. I dropped the calendar and tack, and Meredith, the waitress I had the clumsy exchange with that first day I'd come in looking for work, knelt to pick them up.

"You okay, honey?" she said from somewhere below me.

"Hm? Oh, yes."

"You aren't having another stroke, are you?" she laughed as she put the calendar back in place. "Mr. Mednick's lunch is up. Amelia? You want me to get it?"

"Get what? Oh, no, I've got it, thank you."

Chapter Twenty-Five

I walked to the river early enough to catch the fog rolling in from Arkansas, covering the muddy brown water with a thick white cream. It was a favorite time of day when there weren't any boats yet loading or unloading, so I inched my way down the slick cobblestones. Workmen leaned on bales and boxes they'd soon be lifting and throwing and sipped coffee from tin canisters. They watched me, a strange woman slipping off her shoes to put her feet in the water. It was cool against my ankles and I thought to myself that perhaps this was the same water that Edward floated on, though I knew that was silly.

Walking back, I was filled with excitement for the day. This was a new sensation and I thought it must be hormones, a secret of pregnancy Mother had never shared and I'd never read about in library books sneaked from beneath Mrs. Bowers' nose. My days were full of possibility and I enjoyed my work at the restaurant and getting to know the daily diners and meet travelers just arrived or laying over on their way to someplace else. I saw Edward and myself in each new face, and sometimes I would tell them our story. On days I didn't work, like this one, the hours unfolded like a newsreel and I wondered at what might lie ahead.

There was an old man at the corner of Pontotoc and Main playing his guitar. His right pant leg was pinned up above the knee where he'd lost that limb during the last war. I stopped to listen and thought of Edward and of what he'd taken of me when he left. The man's voice was as rough as the concrete he sat on and in it was more loss than just a leg. He'd come back from war to find he was alone and had grown even lonelier with age.

When you think of me my darlin'
When the nights are gettin' cold
Just hope someday I'll be with you
Watch you grow old

The man had returned with a soldier's heart and, though I was happy that he returned at all (of course I was!), his pleading voice and soft guitar made my longing for Edward all the more difficult to bear. I dropped a coin in his case.

I was late meeting Eleanor and Jean at Gerber's Department Store and Jean and I trailed behind Eleanor like the little girls we felt we were. Eleanor plucked dresses with purpose, studying price tags before returning them to their racks. Enveloped in her trailing cigarette smoke, Jean and I touched fabric and lifted sleeves and hems, but little else. The shopping trip was simply a pretense for us to visit and catch up.

"How are you feeling?" Jean asked.

"Fine. As long as I never stop eating. Soon as I feel the least bit hungry, I'm nauseous. So I don't stop. I have bacon in my purse right now." Jean laughed. "I'll probably gain a hundred pounds."

"You know Dr. Evans won't stand for that. I was told twenty pounds with Vivian and I stuck to it. Of course, it wasn't easy, not with Charlie's cooking."

Eleanor had taken me to Dr. Evans for the initial test. She'd paid for it as well, though I assured her I was capable. She wouldn't hear of it, nor would she accept I knew my own body and what it was telling me. I learned later from Jean that Eleanor had had several miscarriages early in her marriage (another reason for Mama Zaccone to look down her nose) so I let her make the appointment. And I let her pay. It was peace of mind for Eleanor and for me as well.

"Have you heard from Edward? Is he excited?"

"Over the moon. I could sense his joy in the sloppiness of his penmanship. He filled pages with plans for a home with a yard and baseball gloves."

"So it's a boy?"

"As far as Edward is concerned. He says he'll petition Roosevelt himself to turn the entire fleet around if the war isn't won inside of nine months."

Jean laughed and I felt low for lying to her. The truth was I hadn't yet told Edward I was pregnant. I wasn't sure I ever would. Why wouldn't I? I still wonder about it to this day. Oh, how many mornings I sat down at the small kitchen table to write a letter with the aftertaste of morning sickness still in my mouth. I wanted to share my misery and, later, the wonder of it all as my body grew. But I knew Edward had his own misery. And I knew just as I became comfortable with my body, he would be in discomfort. Newspapers shared the horrors of midnight submarine attacks and suicidal airplanes. It would have been inhumane to inject the promise of life into his fear when he had so little control over it. Or so I thought.

"And your mother?" Eleanor said, lighting another cigarette. "She must be beside herself."

"Oh, she is." And she was. Mother wrote to me about God's blessing and family legacy, and in those letters I could hear Grandmother's voice. But the joy within those scented sheets of paper was tempered, I was sure, by her own anxieties of motherhood and her fear, not just for me as a mother, but for my child as well. Where Grandmother lived with an innate sense of privilege simply by being alive and in her station, Mother felt as though she'd never belonged in the Reynolds home.

Chapter Twenty-Six

Working at the café gave me more than spending money in my pocketbook; it gave purpose to waking in the morning and climbing from bed. It brought me out of the cell of my tiny room and of my mind, and into a world where I could talk and laugh with other human beings. And there was another waitress with whom I'd become friends. We were the same age and during the late-night downtime between the 10:15 from New Orleans at Central Station and the 12:35 from Charleston at Union Station up the street, we talked like girls our age. We talked about family and the boys we'd known and those that came in and out of the café. We laughed and carried on, gossiping about women we saw: nothing mean, but just like schoolgirls again.

Christine was from Arkansas, the same rural setting I'd come from, though of different means. Her family were sharecroppers, same as

Lizzie's, and picked apart the hardscrabble dirt of the Ozark foothills for what meagre food they could. To be honest, a pang of guilt shot through my sternum when she described the long winters when she and her mother watched rations dwindle in the pantry. Had Lizzie lived that way? We had so much in the big house — just the three of us — and there were so many nights I refused to eat creamed corn or a cut of meat that looked suspect to me. Were those nights Lizzie's people were hungry in their single room with only a wood stove to keep warm?

Christine knew hunger in a way I never had, which was why, when she met a man in Hot Springs who offered her a better life, she'd jumped at the chance. It was about the same time Edward and I had come to the city that this man stopped at her daddy's truck parked on the side of the road, just down from the baths, to look at the produce for sale. It wasn't much of a haul, Christine said — tomatoes, some melons, okra, and peppers — and what there was was sickly looking. But Christine wasn't. She was young and strong and deeply tanned from working in the fields. And though the work was hard, she was soft with a figure that would take any man's thoughts from produce to lust. He offered her more right there in front of her daddy and when she told me that, I couldn't help but think of my own mother in her parents' diner as they wondered at the excess of the Reynoldses' plantation. It must have looked like the promised land to them. Christine's daddy let her go, and she thought she'd found love.

The man put her up in a coldwater flat in South Memphis, far from his wife and family on leafy Peabody Avenue in Midtown. He was an important man, but she would never say who he was. "He works for The Boss," she said.

"Crump?"

"Says he has the old man's ear." I think she got a thrill out of it, the power. "Says he could shut this city down if he wanted."

"He also said he was going to leave his wife," I'd remind her.

"We'll be together then." She nodded, as if reassuring herself. "Live in his fine house with more rooms than a hotel. I probably won't need to work here then. He probably won't want me to work at all."

I suggested she move into my building where a room had come vacant; it was only a block away for heaven's sake and not the two buses she rode to get to work. But she said he wouldn't like that, and she liked her neighborhood, anyway. It was on a street called Neptune, and it might as well have been on the planet for its distance from South Main.

I shared Christine's situation with Eleanor one Thursday, that day set aside for lunch near her office. They were days I would recount in detailed letters to Edward, from dressing and brushing my hair to the walk through downtown to meet her, the food and lunchtime conversation, followed by window shopping or a movie if she had a light workday. I wanted Edward to know I was at home in Memphis, that I had tamed this wild town and, maybe, become a little wild myself. My worldview at the time was such that walking streets alone to meet a friend, greeting greengrocers, clerks, and sanitation workers by name might be considered wild.

Eleanor talked about work, and the business of cotton futures made my head swim. She sat on the boards of the Ave Maria Guild and a children's hospital, and had the ear of business, civic, and political leaders alike.

"Isn't that Mr. Crump?"

Eleanor leaned back to see the back of the room where, at a large round table, holding forth to a rapt audience of six men, was a white-haired old man. "That's The Boss."

"Who are those other men?"

"Could be anyone. Bankers, politicians, pastors, brokers, movers, shakers — yes-men all. When Boss Crump says it's time for lunch, those in his orbit find an appetite."

"A girl I work with, a waitress, is going with a man who she says works for him. I wonder if he's at that table."

"Going with him? You make it sound like a playground crush."

"Anything but." I whispered, "He's married."

Eleanor leaned back for another look into the distant room. "Doesn't surprise me. Men do as they please and for those men, well, the entire city is their playground."

"She shows up with bruises sometimes. I worry about her. She insists he'll leave his wife and that they'll be happy together."

"They all say that, honey. You tell her that's like waiting to catch a breeze in a bottle."

"Oh, I tell her. I tell her all the time. She says she'll wait and that he's really not mean, just under a lot of stress. I guess Crump keeps his men busy."

"Crump keeps them on a short leash and he waves his liver-spotted hand to make problems go away. You tell her to be careful."

I tried to talk to Christine about it. We sipped coffee as thinning crowds slipped past the window of the Timeless on their way from work to their homes and loved ones. We cried together — me for a husband gone and my "situation," as Christine called it, and she for a love she'd never completely own.

Memories of Lizzie and her plight came to me thick as locust clouds on nights when Christine and I talked. Lizzie had grown up beholden to a family that took her for granted and didn't respect her, all because she'd been taught from a young age she wasn't worthy of respect. The day Christine showed up with a black eye ("A stupid accident," she said), I urged her to get away. "It's better to be alone," I told her, "to learn to love again with someone who will want you all for himself, only you. He's out there, you know that, Christine. Look at these people walking by, each with their own life, someone to love, someone to love them back. Are they any different than you? No. Are they more special than you, more worthy than you? No. Go back to Arkansas, baby. I know it's hard there but go home and start again. Be patient and wait. You're worth the wait, well worth it."

I said those words to her, yet I knew I wasn't just waiting and I felt like a fraud. By urging Christine to go on with her life, I felt as though I were denying Edward in the same way I'd denied Lizzie back in Mourning the day I left and refused to hold her in front of Mother and Grandmother. My life *was* moving forward. In increments of minutes and seconds counted on the big clock of the café, perhaps, but it was progress. Yet I felt time should stand still until Edward was by my side again. Each sunset over the river, every burger I ate for lunch, every sip of wine or book read or movie seen, I believed was stolen from Edward wherever he was, in whatever straits he may have found himself. My hands went to my stomach, a new habit, a connection to my husband. It soothed my mind to run my palms over the cotton fabric growing tight against my skin. That simple action, the sensation and warmth it gave, made me feel closer to Edward.

"Go," I said, "and don't look back. Keep going forward, there's nothing for you here. He's not going to leave her, he won't. You know that."

Chapter Twenty-Seven

> **_Airplanes with Peter, Jean, Christine_**
> 1942
>
> Kodak film instaprint, 7.62 x 12.7 cm
> (3 x 5 in.)
>
> From the artist's private collection.

I'd grown restless and discontent to sit in my room or hold fast to the familiar blocks of South Main. So twice each week, Jean drove us to a local high school, out for the summer, where we sat at long tables in the lunchroom and hand wrote letters to servicemen. The U.S.O. provided items for care packages and we spent hours packaging chocolates and cards and cigarettes. The room was hot and stuffy, the large windows thrown open and fans brought in by an ancient janitor to move the humid air around. Heatstroke notwithstanding, the afternoons reminded me of quilting circles Mother held in the front parlor of our house. Women gossiped and gasped and laughed, and it was the most sociable I recall seeing Mother. I'm glad she had those nights, as infrequent as they were. They were a glimpse into the mind of a girl, one with promise and an eye out for opportunity. A girl who never got the chance to become the woman she might have become.

She would stand on the front porch and wish each guest a goodnight as they left. Once the last one made it to the gate at the end of the drive, Grandmother would pass judgment on everything from Mrs. Taylor's consumption of coffee (with an indiscrete tipple from a flask) and Mrs. Findley's husband to Mrs. Collier's baritone voice and even Mother's dropped stitches. The warmth of friendship and companionship was quickly whisked from the parlor so only the cold of Grandmother's stare filled the air.

But those days filling U.S.O. packages were all warmth. Many of us had husbands, brothers, or sons in the fight and the support of so many women put an energy in the room. I think Jean felt guilty. Peter had ruptured an eardrum as a child and it kept him out of the war. Oh, I know she must have been relieved — as was Eleanor, certainly — but it was difficult to be in a room with so many women keeping their hands and minds busy so they didn't go crazy with worry. As brutal as it is, war brings people together to care for each other — those in harm's way fearing for their lives and those left behind who lay awake at night and wonder at the atrocities of the human mind. I didn't want to be so distracted that Edward slipped my mind, of course, but the comfort I took from those women as we bonded over fear and encouragement was something special I would always remember.

One Saturday, Christine and I were both off work, and Jean and Peter drove us out to Millington where the old horse racing grounds had been fashioned into an airfield to train Navy pilots. We stopped at The Wayside Inn for a picnic lunch of meatballs, bread, cheese, olives, and fruit. And, of course, wine. The Venotuccis owned the hotel that once housed jockeys from around the country during race season and now was home to pilot trainees. The entire ground floor was a restaurant and bar where men in flight suits lounged about drinking coffee and waiting. The waiting of a pilot wasn't like the waiting of anyone else, they were on the ground and what they wanted was to be in the sky. It was much like seeing a bird forage in the dirt, nervous and hopping and always eager to take to the air. The Venotuccis were related to the Zaccones somewhere among the roots of the Italian family tree that forested Memphis. Mr. Venotucci hugged Jean as though she were a daughter, and then hugged Paul. And then he hugged Christine and me, and it was just as warm as Charlie's embrace.

We parked in a field, spread the blanket and laid food out until there wasn't enough room to sit and Jean had to pull another blanket from the trunk. We watched as planes of all sizes came in low to land and others took off. Some, when they came in for a landing, merely touched their wheels down and then, just as quickly, were back in the air and circling the field, at times flying so low over us the wine in our glasses trembled. "Touch-and-go," Peter said.

"Dear?" Jean said.

"That's what it's called, when the planes don't quite land and then take off again. Sometimes it's not safe to land or there are technical problems on the ground or with the plane and it's safer to be in the air."

I thought of the airmen in the bar and their fidgeting and looking out of the windows and up into the clouds. They didn't seem at home on the ground and I wondered if they felt safer in the skies.

"Peter reads everything he can on the battles — ground, sea, and air," Jean said to Christine.

"Will we win?" Christine asked him and it was such a sincere and simple question it elicited only silence at first, as though none of us had considered it ending, only if our boys would return home safe.

Peter lit a cigarette and smiled. "Of course we will. Just look at that firepower." He read several papers every day to keep up with the action and paid more attention to newsreels before movies than the feature itself. Over dinner at Eleanor's table, he regaled us with the advances and retreats until Eleanor told him it was enough of war and time for dessert. We all took Peter's word at face value. An engineer at the nearby International Harvester plant, he was the subject matter expert on all things mechanical, whether it was a cotton picker, car engine, or Panzer tank. Just then an enormous bomber lifted from the ground and banked toward us, casting a shadow that brought night with it. It was so close I could see the pilot looking down and he waved. I waved back. "Boeing's Flying Fortress," Peter said. "They call it 'Grandpappy.'"

We ate and talked and I took pictures of my three friends with the lowering planes in the background. As the fullness in our bellies and the heat of the day overtook us, we all drifted into our own thoughts. I imagined the planes overhead as ships and that Edward might be on one, docking at the airfield and running across the meadow to me. I closed my eyes and saw him as clear as I could see my friends. The tall grass parted for him and butterflies rose all around as they had in Mourning. I put my hand on my stomach and drifted into a light sleep.

It wasn't Edward I dreamt of, but another man. Jean and I didn't only help in the high school cafeteria. When the boys came home, damaged, they needed just as much care, if not more than those in tents and mess halls around Europe. The Marine hospital on Presidents Island cared for the injured as it had since before the Civil War when mariners on the Mississippi River, just a few yards down the bluff, became injured or sick. The hospital looked like a fort and Jean and I were intimidated the first time we drove up to its wrought iron gate and imposing brick facade to volunteer for the day. Inside the hushed hallways, we were shown a laundry room where we folded towels and sheets, red stains impossible to bleach white. It was even hotter than the high school cafeteria and I sat for a bit to rest my legs. "Could she get some water?" Jean asked the nun who'd led us to the room. "She's pregnant."

"Oh dear me, of course."

"Are you okay?" Jean asked, taking the water and handing it to me.

I wiped my forehead absently with the towel I'd been holding. "I am, just tired."

"Why don't you walk the grounds, dear?" the nun said. "Take some fresh air."

Here and there were men with bandaged heads, in casts, braces, eyepatches, stitches, and on crutches walking limestone paths that wound through the manicured lawns of the wooded lot. Military cars and trucks came and went, and everywhere were sentries with rifles slung over their shoulders. I'd made it a point to bring cigarettes and handed them out to soldiers along with matchbooks reading: "The Timeless Café, there's always time for a home-cooked meal." The men were grateful, yet distant, and I felt bad for them, not just being injured, but away from their homes. I asked where they were from as they lit their cigarettes. Norman, Oklahoma. Waco, Texas. Carbondale, Illinois. Joplin, Missouri. Minden, Louisiana. Edina, Minnesota. The mail these boys sent and received to their girls criss-crossed the country. But not one from California, I noted. "Well, get well soon and take care of yourself," I told each of them.

At the bluff's edge was a man in a wheelchair before an easel. He painted the river below and the train trestle crossing the river, heavily guarded with sandbag pillboxes and machine guns on both banks. I tried to imagine Nazi troops on that bridge invading Memphis from Arkansas and shuddered at the thought. I stood just behind the painter and, so focused was he on his work, he didn't notice. Or, I didn't think he noticed. "What do you think?" he said, startling me.

"Oh, I'm sorry," I blushed. "I didn't mean to sneak up on you, it's just so beautiful."

"Thanks. Hard to get the river just right, it won't stop moving." I laughed. "And that particular shade of mud takes almost every color on my palette."

"Well, it's wonderful. The blue of the sky and the green of the fields across the river are very lifelike. But . . . ." I hesitated to point out the omission.

"Yes?"

"Well, you didn't paint the bunkers and machine guns there at the river's edge, just where the stanchions are. Will they be added?"

"No, they won't. There's enough violence in the real world, no need to bring it into art. If this is art."

"Oh, it certainly is. My name is Amelia."

"Roy Carmichael."

I called him Roy. In the service, everyone went by their last name. I knew that on the ship, Edward was "Thorn" and he probably wouldn't hear his first name until he returned home and I hugged his neck and said, as I'd imagined him running into my arms that day in the meadow as the planes roared above, "Edward. Edward. Edward. I'm so happy you're home, Edward. I love you, Edward." This man, sitting in his wheelchair, his hip shattered by a grenade in Italy, didn't have anyone in Memphis to hold him and feverishly whisper his name, so I thought the least I could do, the most humane offering, was to call him by the name his mother would have. "Where are you from, Roy?"

"Palo Alto, California."

California.

An image of Roy and his painting was ripped from my mind as an explosion and shouts from Christine and Jean tore me from sleep. I looked up in time to see a massive bomber tumbling down the runway like a child doing summersaults. Wings clipped the ground and shattered and the fuselage spewed metal like a cannon. The sound was deafening. As the fireball came to rest, time seemed to stop — the breeze quit blowing, birds ceased singing, and I found it hard to breathe. Smoke rising from the wreckage was as dark and fluid as Roy's river, and moments later its stench was carried to us on the wind. When time started again, sound rose from everywhere — sirens and the engine roar of trucks and Jeeps poured from airplane hangars and from the parking lot of The Wayside Inn, MP whistles punched the air before a siren blast deafened us all again.

We were on our feet, helpless in the face of such chaos and tragedy. Christine held me, Peter and Jean held each other. It was "Grandpappy" exploding before us. I'd waved at the pilot as he banked overhead and he waved back at me. I could see him as clear as I could see Peter, as clear as my memory of Roy. My hand went to my face and I felt as though I might be sick. Indeed, my knees went weak and Christine helped me to the blanket. She took the camera from my hands — I hadn't even thought to use it — and replaced it with a cold glass of water from the thermos, but I couldn't get it down. Though it was a tragic accident, most certainly a mechanical failure or misjudgment by a novice pilot, it was the violence of war visited upon us in our own backyard. "Edward," I whispered.

"Shhh, dear, it isn't Edward. It was an accident. It's just awful, but it's an accident and it's far from us. We aren't in any danger, Amelia." Christine pulled my head to her and stroked my hair. Behind us, I could hear Jean weeping. She'd stayed behind in the hospital while I talked with Roy that day and told me later on the drive home that she'd held the hand of a young soldier in a fever dream as he'd murmured over and over, "Pull up! Pull up!"

"Plane crash," the nurse said to Jean in a normal voice, knowing the boy was in a morphine state and couldn't hear anything but his own dreams, his own fear.

And now, here it was. It was the sort of superstition we were well aware of — you didn't speak of death when a loved one was marching alongside Death. The bony hand was just looking for someone to grab and choke the life from, so why mention a name as a hint? Jean had held the hand of death, had soothed it and brushed a towel across his damp forehead. "There, there," she'd said. "It's not happening. It's not real. You're here, in Memphis. You're okay. There, there."

"Can't hear you, ma'am," the nurse said, writing his pulse on her clipboard and moving on to the next casualty.

"Pull up," I could hear Jean whispering. "Pull up."

"Shhh," Peter said. "There, there."

Chapter Twenty-Eight

Life with Edward began in a church, full of promise and love and the security Edward believed he needed from his faith and in his life before he left for war. I had no such faith and, with Edward gone, very little security. And no love other than that of friends and those I considered family like Jean and the Zaccones. Jean, though, was dealing with her own void, a hollowness that ate at the insides of women of that era as they struggled to fill gaps of time between taking care of husbands and children with little else to occupy their attention.

I had none of the comforts of Edward's religion or the attention of any man, so I focused my energy and concern on Christine and her situation. She was eighteen, a year older than I, yet I hovered over her like a nanny, watching for any signs of abuse. I tried to offer her security and hope, the same as Edward's religion had offered him, yet any promise of love and security ended for me, not in a church, but in a restaurant surrounded by friends and colleagues and strangers. It was in my fifth month of pregnancy — Eleanor and I had just been discussing a baby shower the night before — when an angel came to visit and put an end to this chapter of my life.

I saw him as I poured coffee at the lunch counter. It was an action so repetitive, so automatic, that I let my mind wander and my eyes danced across the crowds on Main Street passing the large, plate-glass windows. He wore a crisp, white uniform and caught my eye like a white-capped wave among a sea of brown and black suits. It was a gray day made more so by smog and the blur of speeding cars. I don't know why his sudden appearance felt personal, but my throat closed and I halted my pour right there in front of Mr. Mednick, the jeweler, to watch the angel in white stop and look down at a card in his gloved hand. I stood with the coffee pot poised in mid-air and Mr. Mednick watched it, waiting, as if in anticipation of that last drop of coffee falling from the lip. I believe he might have waited there patiently for me all day had I not set the pot down in front of him. The angel looked up again at the street sign, and then up and down the street. Charlie sat outside by the door where he'd dragged a stool from the counter, he liked to tip his hat to the pretty ladies passing by. He spoke to the angel and was shown the card. Charlie shook his head but the man nodded. When my old friend and boss turned and looked at me through the dusty glass of the door, I felt my knees go weak.

In the small office just off the kitchen, I looked up into the eyes of the uniformed man. He was younger than I'd realized and his bright blue eyes swam in liquid they could barely contain. Though his mouth moved, I didn't hear just what he said. His chin trembled. He handed me the card and held my hands for a moment longer than regulation said was appropriate. Against protocol, he allowed a personal item to escape his lips: "This is my first time. I'm so sorry." He left quickly and from where I sat I could see the kitchen staff quietly watching the scene unfold. All cooking and dishwashing and prepping had stopped and they were crying with me, even Big Bobby with spatula in hand and an enormous tear tracking down his cheek. Charlie went after the young man, I knew, to offer him a meal and hot coffee. He didn't accept, I learned later, and instead fled the restaurant into the murky crowd with his hat off and his head down. I don't know why, but my first thought was, *It's Thursday.* Christine had called in sick and I was covering her shift, otherwise I would have been at lunch with Eleanor and missed the messenger altogether. Later that night, crying into my pillow, I wished I hadn't been there at all, telling myself if I hadn't been told of his death, Edward would still be alive. Had we not spoken aloud of death at the airfield, the specter never would have found me at the Timeless.

Devastated. That's the only way to describe my frame of mind. And naïve. Who would think that no harm could come to her loved one in a war that consumed thousands of souls by the day? Only a young, love struck, and lonely girl. That's who I was. I was seventeen and pregnant, and all I knew to do was curl up in bed and cry until my eyes were raw. Day turned to night to day. I didn't care any longer how the shadows marked time in my room. I no longer cared to eat or bathe or read. Eleanor intimidated the German into unlocking the door and then implored me to eat. The entire Timeless menu was recreated in my tiny room, yet I couldn't bring myself to take a bite. "For the baby," Jean said, so softly and so close to my ear I would've thought it a dream had I not smelled coffee on her breath. I hugged my belly and searched for any connection between that life and the one lost in the Pacific. A rumbling beneath my palms at the aroma of ravioli, spaghetti, steak, and bread so fresh it might have been baked right there in my room. What pleasure I would have taken from devouring that buffet. And in the end, perhaps that's why I refused. Perhaps I should have refused Charlie's offer of a job or the conversation with Roy or a leisurely lunch with Eleanor. Who was I to take pleasure with so much pain and death in the world? How could I take seriously the choice of cannoli or cake when battles raged and those in them had little choice but to fight or die? I had chosen to stay put and not follow Edward to California; would things be different had I gone? Would he be alive today had he taken an extra moment to help me from the train onto the platform in San Diego? To kiss me goodbye among thousands of sailors on that dock in the West? Would the butterfly flutter of my simple movement across the country as we'd originally planned — *We discussed this, Amelia* — have been enough to turn the Zero a half-click into the sea, sparing so many? Sparing my Edward?

I wasn't being rational, of course. Tragedy buries logic along with the dead. I didn't want to eat. I didn't want to see Eleanor or Jean. What I wanted was to be on that train with Edward to California. I wanted to be on the train from Mourning with him, watching a little boy eat my sandwich, tousling his hair. I even wanted to feel the eyes of the other soldiers on me. I wanted to be in the meadow where Edward and I had stolen away and our courtship began. I wanted to be in Eleanor's guest room as a newlywed. I wanted to walk to The Chisca Hotel and into the same room to wrap myself in the same sheets in which I'd last made love to my husband.

Those moments were gone, washed out to sea and sunk to the bottom. Eleanor couldn't return them to me, wafting them in on her cigarette smoke. Charlie's oven couldn't produce the warmth of that first sensation of skin on skin. I was a widow. I was a child of Mourning, my legacy was loss and all I could do was lie still, weep, and wallow in grief.

Edward's body was never recovered. There was no church service. I had no one in that church — bodily or spiritually — that I needed to hear from. But I like to think that it's a small memorial every time I walk to the river and feel the water on my ankles and toes.

Chapter Twenty-Nine

I said Mother and Grandmother each chased Edward away when he first came calling back in Mourning, but that doesn't mean we didn't see each other or spend time together. We had those walks home from school and sometimes he'd sit within speaking distance at the library. He'd ask what I was reading and, almost every time, would say he'd read the book as well. I began to think all he'd done up to that point was read books. He'd take a stroll around the library, come back to the table where I sat, and slide a book across to me. He was training to become a writer. Some Saturday afternoons I'd be sent to the post office to retrieve a parcel or drop off an envelope. I would be out the door in a flash, anticipating seeing Edward there with Mr. Cooper, sorting mail, delivering packages, sweeping up, just about anything that needed to be done.

And then there were those few times we met just beyond the shotgun cabins of Lizzie's people and the tree line to the south, in a meadow of lavender and black-eyed Susans. The tall grass and trees kept us hidden and cut off from the world. Soft grass tickled my bare shoulder and the view of the foothills in the distance so pale green and gray with blue sky above reminded me of the mural in the courthouse. I can still recall what it smelled like when a breeze caught lilac and carried the scent like a kite and what the earth smelled like after a light rain. I'd walk along the dirt road alongside the house where Lizzie had grown up and I'd wave to the people there — Miss Della and Fern, Teeth and his missus if she was on the front porch with him.

Now, I don't say that what happened between Edward and me in that meadow was anything other than what a young, curious girl might get into naturally. No, I was a virgin on my wedding night at the Zaccones' house. But I won't say it wasn't a start, either. We walked and held hands and talked, mostly about his travels and stories he was writing. Sometimes we'd just sit and take in the view, feel the sun on our faces, and maybe we'd kiss. I did let him kiss me. He already had the faintest whiskers and they tickled my face.

Those times in the meadow were few, but I remember them now with great fondness and with a sense of nostalgia for the innocence of it all. It was the meadow and the foothills in the distance I was thinking about as Christine and I sat across from one another during a lull in the crowds at the restaurant. I'd gone back to work sooner than expected. Sooner, certainly, than Eleanor had counseled and then Charlie had expected. But I needed the distraction, the people and their voices. In my room, the voices in my head would not let me be, as they wailed and moaned about loss and love. I tried to sew, tried to read, but the quiet of the room drove me out. So once again, just as I had on the day I went to ask Charlie for a job, I dressed, fixed my hair, put on the same shade of lipstick I'd left on Edward's mouth the day he left, and went back to the cafe as though it were where I was meant to be.

Christine and I drank coffee and she smoked a cigarette, and she told me about the mountains of Arkansas. Her mystery man had taken her to Hot Springs for the weekend, telling his wife he'd be away on business. She gushed about the horse races and the hot spring baths ("We were bathed and massaged together, Amelia!" she said. "Naked as jaybirds right there in front of the attendants.") and the food they'd had in the finest restaurants. She'd finally had her time as the sole woman, the wife-for-a-weekend that she'd always dreamed about. And it had gone better than anyone could have hoped. I didn't see any bruises, no black eye or cuts. He'd behaved like a gentleman, she said. "He truly does love me, I believe that."

"Where did you stay?" I asked, trying to stay engaged though I wanted to tell her she should have just stayed there while he came back. Arkansas was her home, after all.

"Why, the Arlington, of course. Finest hotel in the Ozarks. Mr. Crump has business in Hot Springs and a suite at the Arlington at his disposal, so we took advantage. It was like a honeymoon."

"The problem is honeymoons never do last." I don't know why I said it. The way Christine's face fell told me it was as hurtful as a slap across her cheek. Edward and I never had a honeymoon. Unless you count our nights in the Chisca before he shipped out, we never experienced what so many married couples are blessed with. I suppose I resented her a little, spending a luxurious weekend in a beautiful hotel, massages, champagne, entertainment, sex for days on a whim. I never had that with Edward. I had a train ride, a wedding night in a stranger's home, and then the gift of a hotel stay with the entire weight of the unknown future in bed with us. And we had those moments in the meadow. I clung to those memories but Christine's tales of a Hot Springs weekend washed them out like house paint in the sun. I could sense the color of those moments, but they would never be as vibrant as they'd once been.

Chapter Thirty

I would eventually travel and experience extreme climates in every corner of the world, yet I would never know heat again like a Southern summer, pregnant, when humidity crawled up my body to claw at my mouth and suffocate me. As the days got longer deeper into summer, the only escape could be found outside where the chance of a breeze was worth the energy it took to load cars with picnic gear and drive out to the new Botanic Gardens. We never went to the airfield again to watch the planes "touch-and-go." The memory of the wreckage, the awful noise, the handsome pilot waving down at me as he passed overhead was too much to bear with news of war everywhere and my loss still so fresh. Today, the Botanic Gardens are in the heart of Memphis, but in the summer of 1942 we had acres upon acres to ourselves on the edge of the city. And we needed acres as the Zaccone tribe spread out, walked and ran, and played games of badminton and freeze tag. Charlie — never one to meet a stranger — found a groundskeeper to ask about pests on his roses at home. He admired the blooms of the garden, but his mind was on those climbing along his own back porch. The groundskeeper suggested chemicals and concoctions that left Charlie shaking his head. "Soap," he said, when he returned to our home base of blankets, lawn chairs and picnic baskets, was still the best cure-all. Eleanor lounged with a thermos of iced martinis on a blanket of her own, shared with no one unless she beckoned for a grandchild.

Jean and I walked and I held hands with Vivian until she grew bored with grown-up conversation and ran off to find her cousins. Jean pushed the baby in her pram, pausing our conversation every few minutes to ask if I was okay. "Too hot? Tired? Would you like to rest?" The heat was unbearable and I was surprised by it, having become quickly acclimated each summer as a child when I'd spend sunup to sundown outdoors. It was the pregnancy, of course, that I had not become acclimated to. Still, I was game to push on, but Jean seemed adamant we stop, so we sat on a bench beneath a sweet gum tree. "So hot," she said.

"Nice enough in the shade. I remember hotter days back home when we'd run out of the house first thing in the morning for the pond and jump in without . . ." I heard Jean sniffle beside me. "What is it, honey? Is it the heat?"

"Oh, no. I'm sorry," she took a handkerchief I offered and dabbed at her eyes. "I guess I'm just tired. We were out late last night. I'm just not used to it."

We'd gone to a U.S.O. dance at the high school the night before. I hadn't wanted to go; it felt wrong to dance and laugh without any chance I would do so again with Edward. But Jean had pushed and we'd spent the entire day before decorating the gymnasium and it looked so festive done up in red, white, and blue. Part of me just wanted to see the space filled with people forgetting the horrors and sadness of war for an evening and just *being* with each other. I'd asked Christine to join us, but she said she needed to get home, that there was cleaning to do and her hair to be washed. I knew she'd be entertaining her man. She'd begun to cool on sharing her plans with me, knowing I would just advise her to leave him. "He wouldn't be happy if he drove all the way over there and I was out," she said when I'd invited her to a film or out for a meal.

"Jean, look at me." She busied herself with Rachel, fussing over a bow she'd pinned in her soft, downy hair, but I could tell she was avoiding the conversation. "Nothing happened.

You just danced, there's nothing wrong with that."

"A lapse in judgment," was how she'd put it on the drive home the previous night. But wasn't that the way of women looking to fill the void where loneliness and life's meaning should have been? Eleanor filled it with a career, family, and quiet moments with a drink, and I had work and plans to raise a child alone. But we had no power, no leverage, and no respect outside of close family. I'd never even had that, with Mother's light too weak to shine on another. Grandmother filled her own void with anger and pettiness. Poor Jean had nothing but long days with babies and readying a house for Peter's return from work. But there were too many nights when his work or a poker game took priority. What did she have then? She'd walk around the corner to the Zaccones', but sometimes loneliness is better than in-laws.

So last night she'd had a slow dance with a G.I. And then she had another. Well, I say good for her. I watched her, saw the smile on her face and the way she tilted her head back to laugh when he spoke in her ear. And, yes, I noticed his fingers play across the back of her neck.

"How could I be so foolish?" she said at the gardens.

"I told you last night, you're not foolish. It was just a dance."

"It was three dances!"

"So be it. When was the last time Peter danced with you like that?" Jean gasped and I knew I'd said the wrong thing. But it was true and I knew it, and she knew it, too. The truth was, I felt guilty as well. I watched her dancing with that young man in his uniform and I, too, had a "lapse in judgement" — it wasn't Edward I imagined dancing with me at all, but Roy from the Marine hospital. It was silly, the man couldn't even walk on his own, much less dance. But it wasn't so much the swaying and embrace I longed for as it was that moment of laughter. Roy had made me laugh the day he painted and I watched him, and it had been so long since I'd had such intimacy. We hadn't touched, hadn't even come close, so intimacy is a strange way to think of it, but that's just the way I felt that day. And then later that night at the restaurant when Christine told me she had to get home before her man showed up because he wouldn't like it at all if she wasn't home when (if) he stopped by. "To hell with him," I said and she went to the ladies' room in a huff. In the silence that followed, I thought of Roy. I'd felt as guilty then as Jean did after the dance.

"He probably won't be around to remember it much longer, Jean. He told you he was shipping out today. That memory will die with him." She didn't gasp then but turned her head slowly from her baby to look at me. And the look on her face shook me to my core. I don't know where such a thought had come from or, rather, how I let it escape from my mouth. Lizzie would have spit on the ground to ward off the evil I'd spoken into the world. All I could do was set my jaw and meet Jean's stare.

"How can you say such a thing?"

I knew what I was saying and how I felt. I felt my loss deep in my bones and it worked its way from my stomach into my chest and out into the world. And the world was a hard and violent place. "What you did for that boy was a gracious and selfless thing. Try and look at it that way. He's heading into hell and you were an angel standing on the front stoop to tell him goodbye. You did a good thing, sweetie."

She pulled the bow from Rachel's hair and stood. "We should get back."

Chapter Thirty-One

Two weeks after that day in the gardens, Christine didn't show up for work three nights running. I knew then she'd gone. Though I believed in what I'd said — I knew Christine would be happier without the promise her lover couldn't fulfill, without the fear of spontaneous violence — I still missed my friend. It felt as though I'd sent her away just as I'd sent Edward away alone. I felt as though I were destined to be alone forever as well.

A week later I was working late when a chill ran up my spine. Something wasn't right. Big Bobby had taken the trash out and stopped to talk with porters on break from the station and sip from a pint. There was no one in the restaurant and I stood at the front window where Christine and I had last spoken, watching the cars and trolleys go by outside. Christmas lights were hung around the window and cast a red glow across the linoleum floor and on my skin. I could feel the cold coming in and shivered, hugging my arms tight. It had been raining so the neon and streetlights created a puzzle on wet asphalt. It fell apart with each car wheel, putting itself back together again in the stillness. I turned to see a man I didn't know standing at the kitchen door.

That fear might be allowed into a place where I'd always felt welcome and known only safety was unthinkable. I had my first cup of coffee in Memphis there in the Timeless and was shown the generosity of a city. It's where I was given a job and welcomed unconditionally into a family. And now I would die there, I was sure of it. Why I didn't run then, I can't say. The front door was an arm's length away and had never been locked, yet I turned to face my assailant, this married man so recently spurned by a timid, backwater girl from Arkansas. He breathed heavily and rainwater dripped from the brim of his hat and from his fingertips.

"She's gone," he said. "Happy?"

My hands went instinctively to my belly. "Who?"

"You know who, don't give me any of your shit. It worked with her, won't with me."

"Please."

He walked toward me, slowly. "Do you know who I am?"

"What? No." I lied. After my lunch with Eleanor where Crump had held counsel at the round table, I'd seen the man's face in the newspaper glad-handing and mugging for the camera. He cut the ribbon on new businesses, met with women from the U.S.O. and, they say, just as Christine had, he had the ear of Boss Crump. I thought maybe he'd even eaten at the Timeless a time or two and I wondered if I'd ever waited on him.

"Good."

Later, I couldn't remember just what happened, what else might have been said. "Big man from the kitchen heard the screams," I heard the paramedics say as though through a sponge. "Nearly beat that man to death before a cop happened by. Looked through the window thinking he was seeing a big, black man beating this white woman. I know Bobby, he wouldn't've done such a thing."

The nightstick Big Bobby caught on the back of the head was worth it, he'd later tell me.

Richard J. Alley

MISS INA

Chapter Thirty-Two

"Warm summer nights on my roof as darkness fell over the countryside." Amelia Thorn had drifted away from her living room, out the windows and was somewhere above Overton Park. She looked peaceful and Frank Severs didn't want to bring her back to the small apartment. He checked his watch.

"Amelia?"

"Oh my. I left, didn't I? I do that these days. I don't want to go back, I don't think, but it's beyond my control. Where was I?"

"On your roof?"

"Yes, of course. It was my safe place, I suppose you'd call it today. But there was one night I sat there and, across our garden and the horse pasture, I watched the light dance within the barn. The doors were open wide and the men who worked the fields must have had a number of lanterns lit for me to see it from where I sat.

Shadows passed back and forth, and I wished I could have been included in the fun.

"I sat up later than usual, so I was awake when a lone figure came from the barn and down the long lane that shot through the cabins. It didn't stop at the cabins, nor did it make a straight line, but was more like a moth attracted by light. It was a man and he weaved from one side of the lane to the other, stopping at times to look up at the stars. He was at the edge of our lawn before I realized it was Daddy. And still he weaved — across the lawn, stopped to pet Rebel, one of Grandmother's dogs, and up onto the porch."

"He was lit," Frank Severs said.

"Three sheets, Mr. Severs. It was the only time I can recall my parents fighting. Though it wasn't much of a fight. From the screen door and out into the night, I could hear Mother's voice rising. I don't know if it was his drunkenness that set Mother off or the fact that he was carousing with the field hands, though I suppose it was a mix of the two.

"The next morning I took a cup of coffee out to Daddy where he'd slept on the front porch."

"Put out, was he?"

"That's just how he put it and it was the first time I'd heard the phrase used to describe a creature other than a feral cat or one of the dogs. We sat side by side on the glider, looking out over the mist hanging just above the soybean fields. 'Guess I got put out,' he said, and then he laughed. Not out loud, mind you, but just a chuckle, as if he was letting me know everything would be okay. It's the only time I ever knew of that he got put out, but not the last time he'd drink with the help."

Chapter Thirty-Three

Christine is the only one who is safe.
The thought came back to me again and again like
the chorus of a song in the days following, when
pain and loss released their grip on my mind for a
feverish glimmer of lucidity. I've always allowed
myself to believe Christine did go back to
Arkansas to live in the mountains with her family.
Perhaps now with a husband of her own, tending
a garden and having cast the memory of
Memphis, long gone now, into the wind from a
hillside. She hadn't been there to see what
happened to me and I could only imagine how the
scene must have unfolded that night: an
ambulance screaming down Main Street,
swerving in and out of trolley cars, splashing the
last of the rain onto parked cars. A crowd slowly
gathering outside, wondering at all the blood, the
pregnant woman taken away on a stretcher, the
black man in handcuffs. What would have been

lost on the crowd, unseen the way a ghost might disappear into a solid brick wall, was the white man, disheveled, drunk, and only coming around from unconsciousness after his own beating, being taken through the back door, hustled into a car and secreted away.

Charlie was alerted and he and Eleanor had come running, arriving in time to see the last flickering of the ambulance lights and hearing its screams as it sped away to St. Joseph Hospital on Front Street. They would be left to clean the mess and wonder at what had happened in their happy little café. Guilt mixed with the aches of recovery later, when I realized they must have been beside themselves wondering what had become of me, carried from the Timeless into timelessness.

And what did become of Amelia Thorn?

Before he was carted off, Big Bobby was able to whisper in a train porter's ear, one of the young men he'd been drinking with behind the restaurant. That porter set in motion a string of underground communication that finally reached its destination: Miss Ina. The midwife took me from the hospital early the next morning as the sun began to catch the silver top of the river a block away. She stole me away to her brothel, a one-time hotel just over the bridge in West Memphis.

Miss Ina's twin sons were stationed outside the bedroom door. Each six-foot-four and three-hundred pounds, they took shifts and were told not to let any white men in, "especially if they look like they from the government." She knew Crump's men, once they learned I'd lived, would first go to the hospital before fanning out to pay visits to every midwife and doula in Memphis. Miss Ina kept me safe in her house, sitting at my bedside through a week of delirium. She hovered over me as a new storm raged outside. It wasn't the same rain that had brought Mourning to its knees or the same that had fallen the day Edward left me. This storm was all noise and winter thunder. Heat lightning exposed the room in flashes, exposing grainy newspaper photographs of tragic events. Unconsciousness washed over me and I slipped in and out of darkness, the black-and-white images fading as the air split and thunder rumbled through my abdomen with a shock of lighting between my legs. I writhed and arched my back, pulled at my thighs, ripped flesh beneath my nails. Rolling onto my hands and knees, I choked on blood filling my sinus cavity as the throbbing of a concussion push through my distorted face and into my skull. I bayed at the storm and the pain and the men who had brought me to that place and time.

Amelia Thorn

Dearest Amelia,

I thought I was prepared for anything. With my travels throughout the West and the long, dull commute from California to the Midway, I assumed I was ready for anything that might come my way. I was not. It was my first time aboard ship when those mighty cannons roared. Amelia, it is like sitting on a thundercloud. The ship itself jumps several yards sideways from the blast so that we end up to the side of where we had been. It reminds me of rabbit hunting with Cooper as a boy and the recoil of his .22. It's a small gun, a woman's gun, but as a child it knocked me on my backside. Nothing can ready one for such a blast, for the violence of it. At training, in Biloxi (those weeks away from you were torture!), we practiced our maneuvers, learning what to do in case we end up in the drink, how to stay afloat. We learned how to mop, for Pete's sake, Amelia! So, no, I was not ready and I wonder if I ever will get used to it. In a way, I hope I don't. And I pray that you never know such a shock, my love . . .

The pain was a searing gun blast and pulled me from delirium and from a simpler time. "Crowning, sugar," Miss Ina said. "Doing good now, you just push. You stay awake, miss?" Ina remained calm. She was a cloud, dark and foreboding, floating above me with a hand here, a glance there, nothing louder than a *tsk* from her crooked mouth at whatever it was she saw. And she'd seen it all before — childbirth, violence, fear. Yet each time was like the first, each birth the beginning of time all over again so she took something from each to build a wealth of experience and knowledge and secrets. She tended equally to my bleeding nose and eye socket as to my dilation and water. I passed out and Ina massaged. I came to and Ina implored me to push through it all.

I tried to stay strong, but I called out for Mother and for Lizzie. "This one will be difficult," Ina said in answer, and when a knock came at the door, she hadn't been at all surprised. Sweat stung my swollen eye and in the sharp yellow of lightning I saw the mountain that was Ina between my legs, a long fissure in the plaster ceiling far above me, and something else. A figure behind Ina — a short, white woman just beyond Ina's hunched shoulders. A specter. *Who's there?* I thought but couldn't get the words past my lips. I pushed, feeling pressure all over,

183

all around my body. Thunder, and with one final push, all I had left, I gave in and let go, drifting into the rain that had just begun to fall, hoping to be washed away as I'd been that day at the train station.

I slept for two days straight. The fever of childbirth and shock of violence took its toll on my body so I felt like a sponge wrung dry. When I awoke on the third day, my hands went to my belly where I found only rolling, congealed flesh instead of the taught smoothness I'd grown accustomed to.

"My baby." The words burned my dry throat.

Miss Ina shook her head.

"Where?" I was speaking through a haze of morphine and ether and whatever herbs and oily concoctions that old witch woman had given me. How old was Miss Ina then? She seemed ageless.

"She ain't make it." It was a whisper on the still-damp air and again Ina shook her head, closed her eyes.

"Dead?" I didn't wait for an answer, I was succumbing and felt the familiar pain again in my head. My eyes rolled back. I was unconscious, blessedly and compassionately unconscious.

Chapter Thirty-Four

In those days, West Memphis was a banquet of fast music and fast women, a Gomorrah for Memphians unable to have their vices sated at home. By the carload, they traveled across the Harahan Bridge on weekend nights, their wheels ringing hi-hat rhythms over steel grids. Eager, restless, they poured through the doors of the Plantation Inn and the Cotton Club to kneel at altars to brass horns, piano keys, and booze. Women lost their virginity and husbands lost their families on sawdust floors. Blacks, whites, it didn't matter, West Memphis — the "wrong side of the river," the clergy called it — was one place people danced and drank and laughed together.

Ina's clients ("Geese," she called them. "I hear 'em honking all night this side of bedroom doors.") parked down the street from the brothel,

185

around a corner, or they'd stumble in from nearby honky-tonks. The dog track sent flocks of them, winnings stuffed in coat pockets like so much batting. Others, those with real money, would bring a taxi from Memphis, more than willing to pay a surcharge for crossing the bridge. He'd have the cabbie drop him off down the block. "Here is fine." Wait for the cab to pull away before turning on his heels, tuck his chin into his overcoat, and walk a half-mile for his relief. I marveled that I never saw anyone from my old neighborhood of South Main. Nobody save for one, that is.

Miss Ina grew up under Miss Annie Cook's roof in her storied brothel on Gayoso Avenue just off Main Street in Memphis, raised on stories of "good Miss Annie" the way other children hear storybook fables at bedtime. In the Wild West-era of Downtown Memphis, besotted by yellow fever, she'd sent her girls away for safety, freeing up beds to take in the yellow devil's victims just as the Sisters of Mercy had. That selfless act, which eventually cost Annie Cook her life, nevertheless washed her sins away in the eyes of the public so she was feted in the press and by upstanding women's groups alike. "Savior," she was called. "A saint." But Miss Ina remembered her for what she was — a bold leader. As her moneyed clients hired whole boxcars to move their families out of town, Annie

Cook stood her ground and Ina's mother stood alongside her, her Haitian blood immune to the fever.

Much of the furniture in Ina's home — the chaise and loveseat, side tables, the upright piano, and even the four-poster bed I gave birth in — was from the bagnio of Madam Cook. When her saintly name was invoked in Ina's parlor, where the same heavy, velvet curtains that had hung in the Gayoso home (still smelling of jasmine, candle wax, and perfume), heads were bowed and the madam's name was spoken in a hushed and reverent tone.

During long afternoons, the front porch of Miss Ina's looked more like a girls' college dormitory with books and laughter, cigarettes passed back and forth with easy conversation. It was a sisterhood and there have been times in my life when I've missed those sisters and our time together. We waved at passersby and the men wanted to wave back, that much was obvious, but their wives hurried them along. Ina had her girls dress appropriately and sit up straight on the porch swing, in chairs, and up and down wide steps where we took the air and sun. This was partly out of respect for the neighbors (those who never paid her any respect, not even a nod good morning when she trundled off to market) and partly because "ain't nobody's business what's

187

going on inside this home but ours and our guests," she'd say.

I made fast friends with one of those young women, Betty Lou. Or Betty Ann or Sue — she regularly changed her name. "Only way to be who *I* want to be, when I want to be me," she'd say. The girls kept their Christian names to themselves, whispering them at night to float away through open windows. Mantras from the past alighting on ears miles, whole states, away. More than just our bodies, secrets lived in Ina's house. They ate with us, slept with us, bathed with us, fucked with us. Each girl had her own box of hickory, her own locked safe beneath a bed and dropped into hollowed breasts. Thievery. Whoring. Incest. Loss. Fear. Rape. Revenge. Disease. Murder. Actions spoken with secret names whispered on the wind. Only Ina knew all. She was confessor, catching the wind like daffodil seeds. And those secrets stayed with her to the grave, her discretion as impenetrable as the Colonel's rusted safe back home.

Betty reminded me of Lizzie — young, colored, and with distrustful eyes as though she'd seen things no person should ever see. I never asked Betty what it was she'd seen. In the South in 1943, the horrors a black woman might encounter were vast.

The girls called me Camilla and I was invisible and guarded, a fractured reflection of the outgoing and curious young woman I'd once been. No police came around and no one from the restaurant — no one thought to look for me in a West Memphis whorehouse. No one was looking for Camilla; the trail from St. Joseph's triage had run cold with the first step. It was Crump's man who worried me. He'd know I was alive, that I'd slipped from the hospital like a skink at dusk, carrying the memory of his face. It was in that shadow of fear and paranoia that I began to doubt Christine had gone away at all. I tried to tell myself she was free to make a new life for herself, but then I wondered if that man had gone after her with the same ferocity he'd come after me. Maybe he'd finished the job. Maybe the whole Memphis city government helped him destroy her and was helping him look for me, too. That was the shivering fear that took up residence in the hollow of my soul with pain and with my broken heart. And it's there that I lived for a year.

"Who's Thorn?" Betty asked one day.

The question shook me from the book I was reading, shook me to my core. "Thorn? Why do you ask?"

"You said it when you was down with the fever after the baby. Said it like you was talkin' about somebody." For two weeks following the birth, I'd been delirious with pain and fever and heartache. I slept much of the time but when I awoke, it was with the violence of a storm I'd come to know — one with the same wind, the same rain, the same light charging the air and everything it touched. Ina's sons tethered me to the bed with leather straps on my wrists and rope at my ankles so I wouldn't hurt myself or others. I had stitches still in my face and scalp, two between my legs, and three broken ribs. My face was bruised and swollen so I didn't recognize myself the morning I asked for a mirror.

"Man I knew," I told Betty.

"That man do that to you?"

I thought about my last day with Edward when he'd taken me so roughly in the German's boarding room. It was all relative, his gentle anger tempered by what would come later. "No."

Chapter Thirty-Five

"Girl," I was told. The word struck me with the full force of a train wreck, but that's all I was told. On the day I shook my delirium, I needed answers and I was strong enough to seek them. Let loose from my restraints, I jumped from bed as though shot from a cannon. Pain radiated sunbeams from my insides. I was wild like a river wharf Medusa with hair matted from sweat. I terrorized the home that morning just as the girls sat down to breakfast. I threw dishes and ate food from their plates with my bare hands. My muscles were on fire and blood ran to my ankles, yet I paid it no mind. The porch, that oasis from the goings on inside, that quiet refuge of conversation and lemonade and laughter, became a stage for an audience of neighbors.

"You came from the house like a gale force, swinging the screen door from its hinges, and let out such an unholy scream that cars passing by stopped to see if it might be the end times," Vicki told me later.

"She was just sad," Linda said, always quick to come to anyone's defense.

"Scared the shit out of me. Scared all of us."

"You pulled a cigarette right outta Jenny's mouth, pulled a bottle of rye whisky — the good bottle Ina saves for the geese — and swallowed a mouthful right off, spitting the next all over the porch," Betty said.

"True. We begged you go back inside, but you only laughed at us. Strange kind of laugh, too, not funny, but . . . like a witch. Called us names, laughed at us, blamed us for all your problems, your dead baby."

"We was scared to go near you. Linda scared she might catch whatever you had got."

"Not true," Linda said. "I just felt bad. I lost a baby once, too, you know."

I climbed on the porch banister, they told me, spitting at them and cursing. When Miss Ina came from the back of the house, drying her hands on a dirty apron, to see what the fuss was, it was with just as much force as I'd arrived on the porch. She looked at the street, at the people who'd never paid her home any mind now stopped and looking on as though a circus had set up its big top right there in their midst.

"You get down here this instant," she hissed, for I'd climbed up on the porch railing, my bare feet smearing blood along the white balustrade.

"I want my baby," I sobbed, eyes and nose running so my face glistened in the morning sun.

"This instant!" Miss Ina reached up and took a handful of hair, pulling me from the railing and into the house.

It had been ages since I'd bathed and the smell must have been something awful, though none of the girls mentioned that. Bless them. In a back room, just off the kitchen, Ina had been washing the girls' finery in a tub. Still hot, still full of suds and brassieres and stockings, she shoved me into it. Water and soap sloshed, I shrieked and begged, but Ina held me down until she could tear the clothes from my body. And then she washed me. I calmed down as Ina sat behind me, washing and brushing my hair just as Lizzie had when I was a girl.

Once I was tucked back into bed, hair still damp from the bath, it was Betty Sue (Jane? Ann? Lou? Who was it she wanted to be that day?) who brought me the little box made of hickory, its lid intricately carved with the sacred Mapou tree from her home in Haiti. "You smell like laundry," she whispered, her voice thick with accent and gin. The heavy curtains were drawn so only a sliver of moonlight made its way across the room. Once again I looked into a kind, brown face, wide and bright like the moon itself, half in darkness and half in light.

"What's this?"

"It'll help you relax."

The opium was sticky and black and nothing at all like I'd ever seen before. Its secrets nothing I'd ever known.

"Feel better?" she said.

"Like it's all just a dream."

And my dreams that night were vivid. Lizzie was there, and Mother and Grandmother. There was Daddy on the beach in Palmetto. I heard the click of a Brownie camera and he looked at me and smiled. Edward, in his uniform, was as tall and handsome as he'd been on our wedding day. Eleanor and Charlie, and even Miss Ina. They were all in the meadow where Edward and I used to steal away to spend summer mornings. It was warm and dewy, and everybody was covered in sunshine and butterflies. We were all so happy. Even me. But there was crying and I couldn't find its source. I wandered from the group, feeling the tall grass on my calves and the palm of my hands until it was gone and there were rocks under my feet. They were sharp and cut into my flesh but I kept walking. I had to find the baby. It grew dark and my feet were in water, then to my knees and finally up to my waist. I had to push against a current and darkness set in. It was streaked by a strobing light, and somewhere nearby was a baby that I knew I could save if only I could find it.

I slept through the entirety of the next day and when I awoke the following morning, Betty was waiting with her box. I was kept in a trance-like fog that took the edge from the pain in my head and the pain in my heart. When I was finally able to rise and move around, I found that gin and whiskey from the bar downstairs helped round the sharp edges. I never found the baby and I never again went back to the meadow in my dreams. I would still see my people sometimes, though even they faded with time.

Miss Ina was more than madam, more than midwife, she was a nursemaid to those in the neighborhood who couldn't afford a doctor, or who needed comfort in ways not always legal. It's why they looked the other way at the business she brought in. Ina looked the other way from my self-induced haze because she knew how close we'd been to the police showing up the morning of my ravings. If the Arkansas police had come, certainly Memphis would catch wind. And if Crump's men found out where I was, they'd shut Ina's operation down to get to me. If the drugs were what kept me calm and the memory of all I'd lost, all I'd been through, at bay, then so be it. Ina traded in discretion.

I spent long hours in the parlor, stretched out on the divan with a pipe or a cocktail in hand, and a book. There had been a guest some years before, a door-to-door salesman who spread his visits out, selling Miss Ina on a single volume of the *Encyclopedia Britannica* at each visit, then spending the rest of his time with a favorite girl. The set was incomplete — *A* thru *L* only — the man never returning once his wife found out where he was. Those twelve volumes took the place of the Mourning Public Library and through patchwork moments of lucidity and sobriety, I read them end to end.

The parlor was kept dark in the evenings with lamps scattershot throughout the room. Sepia light cast weak shadows over pallid wallpaper and bathed nineteenth-century furniture in dimness so its age was muted. It became my sanctuary, along with the chemicals, booze, and books. I didn't like the porch where I felt people were watching me and could know my secrets and read the sadness etched into my face. It was my sadness alone and I kept it in my hollowed heart and in a velvet-lined, hickory box upstairs.

Chapter Thirty-Six

Men came and went and, though I saw them nod in my direction and ask for me through smoke and fog, the cocoon I'd created for myself was impenetrable and guarded over by Ina, who shook her head, "Not this one." Still they stared as the young soldiers had on the train and I watched them go upstairs with Betty or Jenny or Claire. They always looked back to catch a glimpse of me where I lay, the fruit they wouldn't taste.

A young man — barely more than a boy — came in one night with a rowdy group of sailors. He was clean shaven in Navy whites and held his cap in fidgeting hands. While his buddies goaded and stood agog at the girls dressed in little more than gauzy silk and heels, he stared at his shuffling feet on the patterned Persian rug, unable to make eye contact with the girls. I took pity on him. I wondered if Edward had had time for just such a visit to just such a house in California before shipping off to his death. I wondered where this young man might end up. I took his hand and led him upstairs to my room.

He was nervous, of course, and a little sad. I sat him on the edge of the bed and pulled his shirt over his head. I let my robe slip from my shoulders. I hadn't been with a man since Edward and wasn't sure how my body, still aching from childbirth and the attack, might react to the physical act of sex. But I could see this boy needed something more than sex, he needed intimacy. He was a long way from home and uncertain in the world.

"Where you headed?"

"California."

"Oh." I was naked by then and the chill night air brought my senses, numbed by opium and drink, alive.

"Then to the Pacific."

"You'll be fine." He hadn't said he was scared, hadn't shown any worry beyond that of performance and the nude woman standing before him, but I said it anyway in answer to a question unasked. I held him, his face to my breast, and rocked gently. If I was his first (and he'd share later that I was), then he surely had no idea it could be so gentle, so loving. I was part lover that night, part wife, and part mother. I was tender and urged him to go slow, to remember the feel of my skin and my hips, my hands, and lips for later. "Take this with you," I whispered. "Where you're going is lonely and you'll want to remember."

Afterward, I held him, relishing the companionship as much as he did, as much as Jean had the night she held the G.I. at the U.S.O. dance. "He's heading into hell and you were an angel standing on the front stoop to tell him goodbye," I told her then. "You did a good thing."

Had I done a good thing? The act had been cathartic for me and was only the beginning. The men I took to bed after that night filled a void the drugs couldn't. I felt whole again and as though each one, with their rough hands (they were all rougher and more eager than the virgin sailor), scrubbed away bits of my past. Each penetration and act (I denied them nothing) worked to erase a small part of my memory, even if it was only for one night, for that moment. When I tired of men, I had the opium, the morphine, the dope that was readily available and whose smell became like incense throughout the house. "I spend a fortune on booze, don't know why y'all girls need to smoke that weed, too," Miss Ina would say, walking through the parlor and fanning the fumes with a dishtowel.

Consciousness was a valley in fog, a meadow at midnight where I couldn't see more than a few feet in front of my face, didn't care to see more than a day ahead. There were more men than I can recall today, and I try not to recall any before the last one. There were mornings I woke alone, wondering at the cash on my bedside table beside a puddle of whiskey. There were mornings a bottle was still there and I'd finish it before rising for the day. I never left the house, not even for the market where the girls walked with Miss Ina, or shopping at Goldsmith's or Gerber's across the river. I didn't go to the movies or to the Plantation Inn. The girls took strolls to the riverside and trolley rides on leisurely Sunday afternoons, but I wasn't a part of any of that. I remained in my room with my curtains drawn or in the parlor and within reach of the bar. Depression pressed upon my mind and being, and it began to show in my face where lines creased my eyes and mouth. Circles beneath my eyes grew darker and darker against my pallid skin. I barely ate, though Miss Ina implored me. "Not hungry," I said, chasing the lie down with gin. A very real hunger became part of the emptiness filled by men and chemicals.

Thoughts of the past, of Edward, became blurred and mixed, so I couldn't discern his face from the others who came and went from my bed. If I concentrated in the moments before opium crawled up my spine to my brain, I might see dress whites and feel uncertain hands, but it was the young sailor I'd shipped off with a whisper and the first taste of a woman on his tongue. It had been my first time for money, and I would shake it from my head just before the pinch of a dream took over.

Chapter Thirty-Seven

"Where is she?"

When bustling around the kitchen, preparing the day's meals for the girls, Ina was a hurricane of activity and scents with pots and pans banging and curses when something didn't go as planned. The oven was always too small, the flame too low, the produce not ripe enough, or one of the girls was in her way, stopping in for a taste of this, a bite of that. It was different than when Lizzie cooked. It wasn't Lizzie's kitchen and she knew it never would be, so she moved like a whisper with an economy of movement. Watching Lizzie, I thought maybe I could cook, too. In the path of Hurricane Ina, I felt my life might be in danger. So I stayed out of her way, seated at a small table pushed into the corner where I sipped coffee laced with rum. She had pies in the oven and the smell of allspice was the only constant carried forward from my childhood. I erased it with a drag on my cigarette and gulp from my mug.

"Who's that, baby girl?"

"My baby." I hadn't asked about her in all those months I'd been in her house. Ina said she died and I'd left it at that, burying my curiosity as best I could. But something nagged at me, fluttering in and away, and my curiosity wouldn't stay down.

"Dead. Told you that." She prepared three birds. Earlier, I watched from my bedroom window as she leaned over the wire fence of the coop, scooped up one chicken after another, and wrung their necks. They flopped and scratched in the dirt before going still. Plucked smooth, she slathered their skin with butter and rosemary, her dark hands glistening in morning light. A third bird lay beside them and got the same treatment though it was small and sickly looking even in death. "Look at that pitiful bird," she said. "Mr. Hobson bartered a half-hour with Jenny for that bird."

"Why's it so small?"

"You ever seen Mr. Hobson's sad, old cock you understand why he traded for that old runt bird."

I laughed, but my question hadn't been answered. I lit another cigarette, smoke mingling with other kitchen smells. "I know she's dead. Was she buried? Where was her body taken?"

"Baby gone, Camilla. Baby gone." She saw the fallen look on my face and her strong hands worked the birds with a fever. Her brow furrowed, worry creasing the smooth skin there. "My Grandmamma was a doula," she continued. "I ever tell you that? Back on the island. Back when there weren't no medicine, 'cept what we made, what we found in the earth and the water. Babies died. Died by the score, just a way of life, and nobody asked what became of them babies. Sad as it was, having them bodies near was bad luck, evil. So soon as they come into the world dead, they was taken away and buried.

"Now, Grandmamma tells of one little body born dead, come out blue as your bathrobe there, was taken and wrapped in linens and prayed over. But just when the men about to put that dirt on it, a cry came out. There was twitchin' and shoutin' and when those men — scared as they was — pulled that body from its little hole in the earth, it was alive as you are now.

"Sound good, don't it? Sound like a happy fairytale story ending? Well let me tell you, that very night a storm blew up. A hurricane came pounding down on my Grandmamma's village like to beat up the band. Homes wiped out, trees torn up by the root, livestock scattered, folks drowned. But that baby, that new baby lived. Mama died, though. Mhm. Mama died in that storm when a tree fell into her room where she give birth and been so sad when told her baby was dead then so happy when told her baby alive. She was right there in that bed nursing that baby when the tree come.

"Now, you tell me, Miss Camilla, how come that baby died then lived, but then its mama went and died? You tell me."

"Well, I . . . I don't know."

"Because some things meant to happen the way they happen," she thrust an oily knife in my direction to make a point. "Some people meant to live, some die. Lord knows why and *only* He know. That mama, maybe she meant to die, but so was that baby. Men should have covered that baby up when they had the chance."

Ina's story was horrible and if I'd had any tears left to cry, if my heart still beat with the same warmth and love I'd packed in my suitcase in Mourning before getting on the train, then surely I would've cried there in her kitchen. Instead, I shrugged. Ina saw it and she slapped a bird and put it in the oven, keeping a wary eye on me. I wondered if I needed looking after. So there was a dead woman, a dead baby on an island long ago. What did that have to do with me? Ina had her god to make sense of it all, but I had nothing. In that moment, at that table in that kitchen, I didn't give a shit why the wind blew one way for some and a different way for others.

Still, though, there was something about Ina's story that stayed with me. Later that evening, with a sweaty, wheezing stranger asleep beside me, I pondered over the island baby and why it had come back to life. Though her story had taken place two generations before, there was a hint in its telling, I believed. A spark ignited in me when she said, "A cry came out." Hadn't I heard a baby's cry the night of my labor? "Hadn't I?" I spoke out loud.

"Wha? Hm?" the man beside me grunted.

"Go back to sleep." Sleep wouldn't come for me and I lay awake sipping whisky to chase away the ghosts swirling around the ceiling above me.

Chapter Thirty-Eight

Days rolled into nights rolled into mornings. Consciousness was born in the shadows and the gray light of day did little to alter the way I saw the world around me. A goose finished, climbed from my bed to dress and I wiped myself clean. He didn't say a word, didn't need to, conversation wasn't charged by the half-hour. No sooner had he left than the door opened again. I dropped the crusted rag into the chamber pot on the floor. As the new man undressed, he told me to turn over onto my belly. It was the voice I recognized first. In the dark, the timbre and menace of it made his unseen face as clear to me as though the sun had suddenly risen.

I did as I was told, my heart beating faster and pumping an awareness I'd known only a handful of times through my blood up to my brain. An awareness of fear and the unexpected made clear. Daddy's death coming so close to me, bad news at the Timeless, the attacker just over my shoulder. The morning Lizzie sat at the kitchen table reading aloud while I stood at the counter making a pie crust. We'd switched places, though Lizzie would grow to be better with books and figures than I ever would at even the simplest recipe. I was enjoying the sing-song of her voice when she stopped in mid-sentence. "Sound it out if you can't see its meaning straightaway," I said, just the way Mrs. Milligan had said to those of us in the second form.

But the silence continued so I turned, my hands sticky with dough (I never could get my measurements right) and saw what had stopped Lizzie cold — a slick, black cottonmouth stretched across the floor. The screen door Daddy meant for Teeth to repair had stuck open again. I had no idea what to do, so I stood stock-still, my hands held aloft and trying not to breathe too loudly. Lizzie sat motionless, her eyes fixed on the serpent, her focus as intent on the problem at hand as it had been on the problem of sounding out the syllables of Proverbs only moments earlier. My body trembled and dough dropped from my hand to the floor. A forked tongue twitched. Lizzie, swift as that tongue, snatched a cleaver from the butcher block and in a single motion severed the snake's head from its body. I whimpered. She kicked the head away as though the two pieces might come together again. For all

I knew they might, I knew as much about snakes as I did pie crust.

Lizzie threw the snake pieces out the door and wiped the mess, then sat at the table. "You need more flour in that dough," she said, and began reading where she'd left off.

I tried to focus on Lizzie's faraway voice as the man entered me with an urgency, again and again until it finally shook me from my catatonia, from the past and the fear. As it must have for Lizzie, my fear grew into anger and I welcomed it. I searched frantically beneath the pillow for the leather hilt I knew was there. I kept it there for the memory of it. It was a memory as sharp as the knife edge itself, the one Edward had kept to remember his father and that he'd used to mark the passage of time when he wrote. "Turn over," I said, though my throat had constricted. "I want to see your face."

"I like that," he said. "No submission for you? Some cunts like to take charge, don't they?"

He rolled onto his back and I climbed astride. I took him into me again and he closed his eyes. Mine were wide. The moonlight shattered the dark across his face just as it had Betty's the night she brought me the first taste of opium. It was him, there was no doubt, the man who had hurt Christine. The man who had attacked me so savagely at the restaurant and, ultimately, driven me to this life. I'd feared that man for a year, never knowing when he might learn my whereabouts and send his goons to take me, to hurt me again, and kill me. That fear had kept me prisoner as much as anything else.

No more.

"You like that?" I whispered in his ear. I was answered with grunts and the smell of beef on his breath. "Look at me." He did. "Look into my eyes, darling. Do you recognize me?" He frowned, this fantasy suddenly turning real, too real for a man who'd done such bad things in his life, whose wife was asleep in their bed just across the river. I gripped the knife handle tighter. "Think. Remember back to the Timeless Café and the waitress there you threatened, the one you beat half to death. She was pregnant. She was me." His eyes opened wide then and he grabbed my throat. He went limp inside me. I had the knife out and at his throat, the tip pressed hard enough for a spot of red to show there. "Take your hand off of me," I said through gritted teeth, and he did. I put my face closer to his so he could hear me. "You took my baby from me," I said and his eyes widened even more. He tried to speak but I told him to shut up. "You took my life from me that night. You get a half-hour fuck for your five dollars tonight, but what do you think a life is worth? Do you know the price for that?" Silence. "Answer me!"

"I . . ."

That's as much as he got out before I pushed the knife into the meat of his neck. He gurgled, his breath coming in red bubbles and a stream of the stuff spewing from an artery. It painted the sheets, the pillow, my skin. And still I pushed. His eyes went as wide as they could before the light inside went out and a filmy gray filled the irises.

I rose and slowly, deliberately washed myself in the bowl. I dressed before opening the door and calling to the room across the hall where the door stood open, "Betty? Betty, could you send Miss Ina in, please?"

Chapter Thirty-Nine

In my last weeks at Ina's — before I became more than a whore and an addict, but also a murderer — I had begun venturing out. Not to public places, but I'd walk instead to the levee and down through the alluvial plains that flooded with the change of seasons. It wasn't like walking to the cobblestones in Memphis, but a slow wade into the water, my feet sinking in the brown, thick sand just so I could feel the water against my skin. Brambles caught the hem of my skirt and driftwood lay everywhere like old bones. Memphis was there across the river. It looked different from my side, quiet and distant. Some part of me thought I could hear the city beckon. A voice called; memories tugged at my body. Those walks began on a Sunday. I remember it clearly, the first day of real clarity since the night I'd been attacked. I'd heard of bodies washing up on those alluvial planes when the river ran low. Whether jumpers from upstream or victims dumped into the swiftly moving current, I never knew. I also never did know what Ina did with that man's body. One would have to assume it was the river that took it, but there were so many ways to dispose of a body in West Memphis, Arkansas, back then — buried, dogs, pigs, fire, or just left in the far-off country for birds and time to do what they do. I never asked, Ina never said. By the time her sons came to my room that night, the sky was already purple with sun. I was washed and dressed and had a gin at the bar downstairs.

It was the night of the solstice, the longest day of the year, they say, when I stood at my bedroom window looking out at the moon. It was full and bright and nearly hurt my eyes to look into it. I looked forward to seeing it against the water. I dressed and gathered a few things, my husband's knife among them, and left the house for good.

MOURNING

Chapter Forty

"And then you came back to Memphis?"

"Well, yes, but you're getting ahead of yourself, Mr. Severs."

"Please, call me Frank."

"A good newspaper reporter unfolds his facts in order," Amelia says. "Chronologically. Let's stay in lockstep, young man." Perhaps she is playing with him. She still has some playfulness left in her old bones, even at eighty-nine. The gleam in her eyes, she is sure, will give her away.

"I told you, Ms. Thorn, I'm not a newspaper reporter any longer. This is for *The New Yorker*. They give us a few more column inches to play with. I'm allowed to stretch my limbs a bit."

"Of course. Now where was I? Scotch?"

"No, thank you."

Amelia Thorn pours herself another sip or two and looks from the window of her apartment to the Brooks Museum of Art where

215

her life will soon unfold before a different, larger audience. She is an artist of some renown and, even more intriguing, of some reclusiveness. This is why Frank Severs is in her home for an interview. Does he want the whole story? He's asked for it and, whether he wishes it or not, he is getting it. Until old age seized her ligaments and muscles in its bony hand, she'd lived a life in the slipstream of the world and, lately, has felt claustrophobic. Amelia enjoys the questions and lingers over her answers — she feels like stretching a bit.

Chapter Forty-One

Ina told me to walk to the river. She told me to have faith. "Go down to the water, into the river until you can't feel bottom. Wait. He will come for you." To be honest, I didn't care if I drowned in the water that night or not. Things would be hot for a while, Ina had said. Difficult for her and the girls. "Men will come for answers." She'd disposed of the body. How? I don't know. For all I knew, it floated alongside me in the river that night. "But it won't last. Them men, they don't want the answers I have. He was a bad man and they know that. He gone and they will surely let him go."

I waded in, as I'd been told, until the mud and silt no longer touched my bare feet. It was a new moon and the night was as black as the water so I couldn't tell where sky ended and the river began. My only horizon was the lights of Memphis on the far side. I was so cold and I

kicked my legs to stay warm and to stay afloat.
Waves lapped at my chin and filled my mouth and
I spat and coughed, choking on the brackish
water. My head sank below the surface and I was
prepared to let go, to allow the water to wash over
me and fill my lungs. *Let it come for me*, I
thought. *Let the storm rage, I'm ready.* I kicked
and gasped, breathing in the night air. I cried. I
grew angry and frightened and felt so alone all in
the space of I don't know how long. I had no idea
how long I'd been in the river or how far
downstream I'd floated when a raft came
alongside me. A tiny black man with only one
arm, improbably strong, lifted me from the water.
I gasped and shivered and tried to thank him but
he shushed me. "Quiet!" He pulled in close to the
shore and pushed us along the reedy bank with a
long pole. His hand slid up the shaft, gripped it
and forced the tiny raft in the direction he wanted
to go. The lights of Memphis had long since
receded and with no moon I couldn't get my
bearings. My life was in the hands of this man and
I let him take me where he would. We floated
with the current, him steering and keeping close
to the bank, when he suddenly and jarringly
turned to the left, taking us into deeper water at
the swirling middle of the river. Out of the
blackness of the water rose a monolith, a steel
iceberg that I hadn't realized was there until we
were upon it and it glared down at us. The raft

pulled alongside and rope netting fell on us from above. My savior lifted me up by my arm and pointed up. I climbed, glancing back only to find he'd gone, slipped away into the velvet night. I climbed onto the deck of the barge and was led to a cabin where I was surprised to find a bag of my very few possessions. Left alone, I collapsed on a canvas army cot and fell quickly asleep in my wet clothes.

I don't know how long I slept. It could have been a night or two, or it could have been a week. The last time exhaustion had overtaken me in such a manner, it followed violence and childbirth. Now I woke in a still-dark room and immediately wretched over the side of my cot. My stomach was in knots and I vibrated with fever. Curled into a ball, I was unable to straighten myself to lie flat. My voice echoed off metal as I cried out to no one, for no one came. Sobbing only caused more vomiting until finally weakness overtook me and I passed out.

When I awoke next (How long, again? A day? Another week?), I was not alone. A thin, bald, shirtless Asian man sat beside me in the weak light of a kerosene lantern and ran a wet cloth smelling of mint and root over my body. "It's the drug," I said, my throat burning with each word. The strange man smiled, gaps in his teeth showing like open passages. "Opium. I need it. Have you any?" He smiled again but only shook his head as he moved the warm and rough cloth down my chest to my stomach, hips, legs, and feet.

He left me there when he'd finished and I fought sleep. I thought of Edward and Lizzie, of Eleanor and Charlie and Ina and Betty. *Betty.* My throat closed as I fought to wail for the pipe she'd first held to my lips. Or perhaps I didn't wail. The darkness had closed so tightly around me that I wasn't sure if I was alive or dead, only that life and death smelled like mint and earth.

I slept.

Tremors like an earthquake woke me. Fever rattled my bones until I thought surely my skeleton would shake apart. The man was there and he crawled onto the cot beside me, holding my naked body tightly to his so his warmth pervaded my skin to my brittle bones, calming me, bracing me against the demons crawling in and out of my skin.

I slept.

Bacon. Toast. Melon. Coffee. It was a dream of the Timeless and the first meal Edward and I had the morning we'd arrived in Memphis. There was even the faintest scent of bleach from the mop bucket kept in Charlie's office where the angel had visited me. Had any food ever tasted better? My eyelids peeled away slowly and light filtered like a candle. I was ravenous. Beside my cot, on the stool where the tiny man had sat before, was a tray with eggs and meat and produce and coffee. I found strength enough to grasp the metal pitcher of water and I turned it up over my mouth, drinking too quickly so I immediately threw it back up. But I wasn't deterred and ate the meal as though it were my first ever, for it felt as if it were.

I slept and woke in regular intervals. There were books and food left at my bedside, and I don't know how much time passed. I didn't care. I reveled in the feeling of my strength and mind coming back to me without the cloudiness of the opium. It had withered me and I was glad to see it go, carried out on the skin of the man who had bathed me and pressed himself to me for comfort. I never saw him again, but I remain grateful.

Chapter Forty-Two

I sat in Mr. Cooper's Jeep and stared up at the Reynolds house. That's how I thought of it, as the home where someone else had grown up. Her name had been Amelia Reynolds and her grandparents were despots from another time — they owned property and people and thought of each in terms of value on the marketplace. Grandmother thought little more of her daughter-in-law and, though she'd held out hope for young Amelia Reynolds, that hope had been ground like bones beneath the steel wheels of a train as it pulled from the station on its way to Memphis.

Amelia Thorn had been born in a Memphis church and baptized by an angel who had taken her hand tenderly in the small office of a café. She was reborn in a whorehouse in West Memphis and baptized once again in the river the night she left.

In the fug of pipe and cigarette smoke fogging the windows, I stared up at the house as Daddy had the day we returned from our trip to Palmetto. I wondered if I was searching its wood plank walls, reflecting windows, and Victorian finials for the same things he had. I searched for any familiarity in the woman I was and the little girl who'd slept and eaten and played in that house. I didn't find it. But I was tired, and Mr. Cooper was antsy. "Amelia?" He was never quite comfortable in the presence of a woman.

Mother held me on the porch as though she were afraid I might ascend into the heavens. Or that she would. We shifted our weight together and the floorboards creaked. Paint peeled on the railing and the window screens were tattered — age was catching up with the house and it was beginning to show in the cracks and crevices of its skin. Mother sobbed and buried her face in my neck and I held her and patted her back, soothing her for the time I'd spent away, so much of it without correspondence. I willed tears to come but they would not and the hollowness inside me became a distraction.

In the front parlor, Grandmother's bedroom had been disassembled from upstairs and reassembled. The old woman was sick and frail, and if I thought she was a hundred years old when I was a child, I was sure she was now two hundred. Claustrophobia followed me from Mr.

Cooper's cramped car to the room, once so large and open, but now cluttered with heavy dressers, wardrobes, tables, chairs, and bedstead. The air was thick with age and with gasses I imagined the dead give off. The quilt covering her body barely rippled with her shallow, sleeping breath as Mother and I stood over her, watching. Mother, I knew, wanted me to pay respects, to genuflect at the altar of the matriarch of the Reynolds clan. Indeed, the matriarch of all of Mourning. I let my eyes wander across the dusty furniture and past the faded wallpaper out the bay window to the oak tree across the yard where Daddy's body was buried. I missed him. I miss him still, and I longed then to run with him down the lane to the barn where he would encourage me to climb into the loft using the rope he'd hung and then jump into the hay bales below. Daddy was uncomfortable in this house and I knew then it wasn't just the stiff, wooden furniture that made him so, but also the stiff, wooden ways of the past.

Mother and I left the old woman to sleep. Daddy's den was dark and oak-paneled with a thick throw rug and overstuffed chairs. It was the most comfortable room in the house still, even with the parlor's damask sofa and chairs, end tables, lamps, and settee shoved into corners and along one wall to get them out of the way for Grandmother's new bedroom. I stopped to look at the massive *Oxford American Dictionary* opened on a table of its own, running my fingers across an open page. Daddy's favorite place had always been a chair by the window looking out over Mother's garden and the barn in the distance. I curled into its leather the way I used to curl into his lap. "I've been to California," I said. The lie came easily.

"I know about the baby," she said. "I wrote to the restaurant in Memphis and that woman wrote back to say you'd miscarried and had gotten away for a bit." I don't know why Eleanor should lie for me but I was grateful. I'd been living within myself for a year, yet had meant no ill will, did not mean to cause any worry to those I loved.

"I went west to clear my head," I told Mother. "It was as beautiful as Edward said it would be. The Pacific is a vivid blue and the sun as gold and large as you've ever seen it. I rented a bungalow and spent whole days on the beach and walking through the stalls of an outdoor arcade. I didn't buy anything, but I believe it was healing for me to be among people and the colors of fabrics and fruits." The lie I conjured sounded appealing and I found myself wishing I'd actually done those things. I thought about traveling to California and maybe down into Mexico to see how other people lived, what they ate, what music they listened to, and how they survived among each other.

When I looked up from my reverie, Mother looked stricken. She clutched her collar and said, "Strangers? You have a home here, Amelia. Why would you go where you don't know a soul? A house to yourself? The beach? You need someone to look after you, dear."

I picked a pack of cigarettes from my handbag, the satisfying *ping* of the Zippo I'd taken from Betty's hickory box filled the empty space left after Mother insisted I need looking after. There was nothing left to say on the matter; in that silence was everything I cared to explain of myself. Mother watched in horror as I blew a thin stream of smoke into the air. The idea of smoking hadn't yet made it to the women of Mourning. Not to the Reynolds home at any rate. I saw myself as a pioneer. "Oh, Mother, I'm sorry. Cigarette?"

"Oh dear, no." And after a long pause: "Thank you."

She looked about for an ashtray as though she didn't have an inventory of the house always at the ready in her brain. Daddy had used the fireplace or simply thrown his butts from the window. I took the saucer from beneath my teacup and dropped an ash onto it, provoking another gasp of distress. "Mother Reynolds is having difficulty taking a breath lately. Her lungs are full of fluid, Dr. Bendel says. Consumption, he says."

"Pneumonia, most likely. Old lungs. Withered. No fight left in them." I turned and blew a stream towards the parlor door.

"Cold?" I said.

"Oh, I've always got a chill. Would you like a sweater?"

"I think I'd like a fire." I got up to go outside for wood, none having been laid inside — not in Daddy's den, anyway — since he'd died.

"Oh, Amelia, let me get a boy to do that. There's a coyote about, it's been seen at the edges of the property. We had to put the chickens up."

I looked from the window to the rack of shotguns above the sofa. "Daddy's Remington would take care of it."

A flame caught readily, the wood brittle and dry, and I stepped back to admire its glow and bask in its heat. Mother closed her eyes, grateful for the warmth as well. "It's easy," I said.

We sat and talked lightly of people from town, old classmates of mine and their parents whom Mother saw at church or market or at the U.S.O. She asked me my plans and I was noncommittal, yet the California lies rolled from my tongue like the Pacific Ocean breaking on the beach. I was saving her, I told myself. Had she known I was beaten, that I was in service to men, she would have perished on the spot, thrown herself into the fire without even a day of rest, having beaten Grandmother to the grave. The house was quiet, the hissing and popping fire like a thunderstorm in the room. The quiet made me think of the Zaccones' home, alive with conversation, laughter, and children's cries. Even of Ina's and the man in the bowler hat who played piano — raucous when the men were about, but quiet and sweet when it was just us girls. Grandmother's piano, wheeled out into the foyer and untouched anyway for years, was silent as a grave. I went back for another armload of wood and the room became even cozier and I dozed into a restful nap.

I awoke to see the pink of the setting sun in the distance, but I didn't move. I didn't want to; it was so peaceful. What I wanted was for Daddy to come in from the fields and hang his hat next to the door before coming into the study to light his end-of-day pipe, sit in his chair, and put his feet up. But he wasn't there and I was in his chair. What I saw instead was Mother coming from the parlor, agitated, shuffling into the kitchen and back again. My stomach grumbled. I hadn't eaten since earlier in the morning on the barge, my farewell breakfast with Mr. Kim. I followed Mother into the kitchen where the black caverns of cupboards opened behind her. She placed a sliver of dried roast and crust of bread on the table. "Where's Lizzie?"

Mother snapped from her anxiety and into anger. "Oh, that girl. She hasn't set foot in this kitchen for days. I imagine she's laid up in her bed with labor. No telling when she might be back . . ."

I didn't wait around to hear the rest. I was out the door like a shot, just as Mother had run to the fields the day Daddy died.

Chapter Forty-Three

One-room shacks lined the dirt road that began at the big house and ended at the barn — a rural Main Street with its own Chisca Hotel and Central Station. I ran, finding my way by muscle memory as the sun dipped lower behind the distant tree line. Mother said it hadn't rained in a month and dust kicked up around my feet. Despite the chill, the door was open, yet the air was stifling inside from activity and anticipation. One light bulb hung from the ceiling on a cord, the only evidence of the electricity Daddy had strung down the lane over Grandmother's protestations. There wasn't a refrigerator or other appliance, no television, not even a phonograph, and I made a mental note to have a radio sent over from town. Lizzie called out when she saw me, followed by a moan of pain. She was in bed, her knees drawn up with only a thin sheet to cover her and attended to by several women who fetched water from the pump outside and dry towels to mop Lizzie's sweat. A bible lay open to Proverbs on the bed just out of her reach.

Her eyes widened when she saw me before the crescendo of a contraction closed them again. It passed and she laughed softly. "Come over here to me."

I sat on a cane-back chair beside the bed and took her hand. "Lizzie. Lizzie," I said. "What is it you've got in there, sweetness?"

"Girl."

"And how do you know that?"

"Don't you worry how, I just do." She laughed again, but it was cut short by pain.

"Coming quicker now," one of the midwives said.

"How is it you show yourself back here on this night when my baby comin'?"

I shrugged and took a towel to wipe her brow. "How does anything happen? A butterfly flitted its wings in China." "Butterfly effect" and "chaos theory" had both fallen within Ina's abbreviated set of *Encyclopedia Britannica*. I don't claim to be an expert, but it seemed my mind soaked up more than opium and gin during those days in her care.

Lizzie just looked at me and licked her dry lips. "I'm gonna get you to explain what you mean to me later," she said before another contraction seized her.

Labor lasted through the night. Lizzie's wailing between pushes must have been heard a county away as those other disembodied cries had on the grave day that gave Mourning its name. This child, though, would not die. The women tended to Lizzie's needs and I jumped in to lend a hand, running to the water pump to ring out the reddened towels, swabbing her forehead, and massaging her back. Lizzie dozed and the midwives and I stood in the kitchen for a pull from roped jerky and an unmarked jug. We shared a pouch of tobacco and rolled cigarettes. When Lizzie awoke, she was ripped from sleep as if from a terrified dream, and the women spoke little but communicated with glances and twitches of the head, and clucks of their tongues.

People call childbirth a miracle, yet what I witnessed that night with Lizzie wasn't heavenly. It was as primal as anything this Earth might produce. It was the same shifting of tectonic plates I'd known myself the first night at Ina's, but this night the shifting created a whole new continent Lizzie would inhabit from now on — motherhood. I'd been scared on my night, as scared as when I was a girl and Grandmother told me about her brothers and sister crushed and drowned in the creek. But Lizzie was strong. She'd taken her strength from I don't know where, perhaps from the women who surrounded her. Perhaps it was a strength she was born with and hadn't even fully understood. I wished I'd been half as strong as Lizzie, that I'd been present and aware and held my baby, as lifeless as she might have been. The fear I'd felt the night the storm came for me and Miss Ina pulled my baby from my body seemed a decade removed, but the cry was still in my ears as though it had only just happened. It rang with a church bell peal and a zeal to haunt me my entire life.

I must have dozed because I awoke in the chair beside Lizzie's bed the next morning, midwives long gone, to purpling daylight and the cries of a very real baby. "You did so good, dear," I said. "Look what you did." I touched the baby girl on the ear, so little like one of Charlie's bowtie pastas.

"It'll be better," she whispered and kissed the fuzzy head.

I bent to hear her. "What's that, dear?"

The baby nuzzled at her breast. "My baby girl. Her life gonna be better. Better than my people, I'll make damn sure of that. No more cooking in the big house, no more cleaning up some white woman's soiled sheets. No, ma'am. She go to school, she read. She get out. *Out*."

Lizzie and the baby slept and I busied myself with tidying up and smoking. I even read a passage or two in her bible. When the baby stirred, I took her and walked around the small room, showing her the sights from the window, though her swollen eyes weren't yet open.

"She's beautiful," I said, handing the bundle back to Lizzie when she woke and sat up. "Does she favor you or her daddy?"

"That old rascal. He wasn't around long enough for me to even know for sure, Amelia." I wondered whether she conceived in this room or if it was in Grandmother's house and the room Lizzie had lived in since she was a girl. Or maybe it was in that old rascal's car, parked at the end of the driveway with the radio blowing blues from a half-state away. I'd wondered myself when it might have happened to me. Was it in those soft sheets of the Chisca Hotel or that violent fuck in the sparsely furnished room while the German woman stood at the bottom of the stairs? I liked to think it was the former, but in the drug-haze of Ina's, I convinced myself only the anger and fear Edward felt before leaving could have killed my baby. I'd been angry and looking for blame, and it landed squarely on Edward's shoulders. In death, I needed him to shoulder that blame so the weight of it wouldn't crush me.

"Over in Europe now," Lizzie continued. "You give me one of them pictures you're taking of her and I'll give it to Cooper to send to him."

"I promise to," I laughed. "She's got your eyes."

"Got your nose," Lizzie whispered.

"How's that?"

She smiled. "Look at that flat nose." She touched her baby there. "Cherokee. Where you seen such a nose, Amelia?"

"I don't understand."

"You know what I was dreaming about just now when I was asleep? Your daddy. Funny, ain't it? I ain't thought of him since you put him in the ground. Not 'til this dream time. Not 'til I saw this nose. Favors a Reynolds, don't it?"

"Lizzie?"

"Amelia, girl, now come on. You said yourself you ain't the same girl left Mourning for Memphis. I never would have told that long-gone girl the truth of it all. Kept my thoughts to my own self all these years and would've 'til they put me in the ground, too. But you a grown woman now. You a widow. You read books, seen a little part of the world, too. You know how it works."

I stared at the baby, at her fuzzy head and pink tongue darting in and out like a lizard's. I studied her nose with its flattened bridge, growing wider at the nostrils, just before Lizzie pulled her to her breast. Stuck in the bag that followed me from Memphis to Ina's and back to Mourning was the very first snapshot I'd taken years earlier: Daddy sitting on a picnic table, his face in profile and a thin cigar between his teeth. He squinted in the Florida sun with his hat pushed back on his head. It had been there all along, right in front of me as Lizzie cooked and bathed me and read aloud — the flattened, Reynolds nose. It was the same nose I saw now on Lizzie's baby. "But how?"

Lizzie took my hand as she nursed, once again looking after multiple people at once. "Your Daddy."

She paused to let those two words sink in, but they wouldn't. As much as I tried to wrap my mind around what it was Lizzie was too circumspect to say, those two words could not be absorbed. "What?"

"Your Daddy, Amelia. He's mine, too."

I stood in anger, shot up out of the chair as though I were going to launch into a speech or launch that chair through the window. My head spun and I started for the door, but that was the move of the little girl who'd left Mourning, running to Mother or, even, Grandmother. I sat, unsure of just what I was hearing, what else it was being born that morning. "How?" It was all I could think to say.

"Your daddy wasn't a bad man, Amelia."

"How can you say that?"

"It's something I know. It's something you need to understand. He took care of my Mama, took care of me. You think Grandmother would just let me move into her home? Nigger daughter of her son?"

"Don't say that, Lizzie."

"Shhhh. It's okay. Your Daddy made sure I had a home here after my Mama left. The only way that old woman and your own Mama would let that happen was if I was help."

My eyes widened. "Mother knows?"

"Of course she know, baby. The only thing she ever made clear is that you was never to know. Guess I'll be put out now."

"I won't let that happen, Lizzie."

"Not saying it's a bad thing."

The revelation of everything struck me like a cast-iron skillet against the temple. I'd always thought of Lizzie as a sister, we were blood-sisters, our fingers pressed together with the prick of a pin on Christmas Day. "She is not your kin," Grandmother had said. There was such force in her words.

"Lizzie," I choked. "Lizzie, I'm so sorry."

"Ssssh, now don't you cry and wake this baby. What's past is past, you understand? We can't change it. I wish there was things we could, sure, but I wouldn't give up my time with you, watching you grow. You such a strong, smart woman now. I want my baby to be like that. I want her to be like you, Amelia."

I hung my head and tears landed on Lizzie's mattress leaving dark circles like rainwater. "We're sisters."

Lizzie laughed. "Sure are. So many times in that kitchen I wanted to tell you. You remember?" She held up her index finger and I pressed the tip of mine against hers. "We family — you, me, this baby."

She followed the baby back into sleep and I wondered what they dreamed of. I wondered if their dreams might be connected now. It was growing dark in the late autumn sky and I sat on the porch smoking, thinking about all I'd heard. I needed answers yet couldn't bring myself to confront Mother about what she knew and why she'd never shared it. Her mourning had lasted for so long and I was afraid knowledge — my knowing — would suffocate her. An owl got an early start somewhere nearby, hooting, desperately searching for a mate on this chilly night. Far down the lane, I saw a weak light fighting its way through a grimy window.

Chapter Forty-Four

Grandmother lay silent, small and frail in the center of her king bed, her skeleton little more than a ridge in the down comforter. Her breathing was shallow and her purplish, paper-thin lids twitched against restless eyeballs. "Grandmother," I whispered and sat in the handmade rocker that had rested bedside upstairs since I was a girl. "Grandmother, are you awake? It's me, dear. It's Amelia." Silence, save for the rasp of life played through a split reed. I sat and watched her for half an hour, watched the moon move into view in the top-most windowpane and its light eventually bathe the patient's face. So much white on white. I rocked gently, thinking of Grandmother chasing Edward from the yard. I thought of him alone on a boat in the blackness of the ocean, looking up at the stars the same way I'd watched fireflies in the fields as a little girl. I thought of the night sky above the Chisca Hotel and my small room back in Memphis. I thought of a day Eleanor and I met at Goldsmith's luncheonette and she hugged a busboy, a black man who had worked for Charlie years before and whom she hadn't seen in so long. The women at the next table didn't bother to hide their disgust at the embrace and as we made our exit, Eleanor brushed against a water pitcher, spilling it over the table and the women themselves.

And I thought of Lizzie. Dear Lizzie. No formal education, no acknowledgment in all these years of who her real daddy was, no chance to play evenly and fairly against the hand she'd been dealt. She waited on this old woman and on my mother and on *me*.

"Grandmother!" I said and moved to sit on the bed, my weight causing her head to shift on the feather pillow.

"Who's there?" she said. Her eyelids fluttered.

"It's Amelia, Grandmother. Back from Memphis."

"Memphis? Why . . . the harm of it."

"Listen to me, I need to ask you something. I need to know . . ."

"Thirsty."

A pitcher sat on the nightstand. "In a minute. Tell me about my Daddy. Did he have other children? Besides me?"

"Oh dear, your father is dead."

"Yes, I know that. But, Lizzie . . . Is Lizzie my sister?"

Silence again. A beetle beat its wings against a window screen and I watched as Grandmother's breathing became more rapid, her eyelids fluttering like beetles' wings until they snapped open. "Lizzie."

"Yes, Grandmother. Lizzie. Is she my sister?"

"Lizzie. Tell her . . ."

"Yes?" I moved in closer, my ear to her cracked lips. "What is it?"

"Tell that black bitch I'm thirsty."

I stood from the bed and looked again at the pitcher and as God as my witness, I wanted to pour it over that old woman. I itched to pour it into her gaping, thirsty mouth to suffocate her. *Let her drown*, I thought. I stormed from the room and out of the house.

In the barn, where I'd visited Daddy and the field hands in the afternoons once their work was finished, I stomped the flooring in the farthest corner until I heard the hollowness I was searching for. Sweeping the hay aside, I wrenched a plank free and plunged my hand into darkness. The glass was cool from the packed dirt. Homemade liquor had been there for years in a collection of mason jars Grandmother would accuse Lizzie of breaking over time as they disappeared one by one. When I held the jar up to my lantern, it looked as refreshing as iced tea.

Most of the shacks were empty, though every now and then a light burned dimly. One of the midwives from the day before sat on her own porch, rocking and smoking. She knitted and puffed, and I nodded her way as I passed on my way up the road, past the tree split in two from a lightning strike years earlier. I stopped at the last house, the one I'd seen the weak light leaking from as I sat on Lizzie's porch after the birth, the one that backed up to a pond with a small dock and a jon boat moored there. "Who's there?" a voice called through the screen door. I could only just make out a shifting shape within.

"Amelia, sir. Amelia Reynolds," I said and my own voice came off the weathered siding, bouncing back to me as that of the eight-year-old girl I once was.

"Amelia? I'll be." The man who came through the door had always seemed old to me, and he looked even older now with skin as gray as his house. His name was Lafayette, though everyone called him Teeth. He pulled a chair from inside the door and gestured to the good, smooth rocker. "Come on up here and thit with me."

"Thank you kindly. Brought you something. If I recall, you had a taste for it when I was a little girl."

"Mmm yeth. Mithter Reynoldth moonthine."

Understanding Teeth was difficult, seeing as how he had none, but the more he talked the easier it became. He was Lizzie's uncle — his wife and her mama were sisters, but she died one night running from Lizzie's house back to her own, hit by the lightning strike that had split the tree. Once Teeth and I settled into a patter, and he'd had a few warming sips of Daddy's liquor, I asked him about his sister-in-law.

"Tessa? Good woman," he said. "Beautiful woman."

"What do you know about her and my Daddy?"

He looked nervous and glanced around, ran his tongue over his gums, and looked back up the road to the blackened, forked trunk. I urged him to take another sip, but he handed the jar to me instead. I sipped and it numbed my lips, my tongue tingled.

"Your daddy used to come around. Never stopped, but he'd come walking through, or on his horse, slow as summertime, and keep on going. Few minutes later, here come Tessa, same direction, into them woods yonder. Just past that stand is a clearing with tall grasses and the prettiest flowers you ever seen. That's where they'd lay up."

I was momentarily dizzy. Was it the moonshine? It was memory, it was the same meadow of lavender and black-eyed Susan and butterflies, where tall grasses and trees kept Edward and me hidden and cut off from the world. I took the jar from him again and gulped. "Did she ever talk about him? About my Daddy?"

"Not to me, naw. But she talked to her sister. Sisters tell everything."

"And wives talk to husbands. What'd she say?"

Again he looked nervous and I took his hand in mine. It was enormous and rough, and his eyes went soft when I put my other hand on top.

"Tessa told my Sophie your Daddy treated her like no other man ever had. Certainly not no white man. No offense, Miss Amelia. Said they talked and he made her laugh. Said they both knew what happened between them couldn't happen nowhere but in secret. My Sophie, she tried to talk Tessa out of it. Tried to make her see what might come of her if they kept on like animals over in that meadow. But Tessa wouldn't hear it, said your Daddy would watch after her, wouldn't let nobody do no harm."

"Did they, Teeth? Did they do harm to Tessa?"

He shrugged and his eyes glistened. He took a long pull from the jar. "She got herself pregnant."

"Lizzie. She's my Daddy's daughter."

"You know?"

"She told me after her little girl was born."

"She make a good mama. Just like Tessa. She loved her baby more than life itself. Your daddy would come around then, after Lizzie, and walk straight up on the porch, right on into that house."

"Did he?"

"He did, mhm. Your daddy didn't give a shit by then. Pardon, Miss Amelia, but it was a sight to see — Mr. Reynolds comin' and goin' like a husband and daddy. I think Tessa was as happy as she ever been. Sophie was nervous as a cat, though. She always was one for seeing things wasn't there in the darkness. Course, sometimes there was things in the darkness."

"What things?"

He retreated into himself and put the lid back on the jar, setting it on the floor beside his chair. He rubbed the back of his thick, scarred neck. "I don't mean to talk out of turn, ma'am. Maybe best if I stop there."

"Teeth, talk to me. Please. I know about my Daddy and Tessa and Lizzie. I know how my family felt about Lizzie. I need to know about Tessa and you're the only one who can say."

He looked to the woods where the two young lovers had met, stared as though he were waiting on a sign that times were different, that safety and security were finally at hand. Maybe he saw something, I don't know, but he began talking without looking at me. "Truth is, nobody knows what happened to Tessa. Just gone one night. Oh, we searched high and low, followed a trail looked like it led through them trees over there, even found a stitch of her dress on a holly bush. But no Tessa. Tried to get sheriff out here. Tried for weeks, even pleaded with the Colonel. He said he'd look into it, make a call. After some time the sheriff rolled on out, took a look around, asked some questions. That's it. Told Sophie, 'She probably run off. Y'all do that, y'know.' 'But her baby,' my Sophie wailed. 'You can take care of the pup,' he said, and drove off.

"Your daddy come out then. Come tearin' ass down that road on his horse and went through every inch of Tessa's house. He went through them woods, into the meadow, and just kept going. Some say he rode clear down to the Gulf of Mexico, down to the water's edge. After he left, the Colonel come down with men and gasoline and lit that meadow aflame. Burned bright, so we all stood at the ready should it catch the barn, these shacks.

"Was weeks before we saw your daddy again, but he'd come around and look in on Lizzie. He held that baby and walked her on out to that meadow where nothing but wildflowers had grown. You ever notice how that patch of land different than anything else around here? All golds and pinks and reds and blues? That's the scorched earth healing itself. To this day it's covered up like a gravesite, covered in color and that's what brings them butterflies around.

"Course, we all knew your daddy's mourning couldn't be allowed to last. Your daddy knew it, too, and he married your mama. Then one day, Lizzie about seven, eight, you weren't nothin' but a baby in diapers, your grandmother come down the road there and right up on this porch, right here where we sittin', and said to get Lizzie, that she'd be takin' her up to the big house for chores. Sophie pleaded but your granny wouldn't hear of it. Lizzie stayed gone." He glanced down at the liquor jar then and slid his tongue over his empty gums. He looked back to me. "Came back around after a while for a visit and Sophie told her to stay. 'Slavery done with, Lizzie,' she'd say. But Lizzie told her Aunt Sophie she needed to look after you."

"Me?"

"Mhm. Said she felt a closeness to you she hadn't felt to nobody since her own mama, though she couldn't have remembered that old girl, young as she was. Now, ain't nobody asked me, but I think she wanted to be near your daddy, too. I don't know when that girl knew what she know, but whatever it was she had up at the big house must have felt like family in some way, even with your old biddy grandma. Sorry for any offense, Miss Amelia."

"None taken."

"Anyway, that's all I know. Probably said too much as it is."

I touched him again on his hand and thanked him, and we sat in silence with the moonshine creeping up on the porch and through our guts. I looked back down the road the way I'd come. "Hey, Teeth, who lives in these houses? The dark ones, boarded up?"

He followed my sightline. "Nobody but ghosts, Miss Amelia."

Chapter Forty-Five

I swept every inch of the wood plank floors. And when I was through, I scrubbed it with a horse brush and soap, carrying pail after pail of water from the pump beside Lizzie's house, the only water source for the ten houses along the row. The midwife watched from her porch, shaking her head at this fool white girl. I scrubbed the floors and countertop, cupboards inside and out, windowsills and glass. I believe I would have scrubbed the ceiling if I could reach. Once I was finished, I brought the furniture — what there was of it (bed, chair, table) — in from the porch. And then I swept the porch. When I was content that there was no longer any trace of the Reynoldses' oppression (Poe's heart thumped with every stroke of the broom) or Teeth's ghosts, and that the living might once again fill the single room, I sat in the rocker on the porch and waved to Teeth where he sat two porches away.

The idea of sleeping under Grandmother's roof after what she'd said about Lizzie was unbearable. So I moved into the shack, visiting the big house only occasionally for food and aspirin and baby clothes scrounged from Grandmother's dusty attic. I couldn't bear to be in the house any longer than it took to fill a cotton sack with bread, cheese, fruit, and salt. I phoned the market from the kitchen phone and had them deliver groceries enough for Mother and Lizzie.

I sat beside Lizzie's bed, mending clothes I'd scavenged as she read aloud from her bible. I only half-listened to those fables, unable to chase the true stories Lizzie and Teeth had shared from my head. She said she wanted her baby to have a better life than she'd had. I wasn't offended by that, of course I wasn't. I was ashamed. I should have seen to it that Lizzie had her own chance at a better life, I should have stood up to my family sooner. I should have demanded Lizzie attend Daddy's funeral, that she be paid fairly for her work and time, that her family's drafty shack be razed and a proper house built.

A boy came around telling me Mother wanted me home, just as I'd been sent by Grandmother as a little girl to collect Lizzie when she wandered. "What's your name, young man?" I said.

"That's Josiah, he's my little cousin," Lizzie said.

250

"Well, Josiah, take this jerky. You hungry?" He was. "And do me a favor and run tell Ms. Reynolds that I'll come along when I get ready to come along and not a minute sooner. Can you do that for me?" He laughed and ran away with his cheek full of the dried, salty meat.

"Your mama ain't gonna like that," Lizzie said.

"I don't really care what anybody likes or doesn't like any longer."

Lizzie narrowed her eyes and looked at me. "What's gotten to you, Amelia? You went away a wondering and wide-eyed little girl, and you come back to us leathery as that jerky."

I stoked the fire in the stove and took eggs from a basket. Lizzie needed to eat. "I'm not the same girl who left here on the day of her wedding. That girl lost a husband, lost a baby . . ." I dropped an egg on the floor and paused before cleaning it.

"What else she lose?"

"More than you'll ever know," I said.

Chapter Forty-Six

I leaned in the open doorway, smoking and listening to mother and daughter cooing behind me. The beauty of the birth and the unexpected ache it put in my heart, along with everything Lizzie and Teeth told me about Daddy, had my head reeling so I'd come to depend on the morning's fresh air to steady myself. The day dawned cool and was slow to awaken as if even the sun and animals preferred the warmth of a family bed over dewy mornings. Those dew drops caught the earliest rays of sun and fragmented them like my thoughts. Somewhere in the distance a tractor rumbled to life, a sound, I learned, still made me sick to my stomach. In all of that stillness, my eye caught a figure on the horizon at the diminishing point of the dirt road. Through rising mist, the figure grew until I could make out a bundle over its shoulder and large box in the other hand. Despite the burden, he walked upright and not bent by the weight. Behind me, the baby sneezed. "Somebody's coming," I said.

"Who's there?" Lizzie whispered.

As he grew closer, I realized it wasn't a "he" at all. It was a woman. She wore high-waisted dungarees cinched tightly with a leather belt, a duster, and a man's wide-brimmed fedora. Large, brown work boots kicked dust up all around her so she appeared to float in on a red clay cloud.

I turned my head halfway, keeping an eye on her. "Lady."

"What she want?"

She unloaded her burden in the middle of the road and set about constructing a sculpture that appeared to have a purpose other than art, though it was indeed beautiful in itself. Three legs of a tripod were driven into the dirt and on this she hefted the box, working quickly and efficiently turning clamps and screws to affix Frankenstein's monster head to the spindly body. It was clear she'd performed this act hundreds of times. Only once she'd pulled the accordion nose from the front of the box did I realize it was a camera. She removed her hat and wiped her brow with a sleeve. Her hair was bobbed and jet black, bangs stuck to her sweaty forehead.

"What is it you want?" I called out, and left Lizzie's porch for the small plot of garden that fronted it. The hem of my skirt raked the ground and I was bathed in an explosion of mint.

"I'll start with one of those cigarettes," she said.

I considered her for a moment before pulling a pack from my shirt pocket and offering it to her. She lit it with her own brass lighter. "Now," I said, "what is it you want on my family's property?"

It was her turn to consider me, and she did, from bottom to top and back again. "Funny, you don't look like a farmer."

"My daddy was."

"Don't look like you belong in that house, either. You look like you'd be more at home in the big house." She gestured back the way she'd come with her chin. A crow cawed somewhere in the trees.

"I'm more at home here. Amelia Thorn." She put her hat back on before taking my hand. Hers was rough and strong.

"Doris Latham. I was told this was Reynolds land. Thorn?"

"Married name. Widowed."

Doris Latham was with the Farm Service Administration and had come to photograph the rural South. "Sharecroppers. You know, the disenfranchised." She'd just arrived from California where she'd documented the Japanese internment camps. "Just awful. You wouldn't believe how those people are made to live."

I looked back at Lizzie's cabin, at the plot of vegetables meant to feed her and her people. "I've never been to California," I told her.

"Shame. It's beautiful — the Pacific Ocean, redwoods bigger than any tree around here . . ."

"Sun that shines like gold?"

"And you say you've never been."

"What is it you're photographing today?"

"That barn. These homes." She was beneath the blackout cloth now and her voice was muffled.

"I take pictures," I told her. The Brownie Daddy bought me in Pascagoula was hanging on a nail in Lizzie's house.

"I'd love to see them."

I told her they'd been lost, burned up in a fire. I don't know why I lied. "Shame," she said, coming out from under the cloth. Her hair was tousled and she smoothed it. "Take a look?"

Grandmother kept photos and letters among quilts and shawls in a cedar chest at the foot of her bed. I rarely entered the old woman's room — it was dark and mysterious, and I didn't like the scent of mildew and must that filled the air; I could never reconcile the notion of laciness and perfume and the private matters of a woman's boudoir with the staid, buttoned-up reality of Grandmother's bedroom. One day she waved me in, calling to me as I passed her door on the stairway landing. I'd been on my way out the door to collect eggs, having recently decided tending to the chickens would be my chore. Fine with Lizzie, who didn't much care for the claw feet or windblown pin feathers clinging to her clothes. Spread across the duvet were squares and long rectangles of heavy paper bordered in white, cracked and tinted with sepia and age. Stoic, unsmiling faces looked up from the bed. Ghostlike images of elderly women dressed in the same high collars Grandmother still wore. Men in Sunday finery, stock still, with eyes caught for eternity darting to the left or right at something unseen — a smoldering pipe just off camera, or a plow left idle when there was work to be done.

I never knew why nostalgia was on display that day. Was it an anniversary or a birthday of some long-dead grandparent or favorite aunt? I didn't know, yet was grateful the pungent cedar chased the odor of age and dust away. It was a day late in spring and I thought perhaps the time of year synced with the historic rains, memories washing over the old woman just as the creek had overflowed its banks and taken the lives of her siblings.

Grandmother took them in, turning one over before carefully picking up the next. She held one longer than the others — a tintype of my grandfather in his Confederate uniform, his beard unruly and eyes stern. I studied Grandmother's face, looking for some hint of affection — a smile, a twinkle in her eyes, a flush in those powder-white and withered cheeks. I had hoped in that instant to see the passion that might have borne my father, that had brought two people together as husband and bride in the first place. The road map of her face, though, remained unchanged. Her lips, pale and flaked, remained clamped shut and her eyes, even in the dim light of her room, were the same coal black as if she were watching something as common as a cur dog making its way slowly across her property.

She laid the photo to the side, though, with tenderness.

The next picture was different. Deep blacks and grays. Five children huddled together, all smiling. Those faces affected her, and a change came over her face. Something had changed in her life, the camera capturing those who would be lost. These were her brothers and sister, and there she was, too, a little girl. To drive home the point, they posed on the back of a wagon.

"Tell me about them?" I said once the tics in her face had become too difficult to watch. A question without an answer. A benign, up-turned lilt at the end of my sentence when what I wanted was to shake the information from her. I wanted details. I wanted memories from the old woman, as immovable as the oak sideboard in the dining room. I ached to take her by the shoulders and rattle the powder from her bones: *Tell me! Make me understand! Talk about love and rain, loss and what aches inside you! Cry! Laugh! Weep with the memory of this photograph!* Yellow light from the window dressing washed over the photographs and Grandmother's face. It was a persistent light in that dark room and I was a persistent girl. "Timmy — did he laugh a lot? Amelia — did she have a favorite doll? Rutger — what were his chores, Grandmother? Please tell me? Talk to me about my namesake!"

That was when Mother happened down the hallway. "Amelia," she whispered. "Come along. Out of there now."

I ignored her but she, too, was persistent. "Come now, run along."

I stood and stared at Grandmother, at the photograph of her long dead family in her trembling hands and the discarded tintype of a Civil War veteran lying to the side. It was the first time I recall feeling pity for someone older than myself.

Chapter Forty-Seven

Lizzy, Baby
1944

Gelatin silver print, 37.5 x 27.9 cm
(14 3/4 x 11 in.)

Courtesy, public collection of
Morning, Mississippi.

I'd never seen the world until I looked at the narrow dirt lane through the viewfinder of Doris Latham's camera. The world I saw then was upside down, but the colors were sharper and my perspective was framed so I could focus. I saw only what was there in front of me and nothing behind me — Edward and his baby weren't within the frame. Beneath the black felt cover, I was safe from everything packed on my trip on the rail line, across a bridge, and downriver. I felt Doris' hand on mine and then something pressed against my palm. It was the camera's shutter. How thrilling to make this picture — to choose the precise moment to press a button and stop the world from spinning, the sunlight from tracking across the sky, a squirrel from foraging, and the seasons from changing. "No rush. Take your time. Be patient," she whispered and it was as though she were with me, swaddled in the black cocoon. I could have waited all day with the fate of the world at my fingertip. I'd seen this view a thousand times as a child, had walked this lane with Daddy and raced with Lizzie, ridden it on my horse and held hands here with Edward. But that day it was as if I'd never stepped foot on the path at all. Something more, I'd never had the control I had just then. Until that day, that moment, nature and those around me — fate itself — had controlled my destiny, where I did and did not go, what I saw, how I reacted. No more. The Earth must have jumped with the minute hand of Daddy's watch in my pocket because at that very moment the sun hit the trees so their greenery shone like emeralds. A crow alighted on the split tree and, just as Lizzie stepped onto her porch with her swaddled baby, I held my breath and squeezed the plunger. The world went dark.

When I left Lizzie's that day, I stopped at the pasture where the horses used to run. Leaning on the fence as I had with Daddy, I thought about the camera. I saw something more than the trees, the bird, Lizzie. I saw that maybe I was ready to feel love again. Beneath the cloth, with Doris' hand pressed to mine and a new light of day let in through the aperture, I believed I could see things in my own way. It had never been that way. I thought of myself as independent when I left Mourning, but I still viewed life through the eyes of my parents and Grandmother, through Edward and then Eleanor, Ina, and the girls. Where had I been? Inside all along, I was coming to understand, and it took looking back at myself, and all I'd been through, from a new lens to get a sense of the real Amelia Thorn.

"Teach me," I'd told Doris.

"Pardon?"

"This. Show me all you know about this camera and what it can do and what I might do with it. Who are you? Where have you come from and what have you seen? I want to know so that I can see it all myself." She laughed at my urgency but said she would and wrote a list of what I would need. I walked from the horse pasture to town to see Mr. Cooper.

Mourning was swaddled in red, white, and blue. Still swaddled in patriotism in the ebbing days of war. The town center was as lively as ever with conversation and shopping, children chasing dogs and the odd goat or piglet shooed into a corral. Everywhere I looked there were women and children — the young men having been swallowed up by the war. The elderly were there, wearing their own war's medals and too-small uniforms in solidarity. For anyone familiar with Mourning's history, the juxtaposition was jarring — children far outnumbering adults. Mourning's bad luck knew no bounds. Drawn to Mourning by the promise of cheap land, settlers who'd seen advantage in tragedy had children enough to fill two schools and fill the air once again with laughter. But no one had been laughing in 1942 when those young boys were leaving for war by the boxcar load. It had become a town of women and the yellow of mothers' and wives' ribbons pinned to collars, mixed with brilliantly colored flags and bunting, fell against a backdrop of black. Far too many widows for one town.

"Why, Amelia Reynolds. I thought you were in California." The sight of the woman in front of me as I left Mr. Cooper's caused me to fall backward into myself, back to what felt like a lifetime ago, yet so real I could taste the bite of gin and opium at the back of my tongue. Camilla

Smithfield Owen — the name I only now realized I'd taken during my time at Ina's. My childhood friend, we'd played with dolls and snickered at teachers from the back row of classrooms. But there was also a flower blooming beside the front porch of Ina's home — a camellia — and I'd always thought I must have seen it when I first arrived. "What's your name, sweetheart?" Betty had asked before I even knew my baby was dead. *Camilla.* It slipped from my lips so naturally that, over time, I came to believe it true. I'd become something different during that year, blossomed, though who would want such a flower in a cut crystal vase on the mantle in their parlor?

"Camilla," I said, and followed my first impulse to correct her. "It's Thorn. I married Edward Thorn in Memphis two years ago."

"The orphan boy? Of course, I'm sure it was a beautiful wedding. How is Mr. Thorn?"

"Dead. He went down in the Pacific."

"Oh dear. Oh, Amelia, I am so sorry."

"And how are you, Camilla?"

"My Robert is in France. Last we heard, anyway. It isn't easy, dear, I don't need to tell you. Times are difficult, even here in Mourning. His pay gets us through most of the month but that last week is lean."

We'd stopped in the sun to talk while her three children — twins the spitting image of their mother as a little girl, and an older boy — ran ahead with their bags of sugary, rainbow treats for a game of tag with two other children. I watched them and their faces sticky with sugar as red, white, and blue as the flag-draped town, and it was then I noticed Camilla's basket with its package of stockings, perfume, bright-white doilies. I'd been to her family home as a little girl when Mother told me not to be rambunctious and take care with the furniture; it had come from their own Confederate lineage and Mrs. Smithfield was as proud of it as any museum curator. I was no sooner in the door than the old woman was reminding me to kindly keep my shoes and the costume-jewelry bracelet Daddy had given me from nicking the sofa end tables.

Patriotism demands appearances be kept up. Families might suffer — a few smaller suppers for the fat Owen kids one week out of the month — but as long as no one was *seen* to suffer, well, then everything was right with the world. "But your land, the apples, certainly they bring in a sum," I suggested. "The need is there, all of those mouths to feed for the effort."

"Oh, Amelia, that was Robert's concern. The boughs are so heavy they sag to the ground, an easier drop for the fruit that's there."

"Shouldn't you harvest?"

She laughed at the idea. "What do I know of farming? Imagine," — she turned to Mrs.

Cochran, who was passing just then — "a woman pruning and harvesting apple trees. Have you ever heard of such, Mrs. Cochran?" Mrs. Cochran had not.

The Owen property was adjacent to the Reynoldses' and as a little girl I'd run through their fields and into the orchard where the canopy darkened the afternoon and cooled me. Truth was, I played more with Robert Owen than Camilla Smithfield as a child. I was a tomboy, preferring to climb trees and swim naked in the pond to playing with dolls and wearing dresses. Beneath the apple trees, Robert and I took our shoes off and stepped on the fruit where it had fallen and rotted, the velvety meat thick between our toes. During the hard frost of winters, Daddy would wake in the middle of the night and rush from the house, joining other men on the road carrying torches billowing smoke and sparks. They built bonfires throughout the labyrinth of the orchard, between trees in checkerboard fashion, flames reaching to the height of the trees in some places. From my bedroom window I could see the fires burning off frost, smoke and mist rising and catching light so the sky above glowed orange. Daddy, Mr. Owen, and the men burned anything they could get their hands on — old pallets, fallen trees, fence planks, hay bales. The scent of tires thrown on to keep the fire burning through the night offended my nose and

I could smell it for days after. So much work went into keeping the trees alive, the fruit bearing and edible, and Mr. Owen always brought a bushel to us as thanks for all Daddy had done to rally the firemen. I believe they were the most delicious apples I'd ever eaten, more so even than Tony's in Memphis.

Leaning on the Owen property fence after my trip into Mourning made my heart feel like one of those rotted fruits. With the elder Owen too old to tend the farm and Robert away at war, there were more apples on the ground than I'd ever seen before — heaped up like autumn leaves, brown, with a cloud of flies hovering over. Squirrels sat on top of the mounds and rats burrowed into them, emerging from the other side slick with juice. As Camilla said, the limbs, unpruned, bent deeply so their bounty touched the mess already on the ground. It sickened me. A way of life, a good living, food for so many, including the boys at war, all turned to trash. The last I'd heard, the Owens had a hundred acres, and when the wind shifted, I believed I could smell each acre's rot. And why? Because farming was not women's work. Because getting her hands dirty was beneath Camilla Smithfield Owen and the station she believed had been handed down through her name and the sieve of legacy. I'd seen it again and again with Grandmother, and the sense of entitlement was a blight on society and was needlessly harming the families left behind during this war.

Chapter Forty-Eight

I ordered the exact camera Doris Latham used, and all of the chemicals, trays, and utensils she'd advised were needed to process film. Teeth's grandson built out a darkroom in one corner of the barn to Doris' specifications and at night the three of us closed ourselves in with Daddy's old truck in the barn and the headlights shining. We looked for any sliver of silver light pushing through and patched the crevices with tar. "Why it gotta be so dark?" Lonny asked.

"Light will ruin the film before it can be exposed properly," Doris told him.

"Exposed?"

"Have you ever seen a photograph?" He had. "Well, it's a product of the controlled access of light. We have to be able to control how much light touches the film so the shadows reveal themselves."

Lonny shrugged and held his hand up, a splinter of light bisecting the palm.

"These chemicals, the film, they're all flammable," Doris told me once we were done and left the room. We stood among the wood planks and hay of the barn like Joan of Arc on the pyre.

"Then I suppose we should be careful," I said, and tossed a cigarette through beams of light and into a pail of rusty water.

For weeks, Doris and I hauled our cameras all over Greenlaw County and beyond, taking photographs of any and everything catching our attention. Convicts paving a road to the east of Mourning at the Alabama line, a connector to the highways that were taking over the country. A crop duster flying so close to fields cotton stuck in its landing gear. Faces of fatherless children in town, waving flags during patriotic speeches and parades, and wives and mothers clutching bibles to their breasts. I took her to the Owen land to show her that side of war, and we photographed the boys I'd hired to work the orchard.

Doris told me I had a good eye as we walked through town where children clambered to get their faces in our sights as mothers turned a wary eye. People were gracious and sat as still as we asked them so we could take their photos. We loaded our equipment in Daddy's truck Teeth had kept running all these years and drove into the

Delta where the sky opened wide and asphalt gave way to hard-packed dirt roads. We were a strange sight — two women hauling equipment that had as much to do with rural life as the Apollo moon missions would later. We were aliens, except I was from there. I was "of" these people and I had a genuine curiosity about the way they lived and survived on the land. I felt I'd been absent throughout my childhood and needed now to be present. For the most part, we were accepted and, once we showed samples of our work, were allowed to capture the work, life, and play of those we met.

Houses were set far apart, separated by fields and connected by little more than wagon wheel ruts. Even here, men were scarce. Some were overseas, of course, but others had abandoned their families long before Hitler marched into Poland or the Japanese bombed Pearl Harbor. Women and children toiled in fields, hoping to make a few cents per pound while also collecting enough for their own tables. Alongside Doris, I captured that struggle and it was good. I knew from the moment I slipped beneath the camera's hood and saw the world upside down, what I was collecting when the shutter snapped was good. It was important. The world needed to see this — every bead of sweat, every tensed muscle, every blister and wrinkle. And those women deserved to have their smiles immortalized as well as they sat beneath sycamore trees to eat meager lunches and pass jugs of cool water back and forth. I tried to stand in their shoes. It was something I began on the train from Mourning with soldiers going off to war. I'd considered that reality the moment the tinny voice came over Grandmother's Philco radio to frighten us with a new world order. But the child, the little boy who ate half my sandwich — what was his story? Was his father headed to war? Would the war last long enough for him to one day be drafted? Either way, the world had changed and it would be his world very soon. And later that night, when I closed my eyes beneath satin sheets, I tried to imagine what it would be like living as a Zaccone in Eleanor's world. I didn't want to become anyone other than myself and yet there was no stopping it in West Memphis. I walked in the girls' shoes, in their clothes. I took those clothes off and took in man after man. It was someone I never could have imagined becoming, and to do so I had to change my name and forget Amelia Reynolds Thorn, forget Mourning, forget Edward and the baby. Forgetting — or denying — was the hardest, but most important part of becoming something else.

But back in Mourning, I didn't want to become, I wanted to learn. I didn't want to walk in the shoes of Doris or the women in the field, I wanted to stay in mine. They were finally growing comfortable, but I needed Doris to take me by the hand and show me her world. That's what I'd taken from Lizzie and what I had in Memphis with Eleanor. In observing and listening, I learned more about myself than I did of those women.

Observing, learning, is what I did that day on the edge of the bean field beneath a sycamore tree as women told story after story. Stories about their no-good husbands, or the husbands they missed with every tendon in their bodies. They told Doris and me about their own childhoods, many spent in those same farms, in those same fields. We heard about grandparents who had been slaves and how fortunate they felt today to be free. *Free.* Working from sunup to sundown, making pennies on the bushel, living in little more than shacks with no electricity, no running water, no plumbing. Still, they considered themselves free.

"Don't you want more for yourselves? For your children?" Doris said. She pulled a lollipop from the supply she carried in a sack tied to her belt and gave one to the little boy smiling up at her.

"More?" they answered. "What more? Drive around taking pictures? Live in Mourning? Jackson? Factory work?"

Freedom was relative. Still, Doris and I hoped our photos might help in some way.

Educate those in power at the very least. Those with the purse strings. Those who might run a wire or sewer along wagon ruts and out to these shacks.

The children crawled among roots of the tree, swaddled in bark, and one found a toad the others chased around, goading it into pits dug quickly with twigs. They laughed and came running when a mother or aunt called to take a bite of apple or a drink of water. Dust covered them head to toe, but they didn't mind. For them, there was too much to see to worry about practical matters. The women, however, had practical matters on their minds and, attuned to the landscape, they looked to the horizon, sniffing at something unseen to Doris and me. In that area of the country, blue covers green. The sky is as big as anywhere in the world. I wouldn't find out for some time, but when a storm blew in, the dark wall of rain still miles away portended danger. Chaos. The women saw it first — smelled it first — and busied themselves with pots and baskets and jugs of lunch, tying them all up into a cotton sack and throwing it over a shoulder.

"Put it all in the truck and we'll drive you home," I said.

"Home? We got to finish this field."

"But, the rain."

"Rain an hour away. Hour and a half. We got time."

Doris and I stowed our equipment beneath a tarp in the truck bed and walked the rows with them, pinching beans from stalks. We kept our eyes on the horizon and the women kept their heads down, focused, practiced. I wasn't scared. The time for being scared of storms had passed. Rains had taken my husband away, washed him into the train station and out to sea. It had taken my daughter with it as well, and I liked to think they were together — baby and daddy — sitting dry beneath a sycamore tree while big drops danced around them. Rain brings life, but it'd taken too much from me. I had nothing else for it to take and was not pressed about standing naked in it as it pelted my bruised and battered body. Perhaps there could be some healing in those big, bold drops.

Sweat fell from my face, and thorns and prickly stalks lacerated my hands and forearms. I didn't complain. We took our cues from the experts and when, at the end of one row, a whistle went up, we threw our sacks into the truck and the women and children piled in back. It hadn't rained in two months, but we had to race as the storm closed in behind us.

Chapter Forty-Nine

Nuances of aperture speed, dodging my hand in and out of light to darken shadows. Newly fixed photographs hanging on a clothesline to dry, faces distant yet familiar looking back at me. What happened in the darkroom was time travel, bringing a world I'd already walked through back to me days later to unveil details I might have missed at the first pass. It was a magician's trick, an apparition pulled from the ether. Doris taught me it was possible to tell a story through a single image.

"Can we take a break?" Doris said. "Maybe get some dinner, have a drink?"

Paving equipment sat outside the roadhouse saloon waiting for the next day when the chain gang we'd photographed earlier in the week would once again shovel hot tar for miles at a stretch. Gravel crunched under our feet and darkness was kept at bay by an overhead light

275

buzzing and flickering through a cloud of moths. Beyond the light was the blackness of night over an open field. The small house that once sat behind the building was long gone so it felt as though the saloon was floating in space with nothing to anchor it.

The clientele were mostly young men and why they weren't in Europe or the Pacific was a mystery. They looked like convicts fresh off roadwork and out of their cells. But there were a few in uniform, on leave, and I was sure their captains would have had them mopping floors for their loose ties, untucked shirts, and rumpled jackets. Those boys were government issued, chewed up, and spit out the other side. They reminded me of soldiers in the Timeless, told by a grapevine there was a free meal to be had at the Italian's in Memphis. They watched Doris and me with the same hungry eyes I'd first seen on the train to Memphis with Edward. Hungrier, even, as these men had been to war and it was in a muddy foxhole or while being tossed across the deck of an aircraft carrier where they'd come to terms with what it was they, personally, were fighting for. Not sovereignty or any government thousands of miles away. No, they'd been fighting for Doris and me and what we stood for — hips and breasts and hot kisses on cold nights. They bought us drinks and we let them.

"Who are you looking at?" Doris said. A middle-aged man leaned against the bar, his suit jacket thrown over a nearby stool and his shirt sleeves rolled to the elbow as though he were about to begin painting the bar. His tie knot had been jerked down and his top button was open. He was in his element, off duty and on the road.

"Just a man. I saw him in town this morning, at Cooper's when I'd gone for the shipment of film. He was nice."

"You spoke with him? Good for you. He doesn't look military. Or farmer."

"He's a traveling salesman, peddling kitchen items to restaurants and bakeries."

"Should we invite him for a drink? He looks lonely."

"We'll let him be."

"Jesus, you didn't bring me here to talk about photography, did you?" Doris said.

I laughed.

"No F-stop lessons? No questions on fixer timing, aperture times? Will we discuss composition over cocktails?"

"Am I so awful? I'm curious — what you do, for me, is an adventure."

"What *we* do. You were already so good and you've been such a quick study, Amelia. You could do this anywhere you want."

"Why do you do it? Tell me that. It's not a technical question, we're just two friends out for drinks and talking about work." The bartender came around the bar and to our booth, bringing a bottle of whisky and two glasses I'd signaled for. A six-piece swing band came in the back and was setting up on stage.

"Why do I take pictures?" She pondered while I poured. "To get away, roam." We clinked glasses and sipped. "And then I bring back what I see. I think those pictures might do some good. Just look at the situation here in Mississippi — men and women, children, living in squalor. Do you think people in San Francisco, in New York City, in D.C., understand what life is like down here? You can tell them, sure, but I show them. It's truth, and that's powerful. Seeing is impossible to ignore."

"Where else will you go?"

Doris shrugged and sipped. "Wherever."

"And your husband, he's still in California?"

"Danny. Yes, we have an understanding — I leave, I come back. What's freedom to roam if you don't have a place to go home to? You came back to Mourning."

"This isn't my home."

"Where is home, Amelia?"

I was struck by the question, struck by my not having an immediate answer. "This was Mother's home," I said.

"Mourning?"

"This." I looked around the barroom, squinting in cigar and cigarette smoke. The music swirled into smoke and the few dancers looked like so much flotsam caught in a cyclone. Mother had learned to walk here, had stocked shelves with her daddy and, when tall enough, churned out malts and taken orders for burgers and omelets. "This room. This was my grandparents' general store. See the bar there? It was a malt shop, and locals came here for their dry goods, necessities, and whatever produce was available."

Doris turned to look, taking in the room as a photographer, a documentarian. She squinted, not from smoke, but to get a glimpse into the past and the ghost of the room as it had been. "I had no idea."

"I haven't been here since I was a baby. I don't have any memories of it from childhood, just a picture on Mother's vanity mirror."

"And yet, there are so many memories. They're sitting right here in the booth beside us."

"I think Mother, when she was a girl, was scared she wouldn't see anything outside of this room — nothing of the country, let alone the world. With every soup can and sack of flour she placed on the shelves, she must have thought she was committing part of herself to inventory as well. When Daddy came along, he held the door open, and she ran."

"Not so far, though."

"No. I'm not sure she ever had a horizon picked out, though. Mine was over the county limits, at least."

"Running from?"

I sipped my drink, lit another cigarette, and smiled at the man at the bar still staring our way. "Sadness. There's an inherent sadness in Mourning that will pull you down and hold you there. If you don't find your will, your legs, before then, you're doomed."

"Like your mother?"

"Like everyone in this bar and everyone looking up at the moon tonight."

We kept sadness at bay with drinks and laughter and stories of her travels put to music by a swinging sextet. Doris Latham was older than I by fifteen years and I was mesmerized by all she'd seen and done. She told me I'd already lived enough for two lifetimes but if I had, then Doris had surely lived enough for four. We'd become close in the time we'd spent together and she regaled me with story after story of her adventures. I imagined myself running alongside her and was sure I could keep up. My two lifetimes, it turned out, had instilled enough confidence in me for four.

It was an alchemy of confidence, proximity, and the warmth of liquor coursing through my body that made me put my hand on hers. The girls at Ina's and I had often taken comfort in each other's beds. We wanted nothing from the other — not power over nor control of each other — but just to be held tenderly in our longing for intimacy without the promise of violence or money. I only wanted to be held that night and mistook Doris' attention, her position as my mentor, as something else. She pulled away.

"I'm so sorry," I said, surprised I was still able to feel shame and embarrassment. The feelings made me angry and I drained my drink.

"No, Amelia, it's okay. Listen to me: lovers are easy to find, it's friends that are hard to come by. You're my friend and I hope I'm yours. And I hope we will be for a long, long time."

Chapter Fifty

Needing cool night air to clear my head, I asked Doris to drop me at the gate and, on the walk back to my cabin, saw a figure on the porch of the big house, backlit by light from the kitchen window. It was close to midnight, so I was surprised to find Mother, alone, rocking in her chair and sipping tea. The afghan across her lap was one from her sewing circle, one she'd made when I was a little girl. She tried in vain to teach me how to work a needle to create the intricate patterns her mother had taught her, and her mother before her. Those patterns, maps of generations, slipped from my fingers.

We sat and rocked for a time, the moon's light casting shadows across the porch. "We went to the roadhouse tonight, Doris and me. The one out on the highway." Of course she knew which one I meant. It was bold for me to say I'd spent the evening drinking in a saloon, but I was far past the point of worrying over my morals or anyone else's. No, the greater sin here was that I went back to Mother's childhood. She hadn't been back since her parents' deaths and it wasn't because she disproved of consumption.

As I was sure the shock of me at a bar lit her body aflame, I fanned those flames with what I said next. "I know about Daddy and Tessa, and Lizzie."

I eased back into my seat and rocked steadily, matching her own slow rhythm. There was a faraway look in her eyes and I could see them twitching back and forth as though she were trying to focus on one of the moths darting in the dim light from the window of the parlor where Grandmother slept. Was she searching the night for an answer, an explanation? She spoke, "Do you know what a dowry is, Amelia?"

Well, of course I did. The story books I read in the library as a child mentioned dowries. But they were things of the past, I thought. And I was unsure how her question related to what I'd said. We rocked and listened to the scratches and calls of animals in the night. My head swam with liquor and I closed my eyes.

"From the moment I was tall enough to see over the lunch counter, I worked in that diner." Mother had never talked about her childhood. I'd been around my grandparents once or twice, but always heard they'd sold the diner and moved to Carolina — North or South, I couldn't recall, to finish out their lives. "One day a man came in, a traveler. So many of our customers were traveling men then, but this one stood out and I can't quite say why. He was polite — said 'thank you,' said 'yes ma'am' — and he had a book with him, Mark Twain."

"Daddy."

"Mhm. Yes, of course. You know Twain was his favorite."

"He used to read to me right here in these chairs."

"He asked how I was, and I don't think any customer had ever asked how I was doing. They told me they needed more tea, more Coca-Cola, pepper sauce for their greens, or another basket of corn bread. But I couldn't recall anyone asking after my day or my health. But your daddy did that day. And he did the next week when he came back. And the week after that." She blushed.

"He'd been down to the coast, he said, looking for a friend," she continued. "He was tanned a deep nut brown, you know, just how he got when working the fields. 'I hope you found him,' I said, but he just frowned and shook his head."

"Tessa?"

"Tessa. But I wouldn't find out about her, or the baby, until much later." She sipped her tea and it choked going down. "And even then, it wasn't he who told me, but his mother."

Daddy went back the next week for lunch. And then the next. He'd stopped searching for Tessa by then, understanding there would never be an answer, not one that satisfied him. Destiny, it turned out, was stronger than love, and Daddy was destined to take over the family farm ("The legacy and heritage of the Reynoldses," Grandmother said) and to push against it would only bring heartache down on his parents and, eventually, himself. "I looked Mourning up in my atlas after that second week and discovered how far he'd come for that lunch," Mother said. It must have been on one of those trips — or on the way back from the sandy beaches of the gulf coast — when Daddy accepted his fate, his loss. That loss wasn't total, though. There was a baby and he would visit Tessa's sister's house to hold her and look into the eyes of her mama, but he also saw his nose there on the tiny face.

Mother was friendly. She was company and a distraction for Daddy. But Grandmother and the Colonel saw her as something else altogether. Sure, she wasn't from money, and even her heritage was questionable. But she was a white woman, unknown in Mourning, whom Daddy showed an interest in. She would do. Once they made up their minds, all that was left was negotiating a fair price. Sometimes, the value of destiny can be haggled against.

"One day, on the third or fourth visit, my mother took herself from the register and asked what his business was. 'Farming,' he said, and she grunted. She knew from farmers. Her daddy had been one, a sharecropper, really, and I guess she wasn't so impressed. I was impressed. We kept a small garden behind the diner, between it and the small house where we lived, and it wasn't easy to grow enough to feed us and our customers.

"The next week, he came in just before closing time and after my duties, as Ma and Pa locked the door before going around back to our home, there he was, sitting on the chairs we kept out front for folks to rest in the shade after a meal. He asked them if he might take me for a walk; they said yes. And, a week later, for a picnic, yes. And then for a drive into the next town where they had the cinema. Yes. And then he asked my Daddy for my hand."

"And, again, yes?"

Mother paused and sipped from her tea which must have already gone cold. She stared into the darkness. "It had already been taken care of. My father and the Colonel had come to an understanding, though they let the courtship play out on its own terms. They would have interceded regardless, make no mistake, but for whatever reason — and I have my notion it might have been an ember of compassion glowing where Mother Reynolds' heart should be — they allowed us the illusion of controlling our own destiny."

Mother fell silent and looked down at the ground, then up to the moon, and I could tell by the way her back bent that the weight of all the space between the porch and the moon was on her shoulders. We sat there, the Reynolds women (I felt more Reynolds than Thorn at that moment) and listened to cicadas. I looked into the darkness where fields were skimmed by fireflies and could just make out the thresher in the moonlight, rusting, succumbing to the seasons since it killed Daddy. Mother had left it there, not wanting it moved even when Grandmother insisted. "No!" she'd shouted in her grief. "No! It stays." It was a tombstone and I viewed it as a monument to the life Daddy hadn't wanted, the rusted dreams that had killed him too soon.

"It's a hell of a thing," Mother said sometime later, and I believe it was the first time I'd ever heard her swear, "finding out exactly what you're worth at such a young age. To the penny."

Daddy hadn't paid, of course, Grandmother and the Colonel had. And over all those years, Grandmother held it over Mother's head. Was still holding it over her. There was no way her daughter-in-law would ever rise in her estimation because she'd been bought and paid for just like the Negroes that worked her land. In Grandmother's eyes, Mother was no better than Lizzie. "That black bitch," Grandmother had said. I believe Daddy loved Lizzie, in his own way, as best he could. And I knew he'd loved Tessa in a way he could never love anyone else. But I also think Daddy loved Mother. And she knew it, too, deep down. If that dowry hadn't been paid, I believe Daddy could have moved away from Mourning to work in that tiny diner, tend the tiny garden around back, and been as happy or happier than anywhere else. I have to believe it, to keep myself sane. I was born of love — if we don't have that, what do we have to live and grow old and die for? I looked to the yellow light coming from the window of the room where Grandmother slept. What had she lived and grown old for? A name? Lineage? Or just to die?

I thought of Daddy in Palmetto, sitting on a picnic table and staring out to sea, and I wondered what he'd been thinking that day. I'd always thought it was envy of the men loading nets onto fishing boats and the days that lay ahead of them with nothing but wind and water and work to be done. He dreamed of simpler things. But was there regret in his eyes? Had I seen that in the way he clenched his jaw as was his habit? And what about Mother in her rocking chair beside me that night? Did she regret ever engaging with the stranger who read Mark Twain and answering his simple, easy-going question: *How are you today?* Did she wish, as an adult with her sick mother-in-law soiling her sheets on the other side of the door, that she'd never slipped, unseen, an extra piece of pie to that stranger, that she'd never taken his hand as they walked from the diner? What might her life be like today if she hadn't? Still in Alabama? Still waiting tables? She must have seen a missing part of herself in me — leaving Mourning to find my own destiny. Maybe she wished she were somewhere else, anywhere else, alone.

"Come with me, Mother." I don't know why I said it. It was impulsive and as jarring to me as it was to her.

"With you? Where?"

I had no idea, of course. But I would be leaving soon and I knew I'd never return. This might even be the last cool evening I'd spend sitting on the front porch where I'd spent so much of my childhood and where so many memories were born. It's where we spent evenings when summer heat drove us from indoors. It's where Lizzie and I snapped beans and talked. Where I watched Grandmother run Edward off the first time he came calling. Where, as a little girl, I danced and played with my dolls. It's where I would wait for Daddy to come in from the fields as the sun began dipping behind the tree line far to the west. And it's the last place I saw him alive. "Wherever," I said. "Away from here, from this house, this town with its death and hollow spirit."

She looked at me and smiled a broader smile than I think I'd ever seen on her face. It lit up the night. When I think back on that beautiful face today, I like to think she considered leaving for just a moment, for just the length of time it takes to smile and for a smile to fade. She was, no doubt, thinking about the porch as well. About long evenings spent rocking next to her husband, and long afternoons watching me dance and play with my dolls. She would even remember leaping from it, clearing the front steps to run out to Daddy where he lay in pieces beneath the thresher. She turned back to the night and stared into the distance at something no one else could ever know. "I couldn't," she whispered. She'd long ago accepted her fate, her station in a life she never had controlled. She weathered it stoically and loved me, and a part of me deep inside respected her for it when she said, "This is my home."

Chapter Fifty-One

After Mother went inside to bed, I slipped upstairs to my childhood room. It was just as I had left it the morning Edward and I left for Memphis. It was just as it had been when I was six and ten and thirteen — a little girl's room. I looked at myself in the mirror, a woman now, and searched for that little girl in her face. She wasn't there.

Sitting and smoking on the roof outside the bedroom window, I thought of those nights I waited with anticipation for Lizzie to run from the back door, down the lane, and to a waiting car. Memories felt like home. *Where is home, Amelia Thorn?* Doris asked. I thought of Memphis and Pascagoula, Palmetto and Ina's in West Memphis. I'd felt at home, to some degree, in each of them. Even California held a place in my heart, the dream of Edward, the last place his feet touched land. Mourning, as well, and my childhood on the farm, riding horses with Daddy, laughing with Lizzie. It was the people in such places that make them home. And each person had their own freedoms, as Doris' was wandering. Freedom for Lizzie was free will, for Betty it was the simple act of choosing a new name. Eleanor found her freedom in stolen moments alone, away from the clamor of career and family and others' needs. Freedom for Mother was found through the front door of her parents' diner and a new life with the Reynolds clan. Freedom for Daddy was something never realized and that saddened me. Whatever it might have been — the love of Tessa, the horizon he stared at in Palmetto — I wish he'd found it.

The roof shingles had absorbed the day's sun and warmed me. Through them, the friction and vibrations of hinges, springs tensed and released, rippled against my body so I felt the front door open more than I heard it. On the front lawn, a shadow slipped from the tree line into a pool of silvery moonlight. Where Lizzie once skipped, a coyote now slinked. Daddy used to take care of danger, protecting the women in his house and the livestock in the fields. But he was gone and I was on the roof, removed from any danger so I could only watch as though the villain were playing across a newsreel. It's how I used to see Mussolini and Hitler, flickering fear and menace just as James Cagney would in the feature that followed. Who was to say where fact stopped and fiction began? The coyote was as silent as those images. The silence of night entered my bones as the radiant heat of the day had and was punctuated by an owl in the distance, the cicadas' hum rising and falling, and, every now and then, the screech of an unknown species. All around the farmhouse — dead, as I'd come to think of it — darkness came to life. The coyote came for death. But then: the creak of a plank in the porch and a shotgun blast ripping the night before silence settled once again. In that silence was chaos and I found it thrilled me. The coyote dropped to the lawn. From beneath me, Mother stalked down the steps, across the lawn, and up to the carcass with Daddy's Remington rifle cradled in her elbow. She kicked the coyote's head. When she turned to walk back into the house, she glanced my way but there was no expression on her face, neither confidence nor fear, accomplishment nor satisfaction.

Chapter Fifty-Two

"I'm from Memphis," he said, though I hadn't asked. He was up and fastening his suspenders, putting his suit jacket on and brushing lint from the sleeves. "Yeah, this is my route. Travel all through the Delta. Been to Memphis?"

"No." I pulled the sheet up over my bare chest and lit a cigarette, wishing he'd float out the door on its smoke.

"Oh, it's nice. You'd like it." Why he thought that I hadn't a clue. "Cafés. Clubs. Department stores."

"Yes. That describes a city. I've always heard it to be crime-ridden, barbaric even."

"Barbaric? Says who?"

"My dear grand-mère." The girls and I at Ina's would occasionally slip into what little French we gleaned from a French-English dictionary on the shelves in the parlor. It made us laugh, feel in control. Frivolity was lost on this man.

"Well, it's not. Not more than any other river town, anyway." He looked misplaced, as though he wasn't sure what to do with his hands, or when to exit. "Anyway, I think my wife is cheating on me. When I travel, I think she has a man over. Or men."

I stubbed my cigarette out. "You can go now." The most compassionate thing I could do, short of putting a bullet in his head, was to show him the exit.

I didn't tell Doris about my visit with the man from the bar later as we sat on the bed of Daddy's truck where it stuck from the barn doors. Our feet dangled. We were teenagers again. "So what's next?" I said.

"I was supposed to ship out from New Orleans next week, document the hunt for German subs off the coast of Cuba. But I'm going home."

"California? Why? Is it because of my clumsy pass? Oh, Doris, I misread signals. The drink . . ."

"Don't be silly, dear. It's time. Time for me to go, to be with my husband," she said. "I've been gone a long time and seen plenty. I seem to have this internal clock — or perhaps it's a compass — telling me when and where to go.

And it's now, it's time to see my way back home."

"To stay?"

"Doubtful. But I miss my little house by the ocean, the Fatsia plants that overlook the porch and the sound of wind chimes. Danny makes them by hand and each has its own voice."

"What about your work?" I held my hand out for the jar and she passed it. The liquid burned my lips, a sensation I looked forward to. I'd taken the rest of Daddy's stash to Teeth when I went to collect the money his nephews had earned in Jackson. I hired them to work the Owen orchard and they'd taken the harvest to sell. Later I stood on Camilla Owen's porch while she cursed me in front of her fat children. "Where is the rest of it, Amelia?"

"That's it. That's your cut."

"My cut? They're my goddamn apples," she seethed.

"And they were rotting. The young men I hired to do the work broke their backs to prune and tend and harvest before all was lost. They deserve the lion's share."

"And what do a bunch of nigger boys need with so much money?"

I stepped into the doorway and she stepped back, pushing a chubby face behind her. "It's their money, Camilla. What they do with it is none of your concern. They'll be back in the spring to tend to the trees and so help me God, if you say anything to them, if you send them away, if you demand more money — if anything other than 'thank you' escapes those thin, chapped lips of yours — I will tell them to burn this orchard to the ground."

I needed a drink after dealing with Camilla and was glad I'd saved a jar for just this moment with Doris.

"Called my agent in New York from Cooper's this morning," she said. "He asked me six months ago to take this next assignment and boy was he pissed. He shouted long distance, asking who in hell could take my place?"

"You're the best there is, Doris. Who the hell can take your place?"

"You. You ship out first part of next week."

"Me?"

"I told him you're as good — if not better — than I am." She drank and a smile spread across her face, and I wonder to this day what she read on mine. I didn't smile, I don't think, though I was happy. It must have been a look of peace, I imagine, as the sense of knowing my place in life, in the world, washed over me. I'd found myself, the coyote slain in the moonlight.

And the very next day I boarded the train, again, to leave Mourning. This time for good.

MEMPHIS

Chapter Fifty-Three

Once again, Amelia Thorn jumped from the cliff face of the Mourning train station platform. Her life looped around and around, and folded back on itself until she found herself in Memphis six decades later, retired, reclusive, her long days spent with books and walks through the Old Forest of Overton Park in the heart of the city, writes Frank Severs. *In the final year of Amelia's life, two strangers took an interest in her, laying her life out in a series of chapters and photographs. She was an old woman then, alone, when Maria Whitaker and I tugged loose the knot of her life. I studied her beginnings to learn how she evolved into who she was; Maria, the end, collecting and sharing a life's work with the world.*

Maria likes to say it was fate that brought her together with Amelia. Like Lizzie on the eve of her first child's birth, Maria couldn't see the chaotic symmetry of attending her grandmother's funeral in Brooklyn, New York, and enjoying the same buffet finger sandwich as a Sotheby's curator who invited her to tour the catacombs of storage vaults nestled in granite and rubbing up against subway lines. He was Egyptian born, his specialty early twentieth century photography, and on his desk, among an archivist's clutter, was a framed reproduction of a photo — a crowded bazaar from his homeland. By Amelia's recollection, she must have taken it in 1949 or '50. Maria admired it and the curator said, "Certainly you know Amelia Thorn?"

"Certainly? Why 'certainly?'"

"She's from Memphis. Legend has it her entire collection is tucked away beneath a restaurant she owns."

"Legend?"

He smiled, Maria told me, adding that the catacombs, kept at a low temperature and humidity for the priceless works kept there, suddenly grew warm. "Well, you'll just have to find Ms. Thorn."

And so she did. As soon as she landed back in Memphis, she went to see Morrie Reese, a photographer whose studio, by coincidence (by chaos?) was a block from the Timeless Café. Morrie Reese sat on the board of Maria's museum and he suggested they take a walk for lunch.

"You know Amelia Thorn? Her work?"

"Sure." Morrie Reese was a man of few words, his images speaking for him. He sipped hot tea brought to him before he even ordered. His eyelids were heavy with age and rested half-closed over blue eyes. He was quiet and philosophical and people who spent time with him said there was a serenity about him that made them feel calm and at ease as well.

"Where can I find her photos? I'd love to see them."

Somewhere, a butterfly flitted and Morrie Reese turned his head to look at the far wall where hung a photograph of an old-world Italian village. It was exquisite with light and shadows and implied movement from decades-old cars and unknowable people walking its streets. It was stunning and Maria Whitaker fell into it. And somewhere below the image of that village, below where Morrie Reese and Maria Whitaker sat sipping tea and coffee, was a basement crammed with portfolios and flat files filled with prints and film and mysteries that, when uncoiled, would reach back to touch a maimed horse bleeding to death on Main Street.

Chapter Fifty-Four

Hector
New Orleans. 1944

Albumen silver print from glass negative,
44.1 x 32.8 cm (17 3/8 x 12 7/8 in.)

Courtesy, New Orleans Museum of Art.

Frank Severs took his phone from his pocket, held it up and snapped a photo of my profile, catching me in mid-thought, my mind rushing through the streets of Havana, the Gulf Stream, and the French Quarter to catch up with my old body. "Simple, isn't it?" I said to him and held up my hand, mimicking a camera. "*Click*. It's almost too simple these days."

Frank was a friend of Maria Whitaker's, a reporter, who found me where I'd cocooned myself away. In my apartment, on the top floor of a building overlooking Overton Park and the Brooks Museum of Art, is where I read and I remembered and I waited. For what, I don't know. Death? Ghosts? I'd grown tired after years of travel, years in the energy of movement and the "aura of other people" as my friend Morrie Reese said was present in everyone, drawing our own energy out like a syringe. Or a leach.

Frank was drawn to the movement, to my travels from Mourning to Memphis to the world beyond. The *why* of it all. The *how*. The *where*. He was a good reporter and a better writer; I'd seen his byline and looked closer into him during my trips to the public library. I wasn't entrusting my life story to just anyone, I'd worked too damned hard to live it. Just as I wouldn't have handed my life's work over to just anyone, but Maria was thoughtful and curious and, as a curator, and a woman, she had my best interests at heart. I trusted them both.

But I'm getting ahead of myself. As I said, I left Mourning a second time. This time for good.

"And you came back to Memphis?"

"Not so quickly, Mr. Severs," I said. "First, I had to see the world."

"You'd already lived a lifetime."

"I had a few more to go. It was time for me to leave. I didn't belong in Mourning. I didn't belong in Memphis, either, not yet. But maybe there was a place for me in the world. I would find out, as Doris had. She said, 'Don't let anybody put a limit on you, not even yourself.' She'd found the world to be her own and if the same were to be the case for me, then I'd have to take that first step to find out. The first step was aboard a train from Mourning to New Orleans, and from there a steamer to Cuba."

I'd never seen anything like New Orleans. It was sweet and sour, wild and cozy, all at once. There were hordes of people, soldiers on leave among them, filling the streets, drinking, laughing, and music everywhere. It was as though the troubles of the world — certainly the troubles of war — didn't exist beyond the cobblestones and Spanish moss carpeting the city. Doris had given me the name of a friend, a painter, who lived in the Quarter and had a sofa for me to sleep on. I arrived at an indecent hour of the night (was it early morning?) and was fully prepared to wait patiently on the front stoop to be greeted by a milkman or paper boy, or however it was New Orleans welcomed a new day. I needn't have worried; New Orleans never said goodnight to the previous day. When I arrived, the second-floor windows glowed and brass horns filled the air. I climbed the steps with my equipment and luggage, and Hector, the painter, greeted me with a hug, kisses on both cheeks as though we were old friends, and a drink. I was passed around the party like a favor, hugged at every turn, handed more drinks, and twirled to music that never seemed to end.

"Bohemians," Mother had said when I told her my destination, and the word intrigued me as much as Grandmother's "heathens" had when she warned me against Memphis. I was in love — not with any one person, but with a city, again.

That night at Hector's was just the send-off I needed. The one I'd had with Mother had been more subdued. "Where will you go?" she said through trembling fingers.

"I explained that, Mother. I'm going to Cuba for work. I don't know where from there."

"But you don't work." The privilege of being a Reynolds woman had seeped into Mother through the years. Grandmother would have been proud of her daughter-in-law, had the old woman not been so near death. "And what about Mother Reynolds?" Mother said. "She's missed you so, leaving again will break her heart."

"Her heart? I'm not sure she's in possession of such an organ."

"Amelia!"

"Goodbye, Mother."

In my childhood room, where I'd once taped the photo of Daddy taken years earlier, I left a self-portrait. It was a straight-ahead shot of me, unsmiling, my pupils ringed with white light as my eyes searched the world beyond the frame. The background was taken up with the Reynolds home, out of focus. If Mother ever found it there in the corner of the vanity's mirror, I don't know. But if she did, and if she looked close enough, she might have realized that, with the big house to my back, my eyes searched for, and found, the home of Lizzie, of my sister.

"Do you live like this all the time?" I asked Hector. Morning light caught him in the far corner of his apartment where an easel, covered with a tarp, had stood like a wallflower the night before. This morning it was uncovered and he stood behind it, stepping into paint, and back out to look, as though he'd never stopped dancing.

"Like what, darling?"

"Like it's the last night ever. Like there's no tomorrow." I lifted my camera from the floor beside the sofa where I'd slept and looked down into the viewfinder to bring Hector into focus.

"But it is tomorrow, dear — there's always a tomorrow and never any way to know what it will bring. But on this tomorrow, you have a boat to catch. Now get up, dress, and we'll have coffee on the way to the harbor. Come along,

Doris Latham will never forgive me if you miss your boat."

Chapter Fifty-Five

I boarded the steamer with only minutes to spare and with a dusting of powdered sugar from beignets on my lips. The ship's captain wore a beige linen suit with vest and a plum ascot. It was a ridiculous costume and not at all captain-like. On the bridge, however, he donned a white captain's hat with its gold crest as though the ability to navigate a ship downriver and into open water was hidden somewhere in that cap's lining. Ridiculous. He smoked a meerschaum pipe and was eager to show me around his vessel, taking me into the engine room where sweaty, shirtless men leered at me and wiped their oily brows with dirty forearms. We toured dry storage filled with bleating goats and sheep that pleaded with me for escape. In the galley, he took a folded knife from his vest pocket, wiped the blade on the thigh of his pant leg, and cut a sliver of cheese for each of us. As we left, he took a wine bladder from where it hung on a nail, angering the staff who had been sharing it. I followed him topside into the warm air and watched as the skyline of New Orleans faded slowly from sight. It was difficult to think of this river as the same water I'd waded into as a young widow, my tears falling to its surface and, I was sure, raising its tide along with the weight of my sorrow. The same river where I'd escaped a life of whoring and where a body, its lungs deflated by my own knife, had sunk to the sandy bottom. In the meandering, violent, angry, peaceful currents there was chaos and there was order. There was life and there was death.

The captain was gallant and romantic, and we drank wine while standing at the railing as the sun dipped lower into Louisiana swamps. He told me about his home in Argentina where he'd grown up on a plantation of rice and sorghum and a thousand head of cattle, yet longed for the sea. "I grew up on a farm as well," I told him.

"You? You don't look like a farmer; you are far too fair. Perhaps you were conjured from the cream of a mother cow's milk?"

He was funny and wanted in my bed. I laughed with him, but my adventure was only just beginning and I found the scent of spicy tobacco from the carved claw bowl of his pipe far more interesting than the man himself. "Goodnight," I said.

It was a long trip to Cuba as we made ports of call along the length of Florida. The captain, tenacious and hungry, did not weary in his advances. His crew, on the other hand, worked as hard at making me feel uncomfortable as they did at keeping the ship afloat and on course. I sensed each man was running from something. The law, most likely — the ship's engines ran on secrets. Tales whispered on deck carried seeds of *murder* and *burglary* and *rape* on night breezes. There were nights I took supper in the galley with the men and then drank with them in the hold after, hidden among crates and sniffing the air for the cloud of Latakia that would give the captain away. I shared stories of my own (taking literary liberty by offering Ina's girls' stories as my own) and they laughed nervously, uncomfortable with a woman's lurid past. But the sailors were emboldened by the late hour, our cramped space, and the liquor they'd stowed away. I carried my own aboard, a gift from Hector, and shared it with them, matching them slug for slug. I was one of them. And like one of them, on those lonely nights at sea, tethered to the long reflection of moonlight on water, they wanted to visit me in my room. I rebuked them all, save for the ship's cat, Roxy, which stretched the length of its body against my legs and slept until the moon was chased away by the sun.

Many years later I returned to the States via the same route, though under a new world order. The Cold War was raging then and I'd been in Cuba shooting a young Fidel Castro as he rallied his people behind worldly philosophies. I traipsed through the mountain jungles from village to village with a platoon of men, caught in the hazy fug of Castro's cigar smoke and incessant chatter. He was charismatic and frightening, but by then I'd been frightened by far worse and I believed, as did so many who'd lived through it, the greatest threat to the world had died along with Hitler.

It wasn't the same boat I returned aboard, nor the same captain. I heard through a friend in the Red Cross she'd been commandeered as a Merchant Marine tanker transporting oil to England and torpedoed in the North Atlantic during the final months of war. "They went into the water and came out covered in the engine oil they'd carried as cargo. There were perhaps a dozen or so in the life raft. This from a mate of mine who survived — lucky son of a bitch was in another raft just outside the slick." We were having lunch at a bistro in Paris and my friend, still on shift, took a sip of gin and placed the glass back on the table, covering it with her nurse's white cap. "Anyway, there was only one flare.

311

Must have been a hell of decision to make — fire it and hope the rescue planes spot it; fire it and risk going up in flames. I imagine they took a vote, but he — your captain — would've had the final say. My mate said it was like the blinding flash of a camera." She gulped the last of the highball. "And that the water boiled from the heat."

My nightmare later that night was of a handsome man with a pencil-thin mustache and oversized captain's hat, his white meerschaum melting to his face as he clenched his jaw tighter, the breath of a scream whistling through perfect teeth. When I awoke covered in sweat, I swore I could smell tobacco.

On my return to the States, we lurched into dock ahead of a storm chasing us from Havana. Modern-day sonar wasn't available, at least not on a cargo ship with questionable papers, but the spiral was never far behind. Sailors are a superstitious breed and blamed me, a woman, for being aboard at all. "Diablo," they hissed, looking astern at the darkening sky, feeling the millibars drop into their bare chests. I hadn't felt threatened by Castro and I'd long stopped feeling threatened by men and their voodoo. We'd either survive or perish, but we'd do it together. If they thought I'd float as a witch, or ascend bodily into the heavens, while they drowned, then they were foolish children. I pitied them as they hurled their undigested breakfasts over the side.

New Orleans was battening its hatches as we disembarked. She would survive, this wasn't her storm. This was Palmetto's. I was on my way there, sent by a newspaper far from the coast to document a storm that promised destruction only seen in a storybook or a John Huston film. *We cannot be responsible for the safety of a woman under such conditions*, the newspaper's lawyers wrote to my agent, and followed it with waivers via airmail for me to sign. I signed their papers and added a few choice words of my own below the signature. I imagine they questioned the frailty of women and the wonder of the English language upon reading.

I looked for Hector in the Quarter, but the woman who answered the door said he moved years earlier and didn't know where. Forwarding addresses weren't common in New Orleans at that time, if they even are now. I remember the party he was having the night before I shipped out — all those young men, none of them serving. Shame, I suppose, was as good an excuse as flat feet for the U.S. government.

Palmetto had grown since Daddy and I spent the afternoon there when I was a little girl. Families, looking for a place to get away after the war, had forced the land and way of life to accommodate their cars, pails, floaties, and need for cold drinks at sunset. The small village I remembered from childhood now extended from the water's edge, across the highway — widened to handle increased traffic — and into where pine trees had been clear-cut to make way. Motels, restaurants, gift shops, an amusement park. I photographed them all because, as far as I was concerned, the neon and tiki huts were the damage unleashed on the area long before any hurricane might make landfall.

But there were still boats moored in the harbor. The view of them and beyond to the horizon was still the same Daddy had enjoyed.

I arrived by train, the last expected for days, and by then vacationing families had scattered. Locals, though — those with nowhere to run — worked to prepare for the inevitable pummeling bearing down on them. The wind was picking up and I stood in the oyster shell parking lot of the diner where we'd eaten. That landmark, and the nearby sea foam-colored motel, were the only recognizable bits of that long-ago day. A shock went through me as I looked to the east and realized I was standing in the spot where I'd snapped the photo of him. That day it had been a Kodak Brownie, not two hours old, and on this day it was a Graflex 4x5 Pacemaker Speed Graphic, dented and nicked and well-traveled, and as familiar to me as my own body. I wiped salt spray from the lens with my shirttail and pointed it toward a couple loading provisions onto their trawler, covering them with netting, and lashing it all down with rope. The man wore dungarees without shoes or a shirt, his skin deeply tanned. A cigarette hung from the corner of his mouth, as did one from his wife's lips. She hoisted boxes to her husband from the dock, muscles tightening and flexing in a sleeveless blouse. Neither spoke, the work took priority. Their speed and efficiency was life and death.

Years later, Maria Whitaker held prints from that day in white gloves and circled her pinky finger around their faces, marveling at the determination and focus found there. "We sat at the diner later that morning and I bought them burgers and beers, and the woman told me they would take their boat two miles east, towards Apalachicola, where a tributary empties into the Gulf of Mexico," I told her. "The surge would make the shallow passage navigable and they'd find refuge anchored as far inland as could be managed. 'The trick,' the man told me, 'would be getting out again before the creek becomes too shallow and traps us.'"

"Kamchatka?" Maria said.

"I didn't mention it, but you can bet it was on my mind. Everything they had in the world was on that boat," I told Maria, and pulled another print from the file. The shutter had snapped open and closed just as the woman's face shifted from determination to fear. Fear came back for me from the past as well, wind-blown over decades. I'd weathered my own storms and saw traces of myself in the woman's face, silver gelatin caught in deep-set lines around her eyes.

Chapter Fifty-Six

Tragedy on the Highway
1944

Gelatin silver print, 37.5 x 27.9 cm
(14 3/4 x 11 in.)

Courtesy, United Press International archives.

I knew I was returning to Memphis to stay. ("Memphis?" my agent said. "Jesus, aren't they still fighting the Civil War down there?") I called Memphis home when I saw Edward off and I'd meant it. I always knew it would be home again even if I had to take a circuitous, meandering route to get back there. I'd seen the good in the world, the beautiful, and met people who would stay with me the rest of my life. I ached to share those stories with Edward and wished I had the talent for writing he had so I might share them with others. I didn't, so I shared them the best way I knew how — through my photographs. I made it a point to be present in the world and to share it with those who couldn't — or wouldn't — explore.

But one can't see only light while turning a blind eye to shadow. It was while peering into darkness that I saw the worst of the world. I was in Korea, where, as a fly on tent walls, I witnessed violence and fear and inhumanity. Women were treated little better than dogs in a war zone, yet my focus stayed true and I am proud of the body of work I produced, even if the images make me ill to look at today.

With my tour up and with gunfire and mortar shells exploding behind me, I boarded a tanker to sail the Sea of Japan to the Sea of Okhotsk and around the Kamchatka Peninsula, a knife blade on the eastern edge of the Soviet Union. There was a soldier aboard, a jazz musician from Kansas City, who had traded his horn with the Bengalese cook for safe, secret passage. He was AWOL; the oceans of the world were afloat with misfits. The cook returned the boy's horn, love more powerful than any payment, and on cool, moonless nights, he played his trumpet low and sad for us. Later, through the thin wall of the cook's berth where the men lay side by side in a single cot, I heard Elvis Presley, the boy who had found fame at the Chisca Hotel a few years earlier, singing through a tinny phonograph about another hotel at the end of Lonely Street.

Kamchatka was a militarized zone and forbidden to outsiders. I was smuggled into its forests by a guide bribed by *National Geographic* to photograph the people living there in stone huts built into the side of the many volcanoes ringing the peninsula. Locals lived primitively and toiled in factories where science turned metal and powder into killing machines. In the evenings, they gathered around open fires to tell stories and share food. Sitting on upended boxes, old tires and fallen tree trunks, they glanced up over their shoulders as a matter of habit, a tic, a recognition of the power there. It was the volcano. Fear — its constant, looming presence — was woven into their DNA so there was no need to discuss the danger they lived beneath. The possibility — the probability — of what might happen had been with them for generations. They spoke more openly about their fear of the Kremlin.

It was early November and my expedition was working its way up the Kamchatka River when the earthquake hit. *Magnitude nine*, newsreels reported later. Trees came down, structures along the banks hit the water with such force a tidal wave sent our small fishing vessel to the other side of the river, wrecking us there. *Nothing can ready one for such a blast, for the violence of it,* Edward had written. Three in my crew died instantly. Instinct takes over in such circumstances. "It can't be taught," Doris had told me the day we'd come upon a wreck along a two-lane Mississippi highway moments after it happened. Doris helped the victims, a family whose car hit a buck bounding across the road, swerving into the ditch and coming to rest on a fence post. My impulse had been to photograph the carnage, an image I later sold to United Press — the first dollar I'd ever make off my photography. "You have that instinct, Amelia. Embrace it. Cultivate it."

The carnage in Kamchatka was far beyond a deer with a broken neck. Beyond, even, the couple's child who'd gone through the car's windshield (he lived), but I'd grabbed my camera just the same to run toward billowing smoke, toward screams of panic and pain in a language I didn't know. As a documentarian, I was forced in a split second to decide whether to give aid or to photograph. History will judge me, but it is because of me history has evidence of the destruction that day and of the souls lost forever. More than two thousand of them. When the first wave of the tsunami hit the mouth of the river, I'd just gone back to the boat for supplies and was pushed upstream with all the force of nature behind it. As if on a rocket engine, we rode the wave deeper inland and up to a higher altitude so when the second wave hit, we were out of harm's way. The second wave, though, pushed bodies with it and floating death met us where my decimated crew and I huddled with villagers. Even as water boiled up beneath us, villagers looked back at the volcano, assuming the inevitable had finally, at long last, come to pass.

Weeks later, safely in the Japanese offices of the Associated Press, the horror of the blank, warped faces silently screaming from underwater haunted me once again. I heard the lowing bleat of a trumpet and saw the twisted lips of the jazz musician through ripples in a pan of developer and the hellish glow of the dark room's red light. I needed to get away from the atrocities of war and Mother Nature. I'd been moving forward for so long, the word "home" — an abstract I'd long been at a loss to define — took on a comforting glaze and, through the viewfinder of distance, was coming even more into focus. Though it would take me another eight years to get there, I did make it back to Memphis.

Chapter Fifty-Seven

On a small Navy outpost just outside Palmetto, we emerged, blinking, from a concrete bunker to open sand, bent and broken sea oats, and seagulls dancing on forgiving trade winds against a peaceful, blue sky. And everywhere else was havoc. Boats stacked on top of each other like Pick-up Sticks in the marina and on land, cars half buried in sand, the highway's asphalt cracked and contorted from storm surge. The diner stood strong but with half of its roof ripped away, as did the motel with its plywood windows caved in. No deaths, thank God.

I hiked to where the highway was whole again and then some, catching a ride on a produce truck into Alabama. I hitched my way into the Delta and jumped a boxcar on a rail line that carried me far to the south of Mourning and into Arkansas. The traveler who gave me a hand up told me he'd been in Korea as well and had little interest in steady work now that the Army was done with him. "Not for everybody," I said. He laughed and said steady work had never really been for him, war or not. He shared a can of spaghetti and I offered him bananas stolen from the produce truck. Sometime in the night, I awoke where I slept on a bed of straw to his hand in my blouse. Edward's knife was close at hand and left a rip in his shirt sleeve and blood running down his arm. When daylight broke, he was gone. He jumped at some point, though I wasn't sure where. Nor did I care.

"Trees? Who the hell wants to look at trees?"

"Maybe decent, normal people do. Stop looking at the work through the agent's, money-colored lens. Maybe after Korea and Kamchatka, protests and lynchings, the store clerks and window washers and shoe salesmen who buy newspapers and magazines need a little goddamn color in their days."

"Okay, okay, okay. Fine. Jesus. How does one even go up a mountain?" My agent had never left the island of Manhattan, not even for vacation. The first time I visited him there, he'd shown me around his city as though we were on safari through the Serengeti. And I'd been to the Serengeti!

"There aren't any elevators as there are in your precious ivory skyscraper, so I imagine I shall walk."

"Walk? Jesus."

I'd called him from a payphone at the foothills of the Ozarks, looking up at Petit Jean Mountain in Arkansas. It wasn't the first mountain I'd come to by that point, of course. And it wasn't even much of a mountain to speak of — as it was only a thousand feet or so, my agent probably walked farther every morning for his bagel and lox. I'd been to Guatemala and the Alps. I'd ascended Mount St. Helens, Etna, Kilauea, and Mount Baldy. In Nepal, I succumbed to altitude sickness, though that may have been the two bottles of gin a Sherpa and I shared in his hut.

So I hauled my equipment, a tent from an Army-Navy store, and supplies alone up Petit Jean via a rutted forest service road that wound through trees and below a canopy thick with pine. The path was clearly marked, yet it took several days to reach the top where the wind was cooler and the valley view's breathtaking with leaves like a patchwork quilt of autumn colors. I'd been through more trying times in my travels and the journey felt like more of a vacation than work even as my boots worked to grip jagged Arkansas granite and slick, red clay.

Chapter Fifty-Eight

A week later, I stood on a crumbling sidewalk in West Memphis, Arkansas, pointing my Graflex up at the four-story, one-time hotel I'd called home for a year. The accordion nose moved out and back but, try as I might, I had trouble focusing through the broken levees flooding memories over me. All evidence of life the old house once held had been excised many years before so empty windows caught the early autumn sunlight to wink back at me. I could recall, if I stretched my memory thin enough, gingerbread detail had once been painted green with red and yellow details around windows and eaves. No one who'd known it as a hotel would ever guess what it would become — a whorehouse — with a wide and inviting front porch teeming with young girls taking a respite from work, catching the breeze, chatting while sipping lemonade, and reading the books Miss

Ina had insisted upon to make our minds as well-rounded as our bodies.

All those years later and weeds poked from staggered and stained concrete stairs where the home sat on an eroding rise from the street. The rotting porch listed and eaves drooped like the heavy lids of a tired, old woman. I snapped and the camera's shutter clicked open and shut.

Travel made going home all the sweeter, Doris had been right about that. My first trip to Memphis had been a direct route from Mourning — from childhood to adulthood — and had ended disastrously. By walking up Petit Jean alone, I believed, somewhere deep down where the voodoo incantations of Miss Ina still echoed, I was purifying myself to go home again. It was nothing Catholic — though it was certainly superstitious enough — nor was it the black-and-white belief of Grandmother's Protestantism. This was something more innate. I was shedding the worst of what I'd experienced. It was a spirituality, Eastern in flavor. But perhaps that was just the taste of Tenzing's homemade Nepalese gin still in my mouth.

A man in a flatbed truck left me there in the street outside the long-vacant and neglected brothel, standing ankle-deep in my thoughts as I had in the rutted mud of Petit Jean. I hadn't even heard him drive away, but couldn't be angry either way, as he'd been kind enough to drive me from the base of the mountain once I hiked down from its summit. Air had thickened the lower I went and my pace quickened, and I felt stronger for having put myself through that week alone with only what I could carry in. It was a strength I'd felt building all along. Where had it come from, though? Had it bubbled up from the well beside Lizzie's house? I'd always thought of Mourning as a place of weakness with its black veil of crushing sadness as I'd described it to Doris in a roadhouse late at night. There was no hope, no future there for a young girl. The landscape promised only rotting crops and dead children, weak mothers and fearful women. Even Grandmother, with her dictatorial ways, was little more than moon shadow on a moonless night.

My strength went back as far as the train pulling away from the Mourning depot on its way to New Orleans. Something stirred there inside me. A changing of the seasons. My time spent with Lizzie and her baby, my time at Ina's, and in Memphis before, was boiling over. I embraced it (schooled by Doris, I knew enough to do so) and I let it warm me enough that winter morning that I removed my sweater. The woman sitting opposite looked horrified and disapprovingly at my bare arms and cleavage, and I gave that look right back to her. I pulled a cigarette from my bag, holding her gaze, and watched as her face went up in the flame of my lighter. It was a fire to be stoked on the steamer to Cuba and my work there photographing U-boat hunters off the coast. It burned brightly with my travels through South America and a glimpse of Antarctica from a whaling ship. Europe and the Far East filled me with confidence and courage, and I created a character for myself as Edward had at his typewriter. I became someone a much younger Amelia Reynolds, taking snapshots of her pony with a Brownie box camera, would have admired, I think. A cross-pollination of Ina, Eleanor, Lizzie, and Doris.

Poor, dear Doris. I missed her and, as I sat in the glow of a campfire on the flat top of Petit Jean, I wanted nothing more than to pick her brain, laugh with her, share a cigarette and a ribald joke. I'd looked forward to her visiting me in Memphis one day and introducing her to the friends I'd made there. But by the time my memories caught up with me outside Ina's neglected brothel, it had been three years since the trawler Doris was on capsized in the Bering Strait. I was in Hawaii when the news reached me on Kilauea, in fact, and stopped in San Francisco on my way to New York. I met her husband; the poor man was lost without her. "She leaves," he said as we drank coffee on the patio of their home. "That's what Doris does, she always has. But she's always returned to me. And I keep looking to the front door, expecting it to open. I walk to the mailbox expecting one of her silly postcards or provocative letters. But nothing's there. She's nowhere now, they never recovered her body."

"No, Daniel, no," I said, taking his shaking hands in mine. "She's everywhere. Don't you see? She always has been. It's her nature. Look at your view. She told me about this view so many times — the blue of the Pacific, the way the sky meets it, the trumpet vine in bloom, the shade of Fatsia leaves. She even told me about the hummingbirds and how, when things were quiet, she could hear their wings beating. 'Tiny heartbeats,' she called them. Look, Daniel. Listen. She's there in all of it — all you have to do is be present. It's what she would have wanted."

He put his arm around me and hugged my shoulder and we stood there together, looking to the sea for those we'd loved and lost. "You're a good friend, Amelia," he said.

"Doris once told me good friends are the hardest to come by."

On the way out the door that day, I stopped in the small parlor where embers of a fire from the night before cooled in the fireplace. He was right, there was something missing from this home. I stood in front of a framed photograph and recognized the figure, naked beside the muddy bank of a pond outside of Mourning. It was jarring to see my younger self there, bare to the world as I'd been at the time, inside and out. I remembered the heat that day and how we'd stripped our clothes and sunk into the cold water, covering our limbs with mud from the bottom, and diving down to wash it off again. It was so much fun, so freeing, so empowering and Doris had caught it all — my confidence and naiveté, my emerging spirit — on film. I reached up to straighten the frame on the wall and left her house.

I walked from Arkansas into Memphis hand-in-hand with cars and trains that sang in my ears, and with the memory of friends made the world over. The Graflex hung around my neck and the large format camera with its tripod was slung over my shoulder. I carried them as Sisyphus had his boulder or Jesus his cross. Those men were doomed beneath their burdens, yet I imagined myself more as Doris on the first morning I'd seen her walking down the dirt lane — tall and proud and strong — a walk full of possibility. Still, my cameras, and all I'd witnessed with them around the world, pressed their weight and sharp corners into my flesh.

Chapter Fifty-Nine

Collective years spent in airplanes and on boats, trains, motorcycles, and the odd camel, showed me what there was beyond the *L* volume of Miss Ina's *Encyclopedia Britannica*. Mine was a lifestyle that hadn't lent itself to routine, but to a sense of shifting sand beneath my feet and of being carried aloft like a kite on wind. Still, when I saw the neon sign of the Timeless Café and the warm, glowing lights from inside, my heart settled into a rhythm from the past.

I looked through the long, plate glass window and took it all in — the linoleum, red-and-white checked tablecloths, and long, wooden lunch counter scarred with age. The booths, as always, were in need of repair or replacement with scuff marks and rips showing in the vinyl. The ancient cash register sat like a monolith on the front counter and the overhead clock like an ever-seeing eyeball just behind it, keeping watch

331

over everything. It was as if I could smell the coffee and warm kitchen grease where butter and bacon no doubt sputtered. I saw myself in that room, too — a young, pregnant girl in a blue waitress uniform with her head swimming in possibilities, holding a coffee pot ready to pour.

It had been so long since I passed through the front door but the sight and smell of the café were as comforting as the porch light on Grandmother's house when I was a child running up the driveway hungry for supper. The tinkling of the door's brass bell had been buried in my subconscious through all my years spent away. Today, it triggered a deep and visceral sense of home and a Pavlovian emotion welled up within me when it sounded. Yet something wasn't right. There were dishes on the tables, many with food still on them in various stages of being eaten. A coffee cup steamed. From behind the counter came the static repeat of a stylus needle failing to find purchase on the inside groove of a record. But there were no people. "Charlie?" I called out. "Bobby?" No answer. I even called for Christine, knowing she was long gone. Her name echoed in the empty room along with the withering bell. It was as if the customers had simply vanished, drawn up through the ceiling or dropped through a trapdoor. Something fluttered in my chest and tickled at the prehistoric fear in my body. I felt sick.

I dropped my equipment but clung to the luggage, wary still of Edward's stolen valise. And that's when I noticed Mr. Mednick, the jeweler, sitting in the very booth where I'd served him meals several times a day. In the same heavy, navy suit he'd worn day-in and day-out, he was just as much a fixture of the restaurant as the bell, the register, the clock, the tablecloths. An empty mug, still turned over, mouth down on its saucer, sat in front of him. He was waiting for coffee.

"Mr. Mednick? Mr. Mednick! It's me, Amelia Thorn. Where is everyone?"

He shrugged and turned the mug upright. Through the window, I saw Madeleine Whitby from the boutique across the street. She waved her arms at me to get my attention. Mr. Mednick, coming to terms with the fact there would be no coffee, no brisket, no asparagus, stood and I handed him my grip.

"Ma'am?" Madeleine called when we'd stepped from the front door. I hadn't seen or, quite frankly, thought of her since she'd come in for an early supper the night of my attack and her voice, too, triggered a memory and made me flinch. "Ma'am? They're gone."

She didn't recognized me and I had no intention of a reunion. "Everyone? Where?"

She walked to the curb of her sidewalk and hugged herself as though it were cold out. "It's

Mr. Z. An ambulance came and carted him off. They all followed."

"Ambulance?" A taxi pulled to the curb in advance of the crowds from the Jackson 1:15 expected at Central Station and I jumped in before leaning back out to call across the street: "Where?"

"St. Joseph!"

"Go," I said to the driver.

I urged him to speed and, at the hospital, threw a handful of bills before running into the emergency room. It was the same lobby I'd been wheeled into years before after being beaten nearly to death. I'd been unconscious then, though, and wasn't sure on this day which way to turn. An information desk lay ahead, attended by a nurse in white uniform. "Zaccone," I said, out of breath, and she pointed to her left and a small crowd there. It looked as if all of the Timeless Café had been lifted up and set down whole in the waiting area. A waitress in her light blue uniform with a pencil behind her ear and order pad sticking from her apron pocket. Mr. Turley, the cotton man, a napkin tucked into the collar of his shirt. Ms. Borden sat beside her son, the haberdasher, and clutched her purse as she had throughout lunch twice every week. Big Bobby and the rest of the kitchen help sat to one side in a section marked "Coloreds Only." He still had his spatula in hand. Jean was even there, in a bathrobe of all things, and holding a small bundle. The only one missing was Mr. Mednick. And then, beside me, the old jeweler appeared, still holding my grip. He'd climbed into the back of the cab and I hadn't even noticed.

The assembled crowd turned as one to look at me as though I carried with me some great answer, as though that answer might be held in the camera still slung around my neck. Eleanor came from swinging doors and the answer they sought, the one we all sought, was written on her face where sadness was compounded by the confusion of seeing me there, a ghost. "Amelia?"

"Eleanor. Dear." We embraced and I felt her body tremble, frailer than I recalled. But perhaps frailness was a condition that had only just come over her on the other side of those swinging doors. She melted into my embrace and I knew instinctively what had happened, the butterfly flutter of chaos I'd felt while standing in the middle of an empty restaurant alighting on my shoulder.

Chapter Sixty

"Do you keep in touch with those you met?" Frank Severs asked. His notepads, pencils, laptop, and phone were spread over the table. He'd become comfortable in my home and invoked eminent domain over my breakfast nook. I sat at a card table and studied the fractured face of a thousand-piece jigsaw puzzle by light from the window. If that face were ever to become whole, in it I would see the bright hues of the Amalfi Coast from the vantage point of the Tyrrhenian Sea's surface. I would be looking at one of my own photographs. What other puzzle makers couldn't know was the photo was taken from the bow of a leaky gondola I'd paid a village boy twenty centesimos to row out and back. We'd waited for a particularly calm day, but one promising the best light. The puzzle maker also wouldn't know that among the figures seen walking the twisting roads and taking in the scenery from their perch high above my boat was a man, little more than a blue smudge now against the red backdrop of a building. I had an affair with this man, a British engineer conscripted to rebuild the bridges of Italy destroyed or damaged in the war. No, all the anonymous puzzle enthusiast would think was, *What a beautiful photograph.* They wouldn't even know it was a photo my agent sold to *Life* magazine and which Mattel Inc., the toy maker, eventually took for their own with no compensation. *É vita.* I brushed a fingertip lightly across the piece with my lover.

I mentioned none of this to Frank Severs. "When I think back on it, it was my time alone that I cherished more than the crowds I found myself in," I said in answer to his question. I found a piece that matched and snapped it in.

"But you must have met some characters."

"That's just what they were, Mr. Severs — characters. As narcissistic as it must sound to you today, here, in this apartment, when I was in the thick of it, as young and as adventurous as I was, the world was merely a film set. And the people were actors in a script unfolding before me as I lived it, in real time. It was freeing. I was unbeholden and every turn of the corner was unexpected. I embraced it all like the nascent hook of a plot."

Chapter Sixty-One

Evangeline. George. Scott. Timothy. Jillian. Rebecca. Edward.

The name stung my eyes. *Edward.* Tombstones lined the green hillside like teeth in a mouth screaming names from the past. *1918. 1899. 1940.* My Edward never had a tombstone. Would I have visited it if he had? He wanted me to go to California and I wouldn't, what made me think I'd be pulled by a marble marker on an arbitrary plot of land?

"Amelia? We're about to begin."

The gash in the ground seemed deeper than it must have been. A dark, muddy yawn with a single tooth at the top. *Calogero "Charles" Lorenzo Luca Zaccone.*

Across the opening from where I stood, Jean sat holding her baby tightly to her chest, using the corner of its blanket to dab at her eyes. The baby was the bundle she'd been holding when I rushed into the waiting room at the hospital. She'd given birth earlier in the week and was on an upper floor when Eleanor called to say Charlie had been brought in. Jean introduced us, baby and me, delaying the moment when I would have to explain my years of absence and sudden reappearance. "Edward," she said. "That's what I named him. Edward." It was her first boy — she had three girls while I'd been gone and had dearly wanted a boy. He was imperfect — one leg malformed and shorter than the other, but otherwise healthy and happy. I bent to kiss him and his butterfly eyelids tickled my cheek. At the graveside, I wondered if she regretted the name, if she wished she'd named him Charles instead.

Later, in the dim light of Eleanor's guest bedroom, I stood at the foot of the bed as I had at Charlie's grave that afternoon, this time reliving a scene from my memory as it unfolded before me. *The woman is stiff, reluctant, though her reluctance is due to fear of the unknown and not any lack of wanting. She wants the man. Madly. He's eager (men always are) but will be gentle. She'd packed her fear in a suitcase for her trip here, yet she is warming to him, pulling him closer now. The act is loving and promises more — a future, a family. As soon as he returns. When he returns. This is their first night together. There will only be one more.*

I hugged my shoulders, looking down at my and Edward's marital bed, wishing for an embrace from that man again. Instead, I slid into the cold satin sheets and lay there with my eyes open, unable to sleep even though I'd been drinking all afternoon and night. Liquor only heightened the anxiety of being in the bed where Edward and I first made love. Though I struggled to remember every second of that moment, every touch of his fingers and lips over the years, I wanted then only to push it from my memory. The nearness, I was afraid, would be too much. I would surely turn to ash.

It had been such a long day and the days and nights since I returned to Memphis were swirling together. One expects a homecoming — a feast and hugs and joy — not death and sadness. On the Zaccones' back patio earlier, I absently twirled a lily from the bouquet on Charlie's casket. He and I had spent so many nights sitting at that very same table drinking and sharing stories. He preferred to drink with company, while Eleanor preferred to drink alone and his kids were always on the move — a bottle of beer carried here, a glass of wine carried there. "Nobody just sits and drinks any longer," he'd say. "Relax. Sip. Sigh. Sip." Grappa, until I found I was pregnant, and then I spent long nights nursing a white wine. Now? Well, what does it matter?

"Mind if I join you?" Eleanor sat and clinked her martini glass to my thimble of grappa. She carried her own lily. "He enjoyed drinking with you. Said you were 'one of the boys.' He missed you."

"I've missed him so. I hate I didn't get to see him again." Why hadn't the butterfly wings of fate pushed me down from Petit Jean a day sooner? What if the truck driver hadn't left me in front of Ina's empty house? I could have taken a cab from West Memphis instead of walking. Arriving one breath sooner and I might have seen Charlie alive. The thoughts scuttled through my mind in the days following my return, but I couldn't give them a home there, having long since abandoned the language of regret.

"After you left, you know he always kept a plate of food for you? If there weren't leftovers, he'd take food from Peter's plate and slip it into the fridge. The end of every week, I'd have to clean the fridge out and scrape it into the trash." She laughed.

"I didn't mean to hurt anyone."

Eleanor twirled her flower and sniffed it, then sipped from her glass. "Of course not. We do what we must to survive. You're a survivor, dear. Charlie knew that. He respected it. I think he saw something in you that perhaps we — you and I — hadn't. Your independence, your strength, your instinct to survive when you stayed behind and let Edward go."

"Oh, Eleanor, if Charlie saw any of that, he only saw me mirror you. From the moment I met you, I wanted to be more like you. I took you into the world with me when I went. All of you, you were with me every step."

We were silent then, sipping and sighing. In the waning daylight, Charlie and Eleanor's grandchildren ran through the yard collecting fireflies. Eleanor watched and smiled at them. The yellow lights shone brighter and, with each blink, another layer of darkness descended. She patted my hand and stood. "It's good to have you home, dear."

Chapter Sixty-Two

To pass the time, I took the trolley downtown to walk familiar streets with my camera, buildings and people appearing anew through the viewfinder. I saw him there. In the faces of men passing on the street, of those awaiting eggs and coffee at the Bon-Ton Café or lunch at Anderton's, those men watching me walk by newsstands and hotel lobbies and nickelodeons. *Edward*. I knew he wasn't there, of course. *Ghosts*. They would never show up on film, could never be pasted into any album or hung in a frame. But those streets were where I'd left him and, I came to understand, where he would always be. It was memory, a longing I'd hoped to leave in Eleanor's guest bed. Memories diluted over years crossing borders and bedroom thresholds now coming back reconstituted, smiling back at every turn of my head. I began considering them a blessing, these memories come so vividly to life.

I wondered if Mother saw Daddy's face at church or in parades as young men were sent off to war. "Mrs. Crawford said she ran across you in town," Mother said one morning as we sat on the porch.

"Bitter old biddy."

"I suppose we're none of us too different," she said.

"We?"

"Widows."

The term had never struck me as a collective before then, certainly not one I belonged to. Me, Mother, Grandmother. And now, Eleanor. Mrs. Crawford wasn't a widow, her husband was on the supply lines, supposedly far enough from the Front in Europe to be safe. "The Lord is looking over us," she'd said to me that afternoon in the Five-and-Dime.

"He must have glanced away while my Edward was in the Pacific," I snapped. Mrs. Crawford would be a widow herself before the war was through.

Those women had all lost more than husbands. Their very identities had died in the metal teeth of a thresher, from heart attack, and by a whistling mortar in France. Whole lineages halted, the widows giving up and lying down along with their husbands. I hadn't. And I wouldn't. I'd tethered myself to Edward and he'd been tethered to little more than the wind. Like a kite, when his parents died and the string cut, that kite had been set loose. The plot of land his family owned was so small it hadn't even piqued the interest of the Reynoldses. When Mr. Cooper investigated years later, he learned the Thorn land had been swallowed whole by Greenlaw County through eminent domain for a public dumping ground. Well, no one had held dominion over Edward. Nor me since he'd been gone, which is why it was more relief than regret to see his face in the crowd. Edward belonged to the back booth of the Timeless Café, to a trolley running east from Main Street, to the shady walk leading to the Zaccones' home, and to a bed in a room at the Chisca Hotel.

But then I began to see the little girl, our daughter. And that unnerved me because I'd felt for so long she was in the world. Edward's kind eyes and soft smile on the face of a child had me turning the other way, changing the course of my path to market or the park to keep myself from grabbing her up and holding her to my breast. But she was uncatchable. She was not tethered to any land, to any booth, or to any trolley car. She was in the wind as well, and the name of Thorn would one day be carried away on that wind for good.

I stood on the sidewalk and looked up at the gothic spires and gray stone of the church. Its

shadowed recesses and colorful glass had once
been mysteries to me and I was sure something
magical would happen on the other side of those
heavy, wooden doors. And it had — I'd been
married there. I had been born into adulthood. My
very own baptism.

I hadn't stepped inside that church since
the day of my wedding, though I'd returned not
long after the angel of death dressed in Navy
whites visited me at the café. A part of me that
day wanted to tell Father Hollahan, the priest
who'd taken two halves and made them whole,
that his union had, in fact, been torn asunder by
war and by his God. Another part of me wanted
an answer. I wanted to know *why*. I wanted to
know what kind of a god takes a half away, allows
wars to rage, leaves a woman pregnant and alone
in the world.

Father Hollahan's attention was focused
on a clinging white rose bush threatening to
overtake the iron fence surrounding a small
garden. I watched him from across the street. He
wasn't dressed in traditional black, no dog collar
that day, but wearing grimy khaki dungarees and
a white undershirt dark with sweat under the arms
and around the neck. He looked like a man, just
an ordinary man, and I saw then what Jean had
seen — the priest was handsome. I could see it
from where I stood in the shade of a maple tree,
watching as his strong hands worked the clippers,

his jaws tensing, and the way he paused to brush hair and sweat from his eyes. The man was strong and healthy and he was right there, safe, tending to roses while Edward and thousands like him lay on the ocean floor, torn and mangled and alone. I couldn't take it any longer and crossed the street in a rage, paying no mind to traffic and cars screeching to a stop, horns blaring.

"Hey!" I shouted. "Hey!"

He straightened at the noise. "What is it? Who's there? Are you okay?"

I stared up at his face — I'd forgotten how tall he was — and squinted against the sunlight. "Tell me why," I said. "Why?"

"Ma'am?"

"You don't remember me, do you? You married me and my husband, Edward. He's a sailor."

"Yes, of course, from Mississippi. How are you?"

I fought so hard not to cry but felt my skeleton crumble at the question. *How are you?* Through a series of sobs and stops, and with the noise of passing traffic, I managed to tell him what had happened to Edward. He took my hands then, held both in his soiled, sweaty palms and began intoning in Latin with his baritone voice. It was a prayer to wash my pain away, to clip it the way he deadheaded his roses so something more beautiful might grow. I pulled my hands from his and put them instinctively on my belly and that's when he noticed.

"Mrs. Thorn, you're pregnant." He snipped a rose, full in bloom, and offered it to me. The aroma reminded me of my wedding day. I took it, looked at it, and then threw it to the ground. His eyes softened. "Is there no comfort I can offer you?"

"From you, yes, but I won't hear anything from your church."

That was the last time I'd laid eyes on Father Hollahan. Staring up at the church's front years later, having lost a baby, whored and hidden, and traveled around the world a dozen times, I didn't know if I'd be welcome inside or not. But I'd told Jean I would be there, that I would be godmother to little Eddie.

It was a week since Charlie's funeral, the baptism postponed after his death. It was to be a day of celebration, yet no one felt like celebrating. But superstitions of the devout are strong and every day Eddie went without his original sin being notated by the Vatican was one more day he might end up in purgatory for the duration. A cheer went up from nearby Court Square, a politician's rally. A bus horn blared, a calliope wailed. I threw my cigarette toward a vine of white roses and entered the church.

The air was as cool as I remembered, as was the holy water I touched with my fingertip to dab on my forehead, chest and shoulders as Edward had. The day of my wedding, I'd worried I wasn't worthy to enter such a strange and holy place. On the day of the christening, after all I'd been through, I didn't give a shit what anybody or any spirit might think. I knew I wasn't worthy, but my perception of worth had changed over the years. Father Hollahan nodded in my direction, recognition in his smile and, as always, no judgment in his eyes. Even as he prayed for me that day in his garden, and as I threw his offering down, threw his prayer in his face, he didn't judge. I smiled and nodded the slightest apology for that flower.

His Latin was as strong as it had been and his voice just as deep. I was asked if I believe in God the Father. What did I know of God other than what he takes away, the misery He'd wrought? I was asked if I believe in the Holy Ghost. I did not.

I wanted to ask my own questions: *Where has God been? Where was He when my husband was blown from the water? Where was He when my daughter was ripped from my womb? Where had He been when I felt the blackest nights of addiction and submission and a pain that might never end?*

Do you reject Satan? I have rejected that demon to his withered, red face.

Those were the thoughts in my head as I held the baby and smiled and nodded because that was what I had told my friend I would do.

Chapter Sixty-Three

The Zaccones had a Zenith radio in the kitchen — an appliance added by Charlie, who loved big band and swing music. Any time of day at the Timeless, customers would be treated to Duke Ellington, Count Basie, or Glenn Miller. He bought the radio for the kitchen at home, fascinated by its size and easy fit on a countertop (the clockmaker in him still appreciated design and function). After the christening, I sat on the patio, catching snippets of music whenever the backdoor opened and closed with cousins and their friends running in and out.

In Grandmother's parlor, it hadn't been a petite Zenith, but an enormous Philco radio whose face glowed green in shaded lamplight. As though pulled by its gravity, we sat in front of the radio and allowed the outside world in. Let in what Mother and Grandmother allowed, that is — news of the Depression, scandalous murders, devastating natural disasters from across the country. Yet, maddeningly, they'd snap its knob, rendering the robot mute, at the mention of the war in Europe and the millions of refugees clamoring for sanctuary. "Not our fight," Grandmother would say. And yet, in front of the radio is where we were sitting when the Japanese bombed Pearl Harbor, making it our war. Mother clutched her collar and Grandmother fingered the gilded edges of her bible. "What did you expect?" I said, and was sent to my room.

Around the Philco was where Daddy and his friends huddled on May 21, 1927, to listen as Charles Lindbergh landed the *Spirit of St. Louis* in Paris, France. It was my third birthday and tables covered with white cloths had been spread across the lawn in front of the house. The old women from Grandmother's church were there, as were men Daddy did business with and their families. When the plane landed, a roar went up that "threatened to break out the windows in my house," Grandmother would say years later. And Mother told me I thought those cheers were for me as, in that instant, I'd blown out the three candles on my cake.

Daddy liked music as much as Charlie, but I believe he enjoyed news broadcasts even more because of his love of stories. He was always reading novels and newspapers, and I wish he could have known Edward, the storyteller, so they might have shared tales.

Twelve years after Lindbergh crossed the ocean, I sat stunned in front of the Philco as news of Amelia Earhart's disappearance filled the parlor's air. "She has my name," I said.

"She was a brave explorer," Daddy said. "Think of the guts it takes to even attempt such a feat. Not many men I know would try such a thing."

"Women have no business setting off on their own," Grandmother said, picking up the pace of her cross-stitch. "Of course she went missing."

"Better to have attempted and failed," he said, but low enough so only I heard him.

It was 1932, the year I turned eight, when we listened for news of the Depression from New York and how the world outside our farm was faring.

We hoped for any news of a break in the long string of bad news but it wasn't to be. "The child was taken from his home in East Amwell, New Jersey, last night," the announcer said, his voice sounding strained and pinched coming from so far away. East Amwell might as well have been a million miles from Paris, just as it must be from Mourning. I ran from school to the library the next afternoon to pore over newspapers for any details of the crime. I knew it would be there, the town of Mourning had a special connection — and a morbid curiosity —

when it came to damaged children. To the dismay of old Mrs. Bowers I read every word I could find on the kidnapping. At night I lay awake wondering where that baby might be, how it could have been taken from the home of someone so famous, someone so accomplished. Charles Lindbergh had flown! As far as I was concerned, anybody who could fly could do anything he set his mind to. The fact that a tiny baby boy could confound him, could be so far from his grasp, was as lost on me as how it was an airplane could stay aloft over an entire ocean.

I was thinking of the Lindbergh baby that day on the patio as Gerry Mulligan's breathy saxophone filled the air, then disappeared behind the door before coming to me again. "That baby died," I whispered. Open, close. In, out.

"What is it you're thinking of?"

I was floating through a daydream — in and out — and Charlie had been carried to me on the music. Charlie, with his great, oval head and fleshy jowls, his baldness and sunspots where hair should be. He looked surprised to be there with me, slack-jawed, but then his face broke into the same warm and welcoming grin as it had the day   we   met.

"Oh," I said. "I must have gone away."

"You're back now. Good," he said. The air around me had gone hollow. Behind Charlie, the waning daylight turned the sky gray as rain approached. "Stay for a while. Drink with me?"

I pushed the bottle toward him and the liquid sloshed, its spirit clinging to the glass. He carried his own glass with him. "He enjoyed drinking with you," Eleanor had told me just a week earlier. "Said you were 'one of the boys.'"

"I wanted to tell you about Doris," I said to Charlie. I poured another sip into my glass, the spirits clinging to my brain and my heart. "I wanted to tell you about the world. It didn't start with Doris, though, Charlie. It started long before, with my Daddy."

He patted my hand and nodded.

"I was just thinking about the Lindbergh baby, I don't know why. I was thinking about my Daddy and the radio, but I remember when he was taken, the baby. Daddy and I spent hours discussing what might have happened."

"I remember when Mr. Lindbergh flew across the Atlantic." Charlie's disembodied voice wafted from the bottle to my ears. The drunk fuzziness made me sleepy. "And I was there when he came to Memphis."

"Lindbergh came to Memphis?"

"Sì, tesoro. It was later that same year. Landed out Highway 51, place called Armstrong Field in Millington. Must have been a hundred thousand people there to greet him. We all wanted to touch the *Spirit of St. Louis*. He stayed at The Peabody Hotel that night, I heard."

It was Armstrong Field where Jean and I had seen the military plane crash. "I had no idea," I said and wondered if my father had known his hero was so close. Had he come to Memphis to see for himself? I'd never heard him say so or heard my mother recount such a trip. I never knew Daddy to leave Mourning at all, other than to go to market, and the trip he and I took to Pascagoula and Palmetto to eat oysters beside the water.

Mothers, fussing over church clothes, shooed their babies inside as the rain began. In the house, adults settled in for games of bridge and poker. In my dream state, Charlie and I kept our seats. "How did you do it?" I said.

"What's that, tesoro?"

"This." I gestured with my arm, sweeping in the house and yard and those left in it. "All this. Family and work, all of these kids and people stopping by all the damn time — in and out, in and out. It's like a restaurant. You were happy if half this crowd showed up for lunch at the café."

He waved the idea away and poured another sip for himself. He was fading with the light and I wasn't ready to let him go. "Niente. It's family, it's nothing to have family in your home . . ." — he shook his hands at me the way he did when his new language failed him and he grew frustrated trying to make a point — ". . . it's

356

why   you   make   a   home!"
        I shrugged and held up my glass for
another pour, but it wasn't going to happen.
        "Why you so sad, Amelia?" The voice
crackled away like a fading radio signal.
        Again I shrugged. "Just reminds me of all
I   don't   have,   I   guess."
        "You feel sorry, that's not the Amelia I
know.   Look   at   what   you've   done."
        I sighed. "Maybe it's seeing baby
Edward. That's wrong of me, I know. Maybe it's
being   in   that   church   again."
        He nodded, his jowls moving opposite
his head. He would not speak to me again.
        "Maybe I wonder what's left, what kind
of life I'll lead. Adventure? Daddy wanted it and
I've had it." I leaned in, my head low so the
liquor's fumes burned my nostrils. I reached
across the table for Charlie's hand but there was
nothing and no one there. Still, I couldn't move
as   raindrops   fell   heavily   on   my   skin.

Chapter Sixty-Four

Bakery
Lucca, Italy. 1946

Gelatin silver print, 37.5 x 27.9 cm
(14 3/4 x 11 in.)

Courtesy, Zaccone family estate.

Morning sunlight filtered through dust-covered windows, giving the room an overcast glow as though a storm were due. The smell was overpowering — food left sitting in the open air, trash piled in cans and unemptied. Somewhere, a mouse scurried through cabinets. It was overwhelming, but I'd been overwhelmed before. Storms no longer held sway over me. I kicked at the tripod, still lying where I'd dropped it the day I returned to Memphis.

"The boys and I have been talking and, well, we want you to take it over."

"Take it over? What are we talking about, Eleanor?"

"The restaurant."

"Surely you're joking. It's yours, it's the family's, one of the boys should take it. Or all of them. Or you, now that you're retired."

"Oh." She waved the idea away, the same wave that had brushed aside the notion that Rose Zaccone might ever consider her a daughter or that Eleanor was tough as nails and the first woman I ever really admired. "I'm just that, dear — retired. And the restaurant never truly was mine. Not even a partnership. It was Charlie's baby, his fifth, I liked to say."

"I remember. I admired that, his devotion to something so singularly. I always wished I'd find something in my life to feel so devoted to."

"Photography?"

"Sure. I was lucky to find it, or for it to find me."

"Maybe the restaurant found you. Charlie built it from scratch, we're asking you to take care of it from here."

It wasn't a decision I made lightly. I wished Doris was still around so I could have asked her. My advisor, my confidant. "She did love a diner," I said to the ceiling where I lay awake long into the night in Eleanor's guest bedroom after the day of the christening. I'd had too much to drink. I'd had an entire conversation with the ghost of Charlie. Laughing at my foolishness, I turned and clutched the pillow to stop the room from spinning. Yet I couldn't stop Eleanor's offer from dancing through my mind.

The Timeless Café had felt like home from the moment Edward and I first walked in, despite all we owned being stolen. Charlie and Eleanor welcomed us into their home. Charlie welcomed boys going to war as though they were of his own blood, never charging them, sending them off with a full belly and warm feeling to remind them of the life they were fighting for and a reminder to come home safe. How many hours had I spent taking up space in a booth, sipping coffee, and reading after Edward left? And Charlie let me. Even as a line formed at the door during the busiest time of day, he never once hurried me along. He should have, Lord knows. And then he gave me a job, my first. Me, with no experience, having been waited on hand-and-foot by Lizzie. The Zaccone boys, as they were known, became men in the back booth where they played cards and sipped from a flask they didn't think anyone could see. They watched women walk by, caught by me in the mirror behind the counter, though they had no idea. They were sweet boys, good men, and were making their own paths in life. They'd survived the war, thank God, and weren't to be chained to any kitchen stove or ledger book. I say good for them, let them explore. I had. And then I came home and things aligned like the cogs of a watch clicking into place, like the shutter of a camera opening and closing.

I was made to feel at home in so many places around the world, from diners to saloons to private homes. I was welcomed in by the poorest, most downtrodden people who fed me with what little food they had. And I'd been made to feel at home at the Timeless as well. I was touched by that. Perhaps I could continue Charlie's tradition, make a new home for travelers who felt out of place.

And yet, I felt out of place. No one had been in the café since the day Charlie died. Moldy food and flies had taken over. But there was something else — it was Charlie's. It was as though I'd walked into his head while trying to become oriented with my own thoughts. Eleanor asked me to take it and take it I would. I swept my arm across the nearest table, sending plates, cups, utensils, and crusted scrambled eggs to the floor. I shoved the tripod behind the counter with my boot and pushed tables to the far end of the room, tipping them first so everything fell to the floor. When I finished, the room was open, the filth and past laid bare. I found a push broom, bucket, mop, and rags. I was reminded of the cabin alongside Teeth and Lizzie, and how I'd spent a day scrubbing to make it my own. It had been the first place I'd felt comfortable since the Timeless, but it wouldn't be the last.

"I wanted to tell Charlie about traveling through Italy," I said to Eleanor after the baptism. "I traveled the length of it twice the first time, from thigh bone to bootheel."

"Assignment or vacation?" Eleanor was interested in my travels, in how I'd balanced my life on the road.

"Depended on the day," I laughed and she did as well, which was nice. Eleanor hadn't cried. Not at the hospital, not at the funeral home where she picked out a casket and headstone, and not at the wake in her home as she'd been bombarded with soft handshakes and cumbersome hugs. Jean and I marveled at her strength. Or her capacity for denial. But neither had Eleanor laughed, so the crack in her face, in her stoic facade, was like a small victory on my part and I glanced quickly around to see if Jean was near. "Italy was rebuilding after the war and I wanted to capture it. A lot of people were displaced or in mourning, and that was hard and needed to be documented."

"You felt a calling."

I thought about that word — *calling.* I'd never felt called to do anything before, not from any higher power. "No, it wasn't divine intervention. Unless you consider Doris Latham a saint, and she and I spent far too many nights drinking and carrying on for me to consider her that. 'Documentarian,' as a profession was handed to me — thrust upon me, really — by Doris."

"She saw something."

"In my work, yes."

"Come now, Amelia, you're too modest. That's the old Amelia, not this new, worldly Amelia Thorn. She saw something in you — your eye, your creative soul, your strength. It was there all along."

"You saw it?"

"I saw something more than the young, frightened bride in front of me. I can't say for sure what it was, but it was . . . something. A bud, perhaps, waiting to blossom. A chrysalis with the first tear in its skin."

I relished Eleanor saying so but felt guilty for her compliments considering all that had happened. It should have been me making her feel better. "I visited Lucca."

"Charlie's home." She put her hand on mine and its warmth surprised me.

"It was beautiful, Eleanor. I walked its circular streets beneath olive trees and everywhere I turned was a photograph waiting to be taken. The age of it was like nothing I'd seen at that point. I hadn't yet been to Germany or England or even the Far East. Italy was my gateway to an older world and I'm so happy to have seen it. I ran my hands along the ancient city walls and could feel Charlie's spirit, his warmth, and I couldn't wait to come back and tell him about it, to show him the photos I took."

"He would have loved that, dear. He missed it so, I know."

"I bought a Leica camera in Rome and the shutter was sticking. There wasn't a repairman in Lucca, of course, but I thought a clock maker could make the adjustment I needed. I looked all over the village, I asked men and women on the street who looked old enough to have remembered the Zaccone shop, and finally I found it. It was a bakery, the only evidence of what had been there the clock above a new sign above the door. It was just like the clock Charlie kept in the café."

"Oh, he would have loved to hear that as well. A bakery, how lovely. The café was an extension of that old world for Charlie, its heart and the comfort people could find there. I think he thought he was sharing a piece of his home, of himself, with customers."

Plaster chipped away but the nail eventually sunk tightly, sturdily into the lathe behind it. "Hand it to me."

"You sure you don't want me to get up on the ladder and hang it?"

"You think I can't?"

"Miss Amelia, I think you can do any damn thing you put your mind to."

"Good, then hand me the frame."

Bobby and I spent the day hanging my photographs around the café and this one — a wide, panoramic shot of the village of Lucca taken from the bell tower of Duomo di San Martino, where I'd gone to photograph its mismatched columns — was the last. From my perch on the ladder, I surveyed the room. It had been three weeks of steady work. The floor was waxed and windows soaped over to keep prying eyes out. Booths were reupholstered, chairs matched, tables leveled so there were no wobbles. The wood lunch counter where Charlie had once repaired watches was taken out and replaced with Formica in a colorful design fitting the modern era. There was no need for the red-and-white tablecloths. Every fixture had been tightened and polished so the overhead lights caught them and they twinkled like stars on the midnight ocean. Around the room, in the style of a Parisian parlor, my photographs hung — landscapes and portraits from Greece, China, Germany, Serbia, France,

South America, and so many other places, especially Italy. I kept the mirror behind the counter, a single pane stretching from one end to the other so the café appeared twice as large as it was. I left the clock as well, a reminder of Lucca and Charlie, to look over us all. I worried it might lose seconds without Charlie there to fuss over it, but what was time? I had no place to be.

"What do you think?" I asked Bobby.

He stood with his hands on his hips, slowly turning to take it all in. "Looks good. Looks different, but good. Modern. Updated. But he's still here, I can feel him."

"Charlie?"

"Yes, ma'am."

"Good."

Chapter Sixty-Five

I didn't want a grand reopening, nothing to smack of celebration as we mourned Charlie. So one day I awoke early, took the trolley downtown, scraped the windows clean of soap, filled salt and pepper shakers, turned on all the lights, and placed a fresh flower on every table. All before the sun came up. And then I unlocked the door and turned on the simple neon sign over the door: OPEN. Bobby was there already, I knew he would be, he'd been coming in daily to scrub every inch of the kitchen. He tightened pipe fittings and stopped leaks, things let go during the busy, day-to-day running of a restaurant. He'd contacted suppliers and a steady stream of trucks had been pulling to the back door for a week to unload whole hogs, greens, flour, eggs, spices by the bucket, butter and lard, paper goods, coffee, and everything else needed to run a kitchen.

Neither of us had spoken of an opening date, but we each knew it to be close.

So, on the morning the Timeless Café reopened — the first morning ever without Charlie Zaccone greeting customers at the door — there was only Big Bobby and me.

At the end of the day, I counted receipts while he shut down the kitchen. Business had been light — far lighter than when I'd been a waitress — and manageable. Bobby and I were a good team. Customers trickled in at first, people from the neighborhood drawn by the neon like flies to honey. Mr. Mednick was there, of course, and he sat in his booth as though nothing had ever happened. I wondered where he'd taken his meals over the weeks since Charlie died.

Jean and Peter raved about the changes. "Papa would have loved it," Peter said, and I was overjoyed. Their girls ran through just as Peter and his brothers had when they were boys, and Bobby fed them bacon and French fries through the serving window. Jean helped herself to pots of hot water to warm bottles for Eddie while Peter walked the perimeter of the room taking in the photographs. "Just beautiful, Amelia. Is this Morocco? Gee, I'd love to get to Africa someday."

It had been several weeks since the reopening and still Eleanor hadn't come in. We didn't talk about it in the evenings, preferring to watch television or read and sip martinis. "How was your day?" she would say, just as she'd asked Charlie every day of his life. I'd watched her back then, at how she never seemed to listen to his answer. He talked and remembered details about customers' orders or the stories they shared, but she had already moved on in her mind. So I saved her the hassle. "Fine," I answered. Since retiring, Eleanor spent her days watching soap operas (her "stories") and volunteered at the Ave Maria Guild, a home for the elderly. Many of the residents were younger than she, and most were either related or longtime friends and family of friends. She knew their names, their histories and, though she took cakes (she still baked one a day) and magazines, gossip from the outside world was the most prized contraband.

And then, one day, without warning, there she was. I was behind the counter, making a malt for Madeleine Whitby from across the street, and when I turned to serve her at the counter, I saw Eleanor standing in the spot where I'd stood my first day back when the restaurant had been deserted. I felt my face flush with anticipation, eager to show her around and hear her thoughts. But her face had fallen and looked distraught.

Years earlier, in an airfield cleared from the Alaskan wilderness, I helped a bush pilot scramble to load his small, single-engine plane with my equipment in time to take off ahead of a storm moving in. "It'll be blinding," he said as we huffed the cameras and portable darkroom from the one-room cabin to the plane. "If it sets in on us, we won't leave. Not until it thaws or we can dig out."

"This is the last of it," I said, handing him a bag and watching as he packed it in, forced the hatch closed and leaned in to twist the frozen latch securely. To the north, a wall of white headed our way. To the south, it was clear blue sky and I looked forward to being enveloped in it and on the way to Anchorage where my agent had secured a hotel room. A hot bath and room service beckoned. In a matter of days, I would be leaving for a job in Hawaii and then, later, to California for a long-anticipated visit with Doris. She and I had traded letters about our mutual distaste of the cold. "Give me a beach bordered by jungle to keep the tourists out any day," she wrote, adding, "Oh, and a drink. That's the coldest thing I want touching my skin."

The pilot turned to me and said, "Well . . . ," and then his face twisted so it didn't look human. He tried to speak but clutched at his chest and dropped into the snow drift that had built up as we were working. The shock on his face was the same I saw on Eleanor that day in the café. So much so that I called for Dorothy, the waitress I'd hired just after reopening. We went to either side of Eleanor should she fall, but she only looked at me as though she didn't recognize me and then to Dorothy as though she were being assaulted.

"What happened?" she said.

"Eleanor, are you okay? Here, please sit. Dorothy, could you get Mrs. Zaccone some water, please?"

"What happened?" she repeated.

"I think you may be sick," I said.

Her lips thinned and her jaw tightened so blue veins showed beneath the thin, brittle skin. Eleanor used to look so strong but on that day she looked weak and frail. She murmured, "I am not sick. I want to know what happened to Charlie's restaurant. Where did it go?"

"Oh, Eleanor. I made some changes."

And then she wept. Charlie was truly gone now, the new Timeless Café echoing the void in her heart. I don't know if she cried for Charlie privately, I could only assume so. But that day in the restaurant, her chest heaved with sobs as she absorbed it, pushing me away when I tried to hold her. "Charlie, Charlie," she said again and again as she fought to catch her breath. I forced myself on her, holding her tightly while customers looked on. All activity had stopped, the kitchen went silent and Dorothy placed a glass of water gently on the closest table. Eleanor's arms hung limply at her side as I hugged her, believing I was holding her fast to Earth so she wouldn't ascend into the heavens with her husband. She spoke to me like a little girl, whispering through her closed throat and lips thick with saliva: "Tables. Plates. Photos. Cloths. People. Glassware." They were mundane, work-a-day needs in any restaurant, but items she'd connected to Charlie. I came to understand from Jean, later, that, though she rarely came into the restaurant, and though she only half-listened to Charlie at night, those one-sided conversations were as regular as the second hand on Charlie's clock. And his voice had been silent for nearly two months. She filled her long days with hobbies and help, yet she couldn't fill the silence of her nights. I wept with her.

But then she focused on another change. Charlie's kitchen staff had been black and the front-of-house help white. That was the way it had always been until I took over. Eleanor's watery gaze fell on Dorothy, her pale blue waitress uniform and dark brown skin. "Why is *she* out here?" Eleanor whispered (thank God she whispered only to me). I'd never known Eleanor to be bigoted. She laughed easily with Big Bobby on those rare occasions she visited. She tipped doormen well and was courteous to men and women of all colors on the street. I recalled the day she hugged the busboy at Gerber's and spilled water on the women who were aghast at such a display. But those busboys and doormen were in their places, I understood then. And I had altered that reality. It was the Sixties in Memphis and everything — and everyone — had its place. Things were changing, slowly, and this was how it happened. If some were left behind, if some customs were buried six-feet down, then so be it. I wouldn't be beholden to the old beliefs and old rules, spoken or unspoken. I'd seen too much hatred and suffering around the world to consider some deserving more than others based on little more than complexion.

It was the first time I'd seen weakness in Eleanor. For that's what her prejudice was. Of course she was grieving and I gave her the benefit of the doubt. She'd walked into a room expecting one thing but found another. She was lost on the map of her own life. Other than their children, the café was her sole connection to Charlie.

Eleanor's metal showed its flaw that day. It softened and buckled, and the full weight of Eleanor fell on me so I was crushed. But I was also unmoved. A coat of paint and polished fixtures were no reason to dilute one's constitution. I didn't say these things to her, I never would, but something changed that day. The axis our relationship spun upon shifted and would never right itself. I loved Eleanor dearly, as I'd loved Charlie, but the pedestal she occupied in my mind crumbled so we now looked at each other eye to eye.

Chapter Sixty-Six

Larry the Pilot
Alaska. 1959

Gelatin silver print, 37.5 x 27.9 cm
(14 3/4 x 11 in.)

From the artist's private collection.

The pilot was dead, of course. His name was Larry and I dragged his body to the clapboard structure where deer and rabbit carcasses were gutted and cleaned. It wouldn't keep the cold out, but Larry didn't need warmth. Out of respect, I covered him with the tanned hide of a deer, its body still hanging above, bound by its hind hooves. I radioed Anchorage to let them know the situation and learned it would be another month before a plane could cut through the ice and snow. I'd have to use Larry's truck with its rusty plow to clear the landing strip when the time came. Until then, I was alone. "You'll have to do the best you can, miss," the voice on the other end said.

There was little to occupy my mind other than the books I'd packed (and already read, some of them twice) and pulp detective novels of Larry's lining one windowsill, condensation from the glass darkening their well-thumbed pages. I did find some girly magazines hidden away, but found the articles lacking in literary merit. There was a turntable — an old Victrola that worked by winding the mechanism inside — and a few scratchy Billie Holiday records. In my solitude, indeed.

Every two days I'd trudge out to the skinner, as I thought of it, to cut a hunk of venison from the carcass. I always greeted Larry warmly, and thanked him when I did. I was pleased to be alive, of course. I shuddered at night thinking of the chaos had Larry's attack happened fifteen minutes later when we were a mile in the air. Despite being alive, the loneliness was of the sort I couldn't ever remember feeling. I'd always been at peace with solitude. I'd been lonely in the dinghy flat on South Main after Edward left, but the possibility for interaction had always been there. In the snowbound outback of Alaska, however, that possibility was nowhere to be found. I was frozen in time.

I was gripped by the same cold once again following the confrontation with Eleanor. Cold seeped into the fissure developing between us. In all likelihood, it had happened years earlier and I hadn't been there to witness it. But that was the point, wasn't it? I wasn't there. Her anger toward me was long overdue and not completely unwarranted. I'd left her world without letting her know where, without the decency of letting her know I was healthy and alive. Trust had evaporated like melted ice.

Chapter Sixty-Seven

I sipped tea and looked from my top-floor apartment at trees exploding in the same autumn colors I'd seen from atop Petit Jean Mountain in Arkansas. There had been the promise of something more those days in the wilderness. It's a feeling only the young know — a sense anything is possible no matter your station or the number of coins in your pocket. Regardless of what you have or from where you come, the next big thing is always on the horizon. It's something I fear I'd lost. It's a feeling I missed. It's the very feeling I'd had every time I waited for an image to appear in the tub of developer when my world was bathed in the red glow of the darkroom. In that image, anything was possible.

As it turned out, anything still was.

"Tea?" I asked when Frank Severs arrived.

"I brought this," he said and pulled a bottle of single malt scotch from a brown paper bag. "To celebrate."

"Celebrate? Is it your birthday? Oh, hell, is it mine?"

"No. Well, it's a birthday, in a manner of speaking, but neither of ours."

We sat by the window overlooking the park and the Brooks Museum of Art far below. It was a cloudless day, the sky brilliantly blue. So blue, I wondered if I could squeeze a drop into my glass to mix with the scotch. It had been a long time since I'd had a proper drink. I was admiring the blue above and the reds, oranges, and yellows below while Frank rooted in his satchel. I secretly hoped he'd pull a pack of cigarettes out, I always wanted a smoke when drinking scotch. Tobacco, like that feeling of inevitability, was something else I missed.

Just as he'd pulled the bottle from the bag with a flourish, Frank produced a manila envelope and slid it across the table. It was dog-eared at one corner and stained with a half-moon of coffee. Surely not the Dunhill I'd hoped for. "I got it from Jack Feinberg," he said. "He was an editor on the short side of retirement when I got to the paper, but he was a reporter at the *Memphis Press-Scimitar* long before that. That's when he was investigating her and dug up the records."

I looked down at this odd gift and back at Frank. "Well, what is it?"

"Do you know who Georgia Tann was, Amelia?"

"No. Is she in that envelope?"

He spoke quickly, propelled by his excitement at whatever discovery he'd found. "She ran a latter-day orphanage. More of a puppy mill, really. Back in the old days — your days — when people were hungry and everything was crashing around them — war, the stock market, polio — she took babies in, took care of them and, in many cases, found new homes for them. Sold them, really. She was a bad person, making a buck off of these kids."

"What does this have to do with me?" I was nervous and sensed the darkening clouds of a storm on the horizon.

Frank drained his glass and poured another two shots. He poured more into mine, though I hadn't touched it since our toast. "In some cases, she took babies from unsuspecting mothers. Sold them, like I said. She was unscrupulous. Amoral, even."

"What are you saying to me, Frank? Quit dawdling and get to the damn point."

"These are yours." He pushed the manila Pandora's box closer to me and I instinctively moved away.

"My what?"

379

"Your records. Well, your baby's records. When they finally arrested Georgia Tann, they tried to find the birth parents, the babies themselves, many grown by then. But you were in the wind — halfway around the world by then. Probably in South Africa from what I can tell from our interviews. The authorities looked, Feinberg looked, but the trail ended in West Memphis. A number of babies were taken — sold, by Miss Ina herself — from right there in her brothel.

"I've been digging through records for weeks but didn't want to say anything until I knew for sure. Now I do. She's alive, Amelia. Your daughter has been this whole time."

Chapter Sixty-Eight

Jean and I spent as much time as possible together after I returned from my travels. The restaurant kept me busy, but I knew enough by then to make time for those who mattered. Jean mattered. We took her children to the zoo and ice skating and let them run among the irises at the Botanic Garden. Jean's face glowed when she watched them, and I was so happy for her and the way her life had turned out — just as she'd wanted. But her smile faded as though she'd been caught thinking something she shouldn't: she felt guilty for her happiness in the shadow of all I'd lost. "Have you thought about trying again, Amelia? A husband, a family?" Her eyes followed Mary Beth, who had discovered a grasshopper and ran to keep up with it.

Over the years, my idea of family had become fluid. I'd made dear friends all around the globe and in my industry. Artists, editors, photographers, journalists. Wayward transients, all. Some fluttered into my life and back out again. Others came and went like a comet, recognizable only by what latitude and time zone I sat within. But others moved with me, if not physically, then in my heart and soul.

I was in Istanbul when a telegram reached me about Mother. It was little more than two months since Grandmother had gone. "I suppose the old woman needed someone to fetch soup and a warm afghan for her feet," I told an uncomprehending bartender. In my hotel room, I wrote a letter instructing Mr. Cooper (for he was the county registrar as well as postmaster) to deed everything — house, servants' quarters, barn, livestock, land — to Lizzie. I wanted nothing of it or of Mourning. I wrote to Lizzie and told her to do with it as she saw fit. And she did, too. She razed the barn and the shotgun shacks she'd grown up in. She split the whole of the property into parcels of twenty acres each to sell them off through advertisements in newspapers from Jackson to Birmingham to Memphis and all the way up to Detroit and Chicago. Those listings sought black families exclusively to purchase the plots. Lizzie kept a fifty-acre plot with the big house on it for herself and burned it to the ground. She even took a picture of the blaze with my old Brownie box camera and sent it to me. In its place, she built a modest home with enough land that she and her family could run until their legs ached and their lungs filled with the freedom she always craved.

"You rescued Lizzie," Frank Severs said. "That must be gratifying."

"I did no such thing. The things she accomplished were far beyond anything I could have dreamed up. I merely pushed the boot from her neck — as it was a Reynolds boot, I saw it as my duty — and she did the rest."

Lizzie had been eager to learn even when we were girls, and still was, sending off for books about real estate and investments. She called on Tri State Bank, a black-owned bank in Memphis, to manage her money. She was so smart and maximized the potential of the Reynolds land to its fullest, realizing a profit the likes of which her ancestors — and mine — never could have imagined. And then she gave it away. All of it. She improved the Mourning Public Library, that institution where she never felt welcomed. She built a community center for her people, and a market, a school where black children were given every advantage whites had. And, finally, to allay long-held fears and superstitions, she had miles and miles of dirt roads paved throughout the county. No more runoff, no more slick mud. And she bought school buses, christening them in memory of her grandfather, whose mule wagon had slid into the creek all those years ago.

Late in her life, visiting the state capitol to wield her considerable influence and power, she lobbied successfully to have the town of Mourning re-incorporated as Morning, Mississippi. A new day.

I found I was tired and sighed at Jean's question before answering, "I'm finished."

"Finished? Well, what do you mean finished?" She was looking at me now, but I was fixated on the grasshopper.

"I'm done. I've had my ride and it was over a hell of a lot quicker than I expected. Done."

"Oh. But . . ."

"Yes?"

"But don't you miss the touch of a man?" she whispered and, in the shade of a tree, the blush on her face couldn't be mistaken for sunlight. Caught off guard by the question, I laughed and told her I'd touched many men. Her face went crimson and she changed the subject. "I always knew you were safe, you know, and that you just had to go away for a while as Christine had. I worried, of course, but I understood, deep down, that wherever you were, you were safe and happy. I told myself that all the time. And then when we started seeing your name in magazines and newspapers alongside your photographs, well, I was just so thrilled for you. Such an adventure. In fact, there were so many men going off to war and so I thought of it like that. You went away for a bit and you would be back, just like those boys."

I lit a cigarette and in the space of my silence, she seemed to realize what she'd said and who would always be omitted when we talked about returning. "Anyway," she said, "thank God you came back."

We were both watching Eddie, who wore a brace on his leg and struggled, yet managed to keep up with his sisters. He was a thoughtful boy, taking time to stop and look at butterflies and goldfinches alighting on thistle. "He's doing so well," I said. "Doesn't seem bothered at all."

"Oh, it bothers him." Jean was grateful for the change of subject. "He's different and kids at school make fun in the way of kids."

"Bastards," I said and stubbed out my cigarette on the bench. I took another out and offered one to Jean, lighting them both.

"I don't blame them, and I know it will make him stronger. More empathetic, anyway. You know, when he was born and I woke to him being placed in my arms, I was so happy. Then the nurse pointed out his leg — called him 'crippled' — and I cried. Peter was strong and soothed me, telling me there was a specialist in the hospital who had already been to see him. Still, I cried myself to sleep that night with Eddie in my arms, and I stroked his lean little leg, massaging it as though I might be able to bring it back to life.

"This wasn't so long after the war and the horror of it was still on our minds. Millions dead. Boys. And I woke in the middle of the night with a start, dreaming that Eddie had been taken away from me to fight. But then a peace came over me there in my hospital bed as I realized that could never happen. Despite whatever else might happen — another war to end all wars, God forbid — Eddie's leg will keep him out of it. Is that selfish?"

As a result of Lizzie's foresight and planning, the land and town once ruled by the Reynolds family became a haven for African Americans. Those who settled there, or who had never left, found a home where they could be productive and happy, and where their children ran and played. It taught me that good can be born from bad, scorched earth can yield flowers and butterflies. For miles around, something missing for so long from Mourning was heard again at long last — laughter.

I watched Jean's boy chase and catch his sister, grabbing her around the waist and the two falling to the ground in laughter. "Not at all," I said. "Keep your kids safe, Jean. Keep them close no matter the cost."

Chapter Sixty-Nine

He held his glass out for us to clink together in another toast. Frank was proud of himself and, I suppose, I should have been grateful. But the knowledge washed over me as the pain had when I was in labor, flooding outward from my middle and tugging my heart downward with the tide. That woman — "Miss Georgia," Ina had called her, it all came back to me now — had been there to help the midwife as she had for so many of the girls, and she'd taken the tiny corpse "for a proper disposal." Who was I to question it all? I was so young at the time, so naïve. Alone and scared and hurting so badly from a beating I'd taken only hours before. Days of morphine and blackouts. The little body — a girl, Ina told me — would have had to have been disposed of. It only made sense to me at the time. And yet, nothing made sense. I'd felt the butterfly movement of life within my body only the day before, I was sure of it. I'd moved my hand to my belly to feel a kick, the flutter of a foot or elbow.

"Kicking?" Eleanor had asked, her tight smile clamped down on a cigarette. I'd even heard a cry, hadn't I? I was sure I had, but then there was the delirium and the thunder and my own cries over it all. I wasn't at all sure.

And now, sixty years later, Frank Severs sat in my living room and told me the other woman in the room that night had taken my baby — that very much alive baby girl — and sold her? Could it be so simple to pull a life back from death? Edward and all of the soldiers and civilians lost in all wars. The men and women of Kamchatka in the tsunami. The young jazz trumpeter, ship's captain, and Doris. Charlie. Kennedy. Dr. King. Were they all packed away in a sealed envelope someplace just waiting to be opened? I didn't know what to do with the information I'd been given. It was all too heavy. The weight of that envelope was too much for me to lift from the table and open. So I didn't.

I hadn't asked for any of this and it angered me that Frank had hefted such a burden onto my shoulders. I stayed angry with him, though I can't imagine why, shooting the messenger and all that. Perhaps it was his prying into my life at all, but I'd given him the key, hadn't I? Long ago, Charlie had chased the messenger in Navy whites down to offer a meal and coffee. I should have taken a page from his book. I just needed time. It'd been so long and was too much to comprehend. The manila envelope sat on a bookshelf, untouched and as benign as any one of the books there. Unlike the books, though, I could sense its presence at night. I started awake and walked through darkness, the only light coming from the museum below to reach the ceiling of my front room where it left patterns of leaves and branches like a family tree. The knowledge the envelope held rippled the air and thumped against my breastbone as Poe's heart had against the floorboards.

I needed time and I took it. I didn't see anyone and I had food brought to my apartment, not that I had an appetite. I refused to see Frank, poor man. He phoned daily. Even sent a letter. He'd always chided me for not having email. I spent whole days looking out the window at the trees and traffic below. I watched shadows and light change across the face of the museum for hours, an old habit of the photographer. Imagine that — I counted my scant, remaining time on the planet by the dance of light and sat idly by while life slipped away.

Chapter Seventy

Of course I knew Josiah Feinberg, the reporter for the *Memphis Press-Scimitar*. He'd been such a regular at Ina's that his rose-tipped penis would be as familiar to me today as the view from my apartment window. If he were still alive, that is. "Feinberg passed away twenty years ago, more maybe? His wife let me go through his records. You should see it, Amelia, an entire basement full of metal filing cabinets. Feinberg kept everything," Frank said.

A wife. More widows. Josiah used to talk about his wife, tell me what it was she wouldn't do. I did it — all of it, and more. But he loved her, he told me that, too. You wouldn't believe how many men talked to me about their wives, their fiancées, their mothers. Just like the traveling salesman in Mourning had. "I don't give a shit about your wife, your mother, your fiancé," I wanted to say to them. But I didn't, of course. They were paying me to listen as much as fuck.

I knew his name from somewhere else, too. I visited the Mourning Public Library when I was there. The musty old building was as much my home as Grandmother's house had been and I wanted to reconnect. I wished I could fade into the stacks, sink into the window seat where I'd spent so many hours exploring the world beneath the proscenium arch of the windows and the stage set beyond that was the Mourning town square. Mrs. Bowers was still there. "Amelia? Amelia Reynolds? Why, is that you?"

"Amelia Thorn. Yes, Mrs. Bowers, it's me."

"I thought you'd given up reading, it's been so long."

"I gave up on Mourning, but it's like a bad habit, isn't it? I relapsed."

She didn't know what to make of that but stamped a book she had open before showing me to the basement where the region's newspapers were kept. Librarians are just hoarders when you get down to it, afraid to throw anything out as though history might erase itself were they not at the controls. I dug through the stack of *Press-Scimitar* newspapers from Memphis until I got closer to the date I was looking for and then I felt like a prospector digging into a vein thick with ore. Moving back and forward in time at the same time, I scanned the front pages and Metro pages with dust in my eyes and nose. I sneezed and it echoed in the cavernous room. No one was there to bless me and I was grateful. Four paragraphs, six pages in and five weeks out, presented themselves to me. The motherlode. *A body, hung up in fishing line and a downed tree, was fished from the Mississippi River and is believed to be that of a man in the employ of Boss E.H. Crump.* The byline belonged to Josiah Feinberg. *Looks like a suicide*, the police captain was quoted as saying. *We get a lot of those around this time of year.* There was no ongoing investigation, I was in the clear.

Anyway, that explains why the records of my baby didn't make it into Josiah's newspaper, the source was far too personal, and too telling. Had he known I was in Georgia Tann's records, would he have searched me out? Would he have been able to find me in Kenya or Venice or Christiforinika? I'd been as hidden from the world in West Memphis as I'd been while wandering the Eastern Hemisphere.

Chapter Seventy-One

My finger slid easily beneath the sealed flap and gave way without effort, the glue having long since lost its strength. I'd moved it from the living room shelf to the nightstand beside my bed. There, I believed, I might dream about the information it contained. It had been many years since I'd dreamed of my daughter, of that awful night and the loss born with her. I'd been set free, I felt, cured of the fever ache of sadness. Frank Severs brought it back to me and I tried to fight it off, I did, but the connection proved too strong. I'd grown weak again in my old age and could no longer fend off the fever.

Before pulling the contents out, I closed my eyes and ran my palm over the envelope as though a genie might appear, as though all the answers I didn't even know I had might pop out. Inside was a more formal-looking page than I'd expected. And that's all it was, a single page. I had never considered the exact date before, never affixing a birthday to what I'd lost, yet there it was, the date. "Tennessee Children's Home Society" was in block letters, followed by her name: Georgia Tann. The body was a too-long paragraph of homespun legalese and there, at the bottom, filled in with a flowing script were two names and, simply: Baby Girl.

Baby Girl. My hand went to my mouth, stifling a sob. I tasted the dust and age of the document on my fingers and fought to stay upright. Giving in, I sat on the edge of my bed, heaving thick sobs that rolled from my throat. The lost time welled up inside me and sprung forth, wracking my body so I felt the physical pain I'd endured for my year of exile, my penance. I felt again the pain of the night I was beaten and bloodied. I felt the pain of childbirth and my insides fighting to get out. I lay back on the bed, covering myself with the heavy comforter and lay there, alone as always, crying and convulsing until sorrow overpowered me and I drifted off. Just on the other side of sleep, I gripped the paper between both hands as though I were afraid it might flutter away.

When I awoke the next morning, light streamed through the windows. My first thought was the dreams I'd willed to come had finally done so, but as I moved, the crinkle of paper gave me a shock. Holding it above me as I lay on my back, I read it again. The notation at the bottom right corner had escaped my notice and the sight of it almost made me wretch so I had to sit up to keep from choking.

300 dollars
IF percentage 10 (30 dollars)
PAID

IF. Ina Freeman. Miss Ina sold my baby girl to Georgia Tann and, for her services, received a fee of thirty dollars. The realization made me nauseous. It made me angry so I questioned everything — her loyalty, her story of the dead baby come to life on her island. In the drawer of the nightstand beside my bed was Edward's hunting knife and if Ina had still been alive, I surely would have gone to her and cut her throat. I would have slipped her lifeless body into the water as she had with Crump's man and turned my back as she sank to the rank river bottom. Miss Ina saved my life, I never doubted that, and for that, I considered her a saint just as she had the madam Annie Cook. But Ina took life from me beneath that same roof — cut the umbilical cord that connected me, not just to my baby, but to Edward as well.

The lobby of my building was a world of dark mahogany woodwork and plush furniture. Absent any organization in their lives, save for arts-and-crafts or bingo, the residents assembled there each day late in the afternoon. There was nothing scheduled, yet they filed from elevators like Peabody ducks. A week after I opened the envelope, Mr. Showalter sat at the glossy black Bösendorfer piano and played his way through the Cole Porter songbook. A small, stemmed glass of Campari rested above the keyboard beside a book of music. "They say Oscar Peterson once played this very piano," he said. I sat beside him on the bench with my back to the keys so I looked at the room and the seniors scuttling across the parquet floor, mindful to an obsessive degree of the curled edge of a Persian rug. A silvery legion armed with walkers and canes, and the fear of gravity in their hearts. "Of course," he continued, "there's no way to prove it. Perhaps this piano once graced the stage of a concert hall where he performed. Or OP was walking down the street in New York or Toronto and saw it in a showroom, pulled by its beautiful, glossy finish and gaping maw. Provenance is a tricky thing to prove. So many stories in the world, anecdotes . . ." — a flourish on the keyboard — "lies."

"I photographed Oscar Peterson at his home in Canada. I can't even recall who it was for — newspaper? Magazine? Nor can I recall what it was he played."

"You make my point for me, Amelia. Memory is a tricky thing, we remember what we want to remember. It's a protective mechanism. It filters out the bad."

I sat and listened to his rendition of "Begin the Beguine" and wished I had my own flask of Campari hidden away. "What did you learn, Lieutenant?" Philip Showalter was a retired police detective from Detroit who had moved to Memphis to be close to his daughter and her family. The badge was a calling card despite the city, connections based on brotherhood. Without missing a beat in the song, he slipped a hand into the left breast pocket of his canary yellow blazer and produced a folded sheet of paper. I glanced at the name and address, surprised to find it was only a few miles from where we sat.

"Be careful, Amelia," he said. "The past is memory and, well, we know how unreliable memory can be."

Chapter Seventy-Two

In the mid-Sixties, I reimagined the Timeless Café as a coffee shop with live music — folk singers, mostly, and some poets, violinists, one accordionist, though I told the young man I couldn't abide that sound another night. He understood. It was as lively and as Bohemian as anything you'd find in Greenwich Village and reminded me of the night I'd spent in the dreamy air of Hector's New Orleans lair. The hair was longer and clothes more casual — torn in places, fringed in others — but the energy was the same as it had been in Charlie's day. The machine of commerce still thrummed and the machine of war churned, gnashing its teeth on young men of another generation. This war, however, didn't even have pretense enough to save the world from any inherent evil. It was political. But boys died just the same.

The Timeless was family. When Big Bobby's nephew, Red, took over in the kitchen,

Bobby told him, "Look after Miss Amelia, you hear." And then he whispered when he thought I couldn't hear, "And keep that back door locked so trouble don't get in." Red came to me when his son got his draft notice. He knew I'd once escaped, though he didn't know the details, and asked for help. His boy was timid and bookish, and so slight he used two hands to push the kitchen door open to go see his daddy. I'd seen what war wrought and I saw so much of the young, soft trumpet player from Korea in Red's son. I couldn't bear to see him twisted and bloody beneath a sea of violence. So we hustled him out the week before his draft day and when the inspector from the board came around looking for him, I played dumb. Unlike the messenger in white who had come for me, this man was not offered a free plate of food. The others were. They came into the café on their way to the great unknown and, out of respect for Charlie and his policy, they didn't pay for their meals. Not here, not ever.

My old agent tracked me down and tried to pull me out of my self-imposed retirement. He said I was being asked for by name to go over on troop deployments, fly aboard choppers for rescue missions, document the humanitarian aid going to families even as gun battles raged on. I declined. I'd seen enough of the horrors of war that I didn't need to immerse myself in it again. It was a younger woman's game and I was happy to leave it to them. "A diner? Pancakes and bacon and malts and shit? Jesus Christ," he said. I invited him down, told him lunch would be on me. "And leave my island? For the deep South? No, thanks. Take care of yourself, Amelia."

A few years later I'd be pulled from retirement with the wail of an ambulance siren and the wailing of a people. I didn't hear the gunshot but left the Timeless at a run along with a crowd of people on the sidewalk. At the Lorraine Motel, Dr. King's body was being loaded into the ambulance. As whispers punctuated the air filled with police sirens ringing throughout the city, the realization of what had happened made my knees weak. I looked down to see my camera in hand. It had been a reflex, muscle memory leading me to grab the Leica I kept in the office. I pushed through the crowd to capture images of a white sheet and gurney, stricken faces on the balcony and in the people running this way and that.

Red slashes of light cut through the darkness later as the images appeared in the tub of developer. I called my agent, who was glad to hear from me, but his voice was hoarse with sleep and sorrow. The pain had been felt across the country and up to his island. It would be days later when I'd learn the fatal shot had come from the same small room I'd lived in when Edward left for war. How many lonely nights had I spent staring out the window, down the slope of lawn at the people coming and going from the Lorraine? The thought sickened me.

Not long after, Big Bobby came to me with an idea for a restaurant in North Memphis where he'd feed shift workers from International Harvester and the Firestone tire plant. It had been a lifelong dream, he told me, and he needed it now more than ever. "Too close," he said. "I don't know I can go on with my day to day a block from where . . ." He couldn't go on but I understood. When the money came in for the pictures I'd taken that night, I gave it to Bobby. I didn't want it and I wanted to see his dreams play out.

His place was comfortable and the food as good as I'd come to know he could cook. The café was in a strip mall development on the site of the old Wayside Inn at the end of the airfield where Jean, Peter, Christine, and I had watched the B-1 bomber crash, and where Charlie, in a fever dream, told me Lindbergh had landed years earlier.

Though I was old enough to be their mother, I enjoyed the energy of the young people who hung around the Timeless in the days of flower power. Their world views, sexual freedom, and whole-hearted dissent was liberating. It spoke to me and I envied them their

401

age at that particular moment in time. When Edward and I had our first Memphis meal (I was a blushing virgin bride-to-be!), there'd been a palpable, workday energy with people rushing in for a half-hour lunch, rushing off to catch a train. Responsibility ruled the day. But in the Sixties, the hippies had more time on their hands, whole days and nights. Time to sit and argue philosophy or art criticism. Certainly different than the way I lived my life — crossing off the next thing on the list, exploring around the next corner — yet thrilling in its own way.

Jean came around to sit at the bar, drink coffee, and laugh at the fashions and conversation. Her kids came around at night to hear music and smoke pot. Oh, I didn't tell Jean, they trusted their Aunt Amelia. And I reveled in the independence of her girls, the energy, the promiscuity. They blew off steam on those late nights but they were going places, places far away. Eddie rarely came around and when he did he preferred inspecting the kitchen, limping through the swinging door to spend time with Red.

Chapter Seventy-Three

"Is this even legal? I could be deported."

"Quiet, you. I'm looking." I sat in the back of the taxi and peered over the window. I had shrunk into my age so much I barely had to crouch to remain unseen. Ivan didn't crouch at all, not the best costar for my noir adventure. "Must you smoke?" He was Croatian and smoked Muratti cigarettes from Turkey sent to him by an uncle there. I once traded a carton of Muratti for a ferry ride across Lake Eymir in the Ankara Province. The ferryman's wife kept a kettle of fish she caught on the trips back and forth and many had died in the heat. The tobacco scent still reminded me of the stench of dead fish and I told Ivan so. "Why can't you put that out?"

"You aren't even paying me to sit here, Amelia. We move, meter runs, you pay. We sit, you tell me, 'Stop meter!' You don't pay."

"Cry me a river," I said under my breath. My old eyes were still strong and I watched the couple as they walked toward me from the far side of the pond in Chickasaw Gardens. Their home was nearby and as Ivan drove past it I was warmed knowing my daughter lived in such a place. It was stately and with two giant magnolias in the front yard, just the sort I used to climb as a girl in Mourning. Would I have been happy with such a home? There were times — on a train through Austria or while taking in the colors and scents of a bazaar in the Mid-East — when I wondered to myself what dull pattern my days might have followed had Edward made it home from the war alive. A comfortable house, a kitchen in which to cook meal after meal for my husband and kids. Would it have been enough? Would they have completed the jigsaw puzzle of my soul? Early on, I had my doubts, and as the days and years unfurled and railroad lines stretched out in front of me, those doubts grew into certainty. And over time, I grew less and less ashamed of that feeling.

But later, I did want a home and needed space after my confrontation with Eleanor at the newly reopened Timeless Café. It was a home I was thinking about one day as I leaned on the lunch counter, drinking coffee before the next rush. I was considering my options when a mighty crash shook dishes and rattled mugs.

Across the street, a plume of dust obscured much of Calhoun Street, from Pantaze's Drug Store to the train station across the street. I went to the door with Dorothy. "What in blazes?" Gloria, another waitress, said from behind us.

"A bomb?" Dorothy offered. "Did a trolley explode?"

When the dust settled, we saw two men leaning from the second floor of Pantaze's, wiping their brows and looking pleased with themselves. Aldo Pantaze stood cursing them so anyone within two blocks could hear. From the second floor, they'd pushed an enormous chunk of metal through a hole in the wall to the sidewalk below, where the weight of it shattered concrete. As the dust cloud rose beyond the second story, I noticed a LEASE sign in the window. "Mr. Pantaze!" My voice joined the chorus of curses as I headed across the street.

The upper floor of Pantaze's Drug Store was long and narrow with dusty wood floors that sloped to one back corner. Walls were brick with sturdy shelves holding the alphabet — metal As and Ns and Qs of every conceivable size and style. The second floor had been home to a print shop, and it was an offset press the workmen had dropped to the sidewalk. Everywhere, counters, cabinets, and fixtures were being ripped out and naked wires spilled from holes in the walls. Windows rose from the floor to the double-height

405

ceiling and an iron staircase spiraled up to a loft in the back where office furniture, piled high with ledgers and calendars dating back a decade and more, cluttered the space. It would have been a wreck to anyone else, but to me it was something different altogether. "I'll take it," I said from the office. "Mr. Pantaze?"

He was on the main floor, still swearing at the workmen (they turned out to be his sons) who had shoved the machine to its death. "Eh?"

"I said I'll take it."

"Take it?" He looked around at his property. "For what?"

"For a home."

Again he looked around, then to his sons for clarification. They shrugged at him and he, in turn, looked to me and shrugged.

I found myself once again sweeping and scrubbing, as cleansing to me as it had been in the cabin in Mourning and then at the Timeless. In the loft, clear of desks and desk chairs and filing cabinets, I put a bed and bureau, a nightstand and a small table by the window.

Edward would have loved it. That was what I thought as I walked through the apartment once everything was in place and the hole in the wall sealed up. He could have written there beneath the window and we would have had coffee overlooking Main Street. There was no wide front porch and no scent of allspice, no magnolias in any tidy front yard, but it was just the space I needed. It was the first true home I'd had since leaving Mourning to be married. Until then, the most at home I'd felt had been in the stateroom of a ship, a train's carriage, and the noisy cabin of an airplane. I loved to sleep beneath stars with a campfire smoldering nearby and, of course, a hotel room would forever call to me. But the room above Pantaze Drug Store was mine and I decorated with photographs and paintings of artists I'd met, and a selection of the metal typesetting letters arranged on shelves among books accumulated from Burke's Book Store at the other end of downtown in the Pinch District. The apartment was large enough to devote one end to a small photography studio, where my large format camera sat atop its tripod to catch natural light as it moved across my world.

Sunlight dappled through branches of oaks and dogwoods and reflected off the pond's surface to sprinkle the couple as she leaned into her husband as I did with Frank Severs on our walks. It wasn't to hold herself up as it was with me, she only wanted to be closer to him. They held hands. They laughed. I lifted the camera to my eye, resting its enormous telephoto lens on the cab's doorframe, and waited. From behind the couple, three children scampered. I waited until they were in the frame, the woman's hand went to the tallest boy's head, and I clicked the shutter. It was a clear day with autumn in the air and the sweet smell of magnolia was strong enough to break through Ivan's fug. I wiped a tear. "Drive," I said.

I took the camera back to the Memphis College of Art, a mid-century modern building in Overton Park within reach of the Brooks Museum of Art. The camera and lens belonged to Colleen Chockley, an instructor in photography and design. I'd been asked to speak once or twice to her introductory photography class years earlier. Me, a Luddite who had to borrow a digital camera and have someone else download and print the image. I hadn't known what to say to the pimply-faced children staring down into their phones. They didn't know an F-stop from a STOP sign and I'd never walked in their shoes. I learned all I needed to know from Doris Latham in Mississippi's red clay ravines and on a trawler full of fishermen searching for periscopes in the waters between Cuba and the West Indies. I set up makeshift darkrooms in hotel bathrooms and oily corners of airplane hangars. But we all start in the same place. I mean, the very beginning, feeling the camera's smooth body against our cheeks and letting light fill our optic lenses. It opens us up to a world we'd never know otherwise.

The students had to have known the magic as I had or they wouldn't have been there to learn how to control the magic. Because that's what photography is — magic. It's the ability to stop time, to keep the world from spinning for just a second, and then forever. It happened to me on a dirt road outside a shotgun shack. Though I'd been down that lane a thousand times, I'd never truly seen the wood of the shack, the way it blistered and peeled, and how many shades of gray it was. I'd never seen the grass and brush so green or the way red berries popped with color. I'd never seen a bird stop in mid-flight. And until Lizzie stepped into the frame with her baby, I'd never felt my heart leap with such joy. *Click.*

So that's what I talked about to the kids in sneakers with buds of music in their ears. I told them about the decisive moment that Henri Cartier-Bresson suggested is within all of us. It can't be taught. So I didn't teach, I suppose, but urged them to find their own moments. I urged them to be *in* the moment, *of* the moment, wherever that moment might be. I had. All around the world, I'd made time stop and, in those moments, with each snap of the shutter, I came to know, just a bit more, just who Amelia Thorn was.

"Newlyweds? At their age? I can see how in love they are." Colleen sat at her computer and we both watched my images slide across an enormous flat screen the size of Grandmother's Philco. Colleen had a side business shooting weddings and engagement photos, a facet of the industry that never interested me. I knew the fragile filament holding those gold bands together, binding two people into one, and worried my camera might expose that fragility.

"No, they've been married their whole lives," I said, marveling along with Colleen at the love the two had for each other. "I just wanted something to remember them by."

Chapter Seventy-Four

Frank and I spent the day at the Brooks Museum in one of the hushed halls holding my work, my life, hung on walls so I could flit from memory to memory. "What's it like, Amelia, walking among all these old friends?" They were all there, it seemed — the broken horse, Tony's mother at the produce stand, Lizzie and her baby, Hector in New Orleans and Larry in Alaska, the car wreck in Mississippi, and a bakery in Lucca. Old friends and unforgettable tragedies — the war dead and wounded, watery faces in the Soviet Union, and Dr. King's lifeless hand dropped from beneath a sheet. So many memories racing back to me.

It was a private showing for Frank and me, though there was still work going on around us, more fuss than I cared to have made over me. Across the room, Maria Whitaker and an assistant made last-minute adjustments to descriptive

411

plates. "Will it be ready by tomorrow?" Frank called to her.

She looked back, a bit frazzled, I'm afraid, with a clipboard in one hand and a pencil behind her ear. "It will have to be," she said.

"It doesn't have to be," I offered. "I've waited this long." They both laughed, but I'd stepped away from Frank and was caught in an image just inches from my face. I'd forgotten how muscular Edward had been. Furrows of the hippocampus shield us from details. The photo reminded me of his physicality, the hardness of his body from laboring in the Conservation Corps and with Mr. Cooper. Life was different then, far different in the Delta where a strong back and legs were more important than book smarts. But Edward had been smart as well. He was whole and it was that wholeness I believed I captured in blue morning light filtering through the window of our Chisca Hotel room. I'd forgotten about this one and wasn't sure I would have allowed Maria to hang it if I'd remembered. But here it was, and I was willing to let fact replace recall.

"I'm afraid I've dredged up a part of your past you'd buried. I'm sorry for that."

"You were just doing your job, Frank. And doing it quite well, if I say so. I opened the door and my heart to you and you made yourself at home, as you should have."

We walked together through the Old Forest of Overton Park after leaving the Brooks, where it was warm but weather reports promised the mild temperatures wouldn't last. He was kind enough to shuffle along at my speed, leaning in together as the couple at Chickasaw Gardens had so I might keep myself upright. Much younger people passed by in neon-color running shoes and on high-tech bicycles. "Have you given any more thought to my suggestion? To inviting your daughter to the show?" It was a suggestion made after giving me the envelope, as I sat staring at it, unsure if I would even open it. "I mean, why wouldn't you? She's so close. It's amazing, really, when you think about it. Sixty years and she lives just down the road."

I didn't know what to tell Frank; he'd worked so hard to get my story right and to track down the truth about Ina and Georgia Tann and what they'd done to me. "I'm not even sure I'll contact her," I said.

Her father (the word stuck in my throat) had been a dentist, her mother (even harder to say), a homemaker. The would-be daughter of a single mother taking refuge in a whorehouse grew up in private schools and married the year she graduated from Loyola University in Chicago. Her husband was in banking, she'd been a nurse at the children's cancer hospital before taking early retirement. They had three children

413

and five grandchildren. Captain Showalter's connections were strong and I shared most of the information with Frank, but not the last bit. It was none of his business. "There's something else," Showalter said, stopping mid-song to grip my forearm as I stood to leave. "Alzheimer's. It's early, but it's there. I thought you should know."

"Jesus."

I worried over the chaos I would bring into that woman's life — into the life of her family. I'd waited until her grandchildren were in the frame to snap the picture, I knew that was no accident. It was my decisive moment. Her life was full and I was afraid the slightest flutter of a breeze might tip it to overflow. How much longer would she have before the disease erased everything? Who was I to confuse things?

"You seem lost, Amelia," Frank said.

"Just hold onto my arm and I'll find my way back. You wouldn't leave an old woman alone in the woods, would you?"

Frank laughed. "Of course not. Would you like to get something to eat? It's getting late."

We'd made the loop back to the Brooks and I looked up to see my apartment window through trees from where we stood. So odd to see from that vantage point, as though I were looking back at myself. "No," I said. "No, Frank, I need to go home and make a phone call. I'll see you tomorrow? I'd like to have lunch with you before the reception."

Chapter Seventy-Five

As Frank and I drove downtown for lunch the next day, I could sense him looking over at me, could feel the anticipation in the car with us. I let him wonder. "So you won't tell me? I'm just your driver?"

I shrugged, feeling playful. "I told you, we're going to eat."

He drove with his wrist draped over the wheel just as Charlie used to and leaned away, into the door, as though he were uncomfortable with me. "Well, you look very nice."

"Thank you. It's not every day one has her entire career nailed to a wall for people to judge."

"No, it isn't."

As his car covered familiar blocks, the landscape played past like the flicker of a newsreel. It was a film I'd seen many times, though it had been remade and the unfamiliarity was disorienting. "That's where Anderton's was," I mumbled.

"Anderton's?"

"Eleanor and I ate there every week. She worked in that building, there. The Warner was up the street, where I'd go alone some evenings for a film. Where was Goldsmith's? There. It's gone, too." I thought I could hear piano music from a second-story window, the clip-clop of horse hooves, and feel the smooth, brown skin of bodies on Beale.

So much of my past haunted these streets and doorways, nostalgia a comfortable companion. I'd been coy with mine and now I relented a bit. "We're going to pick up a friend after lunch. I wanted to look my best for her."

"A friend? Amelia, is it . . .?"

"Watch the road, Mr. Severs," I snapped.

It was Eddie who waited on us at the Timeless Café. "This is my friend, Frank Severs. He's writing a newspaper article about me," I said.

"Actually, it's a magazine story. And it'll probably be a book when I'm done."

"Aunt Amelia does like to talk," Eddie said and leaned down to kiss my cheek.

"I do hope you and Bob will be at the show tonight," I said.

"We wouldn't miss it. And of course we'll be bringing Mama."

"Oh good, it'll be so nice to see her. I miss her so."

"And she misses you. Talks about you all the time. You know you're welcome for dinner any time."

"Oh go on, Eddie, you know I don't leave my apartment."

"It's really quite amazing, Mr. Severs. Intrepid adventurer Amelia Thorn has traveled the world, yet I can't get her to my house across town for a simple family supper." And then to me, "Would it help if I promise Bob will cook?"

"Couldn't hurt."

We sat in the same booth Edward and I first sat in so long ago. It was my booth; Eddie even had a small brass plaque with my name affixed there. Two booths away was a much larger plaque with ELVIS PRESLEY inscribed on its face. "He preferred to sit at the counter so we could talk," I told Eddie when he had it mounted.

"I can fit more people into a booth," he said. Eddie always did have a better head for business than I had, he was more like his grandfather. The Bohemian coffee bar had been whimsy, but it would never have been sustainable.

"He came to me and told me he was interested in the restaurant," I told Frank once Eddie had taken our orders to Red, who was still working in the kitchen, too stubborn to retire just as his uncle had been.

"So you sold it to him?"

"Hell no, I gave it to him. It's his birthright, I was only taking care of it for a while."

"Just as you gave your life's work over to Maria to show to the world? Don't you see, Amelia, that work is your daughter's birthright."

"What do you see in those images, Frank? I see history. I see time, and it belongs to everyone. I'll be dead soon, what do I care what happens with time after that?"

"Don't you want to consult?" Maria Whitaker had asked me when I handed the storage keys over to her.

"I trust you," I said. "I took them, you tell me which ones are good."

I'd been as comfortable handing my work over to Maria as I had been handing the café over to Eddie. "What do you think that says about me?"

Frank thought about it, chewing on bacon and sipping coffee. He spoke, but I was finished listening to him. I'd walked the gallery where memories opened up wounds and rubbed nerves raw again. I laughed at some and choked back tears for others. To the gallery visitors, those photos would tell the whole story of the life of Amelia Thorn. But to me, they were only part of the story — snapshots in every sense of the word. Borders of photos make a prison where I am doomed to live each moment again and again. I never wanted to live a moment. I wanted a life. I never dreamed in black-and-white, I wanted color. I wanted sound. I wanted to taste and feel and smell. That's why I left time and again, as Doris had taught me to do. I returned on my own terms with the freedom Lizzie craved. *Where is home?* Doris had asked. Within the borders of every photograph I've ever taken. Within the movements and voices of every woman I've ever known, for each stage of my life was ushered in by a woman. Mother and Grandmother as I left Mourning for married life. Eleanor after Edward left. Miss Ina. Doris. At every turn, every change of season, I was reborn and birth relies on women. It's their strength that stays with me. Even the quiet, subtle strength of Mother, who stayed with Daddy and loved him though he loved another. I've taken something from each of them and secreted it away deep inside so when times were tough, when decisions unclear, or when patience might be a virtue, I could open that box to look through memories, advice, actions, and the characters of those who came before me and select just the right talisman to see me through. Happiness, pain, sorrow, loss, courage, adventure, the unknown. The women of my life drew the map to see me through each region, every stage.

I won't say I traveled unscathed — the scar tissue of my soul is a map of its own — but their wisdom and experiences whispered in my ear when I stood at a fork in the road. Destiny? Sure, I took those reins, yoked to bulls and bullish men and their bullish ways. And my arms screamed with the pain of gripping them and steering and stopping. And when I wanted to let go, when I dreamed of that wagon full of my own experiences and memories overturning into a swollen creek, when I hoped for a violent end to bring an end to a difficult life, I heard the voices of Lizzie and Jean and Betty Sue and sad, lost Christine, and I knew I carried them in that wagon with me and it was for them I stayed on my path. Their collective voice, as age caught up with me, was the soothing opium, the release of childbirth, and the satisfying click of a camera's shutter. Their memory and all they, and women everywhere, have given to the world, to me, is the sum total of my life and work.

What Frank Severs would eventually write about me was true: *Amelia Thorn went into a world of chaos and she survived.* But what he didn't understand about this timid girl from Mourning was what the world could never have known or expected — I *was* the butterfly, I *was* the chaos.

421

Across the street, Frank pulled the door closed, silencing the noise of traffic left behind, and the air inside was as hushed as the gallery at the Brooks had been. Inside the train station it was 1942 and everywhere were people, their shoes scuffing polished concrete floors and smoke swirled through low autumn light coming in windows. Shoeshines snapped rags and babies cried. Arrivals were called out. Soldiers tipped hats and their girls dabbed at tears. Ghosts, all of them. Standing at the foot of the grand staircase, I saw myself descending, arm-in-arm with Edward, my face eager to catch every detail, to remember every sight and sound.

My daughter had her own life and it looked to be comfortable and fulfilling. She had a long marriage and children of her own, grandchildren who adored her. Her life was not mine. Her family was not mine. I'd traveled the world with my children, their names exotic — Graflex, Hasselblad, Leica, Kodak — each with a personality of their own.

And I had Lizzie, my true family, my sister, my friend. She'd cared for me, laughed with me, cried with me. She was who I wanted to share my work and my life with. And through lives tied together, through time and space, there she was. The crowds, shoeshines, travelers, all of those ghosts fell away so there was only Lizzie, so real and so much older than I'd ever known her but as beautiful as ever, in a wheelchair pushed by her great-granddaughter. With Frank holding fast to me, I bent to kiss and hug her, and we cried, two old women folded into each other. In her withered, palsied hands she held a photograph and lifted it for me to see — our father, sitting on a picnic table and looking out to sea, imagining the possibilities.

EPILOGUE

The old woman's grandchildren visit. They are young and energetic and beautiful, and she enjoys having them so close. They were told to visit by their mother, the old woman's daughter-in-law, but she doesn't know this. She just knows there is an energy in the house and she likes the picture in a frame the youngest brings to her from a shelf in the living room. There is so much the old woman doesn't know, so many holes in her memory like pieces of a puzzle slipped from the table.

There are moments from her past, secrets eaten away by the disease as though they never happened. The flirting and single, passionate kiss stolen by a doctor at work she never told anyone about. It's gone, it never happened. Her husband's favorite cufflinks passed down through generations that she accidentally brushed into the garbage disposal. He thought them lost and she never told. It never happened. Of course

424

she can't remember her birth, or the woman who secreted her away across the river. Nor can she recall the couple who came two days later to take her to their home. They never told her she was adopted. It never happened.

And the old woman can't remember the day, five years earlier, when a package came to the door. A manila envelope with no return address and a single photograph inside. She couldn't know the photographer died a month after sending it. All the old woman knows is that with her in the photo are little children in brightly colored sweaters, and they're laughing. Her gnarled fingers play over their familiar faces. Her mind is childlike now, curious and searching, and her eyes find what not even the photographer noticed through the powerful lens — a butterfly alighting on her shoulder at the very moment the aperture opened and light flooded in.

— END —